Praise for Frances Fyfield

PERFECTLY PURE AND GOOD

Frances Fyfield

BALLANTINE BOOKS • NEW YORK

Copyright © 1994 by Frances Fyfield

All rights reserved under International and Pan-American Copyright Conventions. Published in the United States by Ballantine Books, a division of Random House, Inc., New York. Originally published in Great Britain by Bantam Press, a division of Transworld Publishers Ltd., in 1994. First published in the United States by Pantheon Books, a division of Random House, Inc., in 1994.

Library of Congress Catalog Card Number: 93-40244

ISBN 0-345-38279-X

This edition published by arrangement with Pantheon Books, a division of Random House, Inc.

Printed in Canada

Cover photo © Frank V. Blackburn/Windrush Photos, England.

First Ballantine Books Edition: April 1995

10 9 8 7 6 5 4 3

To the esteemed
Charles William Fyfield OBE
—otherwise known as the uncle
who enriches life.
From a niece, with love.

PROLOGUE

It was an ordinary place. People lived and died in it. On Sunday mornings in summer, some of the men who lived nearest gathered on the quay to gossip. News of death was underplayed; views of life, casual. For most of them, like Stonewall's new father, who did not frequent the pubs unless driven by a louder-than-usual row indoors, the occasion was a mixed relief. All of them made it look as if they had met by accident. When they dispersed, they did not arrange to meet again, same place, same time. That would have been some kind of admission, as if they needed one another. Which they did, but could not say.

The overgrown village of Merton on Sea boasted a population of eight thousand, doubling in summer. The high street formed the undulating backbone of the village, flanked by alleys and uneven cottages spreading out like crooked limbs. The main thoroughfare, too narrow for the dustbin van, wound uphill away from the quay into an almost elegant square surrounding a green. Here, where the merchants in wool and grain had lived a century before, the houses were large and ponderous, governed by the Crown, Merton's only hotel. The town-cum-village, large enough to form a metropolis on this underpopulated length of the flat East Coast, fizzled out further inland beyond the council estate and the church, the last cottages giving way to rich farmland with never a hill in sight.

1

Merton was a conurbation which had grown on trade and fishing, been eclipsed and grown again without the benefit of planners or preservers, so that the visitor's abiding memory was one of obstinacy rather than beauty, haphazard charm rather than style. If Merton had aspirations, they were humble, a desire for consistency rather than change, an understated pride which could never see the point in the newfangled, a sense of order which would always defy chaos and a self-sufficiency made necessary by isolation. The inhabitants were ruled by good sense, kept promises to one another, did not mind their own business and only fleeced the holiday-makers enough to make a modest living. They neither noticed nor cared how the blatant vulgarity of the quay's front marred the Victorian splendour of the rear enough to deter any serious follower of taste. The people who lived in Merton liked it the way it was.

So did the holiday-makers and holiday-home owners. Those of lesser luck or affluence, unable to face the forest of bed-and-breakfast signs, where the landladies made no concession to foreign habits, rented a caravan on the camp site a mile from town, reached on foot by the raised causeway along the sea defences. This path, hiding the road on the landward side, ran alongside the wide inlet which led to the busy public beach, the lifeboat station, the pine woods and the miles of unadulterated sand which stretched west. Sometimes, where sea joined inlet, seals would play. There were beach huts, mostly old and crooked, flanking the woods.

At high tide, Merton became part of the sea. The inlet filled with water deep enough for the passage of small steamers which occasionally anchored, along with fishing vessels and an increasing number of pleasure craft of the less expensive variety, hobby boats rather than yachts, in keeping with Merton's obdurate lack of style. At low tide, the view altered dramatically. Gazing seaward from outside the amusement arcade, there was nothing beyond the car park but boats listing sideways and sand banks topped with reluctant vegetation in a vista of browny-green land, full of hidden detail invisible to the eye. People parked on the quayside car park, peered down at the moored boats, saw the same flat view to the east, and ate hamburgers with onions from the arcade or fish and chips from one of three sources. In July it was something to do. Merton's entertainments were not otherwise sophisticated.

The men on the quay on Sunday mornings gathered thus only in summer: in winter you could scarcely stand out there. Male gossip was more restrained than the female kind, and only the youngest men ever dared venture a remark on the girls passing by, reserving any unkindness for strangers only. Stonewall's stepfather never felt quite comfortable standing there on the edge of the water, particularly if the tide was down and all that stretched into view was the peculiarly inviting, earth-and-sand-smelling channels leading out to the sea. He never stood there without thinking of himself as a kind of pretender, a man who kept secrets. When one of the lads gave a low wolf-whistle, he could only quiver with embarrassment, think of the woman he had watched, two years before, drunk and scarred, staggering along on her unsteady way out for a morning walk down the creeks. Or rather, he had not watched; the boy with him, little Stonewall, had watched, pointed, sniggered and been cuffed gently round the ear for his rudeness. They had watched her go down the high street, bypassing the medical centre although she looked as though she could use a doctor, then seen her grinning at her own hideous reflection, first in the shop windows, then in the water. The man still shuffled when he thought of that, shuddered when he thought of what happened next after they'd gone out

in the boat. Poor Stonewall had hated the water; he
had to be forced to learn because no-one who lived
as close to it as they did could afford to shy away.

'Nice day for it,' one of the men would always remark, never specifying further and never being
asked, while Stonewall's stepfather wished that the
sea would come back and obscure the vision of his
mind's eye. First that woman with her cloud of red
hair, Mrs Tysall he had later learned, looking so
drunk and so tired, teetering out over the muddy sand
in her unsuitable shoes, a real townie; and then the
same woman, without shoes and without life, lying
with her hands twisted in the sea heather up at the far
end of the creeks, her mouth full of sand, her red hair
damp and matted, a smell beginning to rise from her,
still mainly the smell of the sea, which reminded him
of sex. Saw her living one day, found her dead the
next when out on another outing with that miserable
kid, Stonewall, that parcel of skinny, asthmatic baggage which came alongside his beautiful widowed
mum, and had to be taught to understand the tide.
    Stonewall would scream whenever he was put in a
boat and rowed up the creeks to find a place where the
water formed safe and shallow pools, but once there,
the child changed tack completely and became calm,
ready to play and sing to himself for hours, leaving
the man he would not yet call Dad free to dig for the
lugworms he needed for bait. The relief when Stonewall stopped crying was always tremendous. The crying, a breathless keening, always made his stepfather
sick. If he did not get this boy right, the whole edifice
of his marriage would crumble, he knew it like he
knew the time of day and he knew these creeks. Silence down here, a sense of contentment and the brink
of a breakthrough with the boy; peace.
    Until he had turned to one side, seen that red-haired
lump with her long brown legs spread and her heavy

skirt plastered with mud. Two years of Sundays had passed and he could still feel the panic now, like a mouthful of salt water. Remembered himself thinking, The silly bitch, how could she do this to a boy? Lying there, obscene in death, her head half embedded in the bank, her hands raised above, twisted into the heather as if to anchor herself there. Waiting for a child to find her and begin the screaming nightmares all over again.

No Merton-born man travelled ill-equipped and, besides, he had come prepared to dig for bait. Inside fifteen furious minutes, using his spade and closing his ears to the sound of sloppy sand on dead flesh, he had buried her, right there in the depths of the bank, just before the boy came back from the pool. He had meant no harm, he had meant for the best. Let someone else find her; someone unburdened by an hysterical child and a heavily pregnant wife. Let the tide hide this red-haired bitch here until tomorrow when he was at work and the boy was safe. Let it hide her, preferably for ever.

From that day on, though, Stonewall had stopped his screaming, took to the creeks like a duck. It seemed that some god somewhere approved.

'Found another body, they did, so I heard, off Stookey,' one of the men said, covering a gap in conversation, while a thin thread of smoke from his cigarette drifted upwards. Stonewall's dad jangled the coins in his pockets to hide his own discomfiture. The friendly coast yielded three or four bodies a year, swept from God knows where. Mostly men, overboard from a tramp steamer, big men, rarely identified, the homeless of the sea. A corpse was always a matter of remark, but hardly news any more and never in front of the children. Sometimes it was difficult to tell how long a man had been in the water or rotting in the sand where they were found. Mrs

Charles Tysall had taken a whole year to surface, as
far as anyone knew. Unlike the indigent sailors, she
had been identified, her death the subject of specula-
tion, her strange reappearance the stuff of long,
public-house and hairdressing-shop debate. Stonewall's stepfather had never said a thing: he had been
either too wise or too shocked. A body was only a
body. He had his own kin to look after.

The guilt only lingered on the Sabbath, when he
thought of that woman's husband coming back to look
at her after she was found. Stricken by grief, walking
out over the sands to see where she had lain, never
coming back. She would have been a beautiful woman
once, before she had acquired that dreadful, lacerated
face. Someone must have loved her, ached for her,
yearned for her in the year she had lain buried before
the freak storm broke the bank and sicked her up.

That Charles Tysall had indeed loved her in his
vile obsessive way, was something his wife Elisabeth
had never doubted, but the nature of the love had
been as cruel as the tide, requiring the same complete
possession of everything it touched, punishing insub-
ordination with violence. She had played for attention, misunderstood the nature of the madness,
flaunted her red hair and her own perfection. Therefore, in complete accordance with his own logic, it
had been entirely justifiable to beat her into submis-
sion, beginning with the face.

The men on the quay knew nothing of this, then or
now. Nor what Elisabeth had thought while lying
there with her hands self-imprisoned among the
heather, waiting for the pills and the gin to work and
hoping this would be revenge on him, and then,
thinking too late, of what she might have left. Thinking of how she should not be doing this, dying without a whimper or a warning. It was so unfair to
whoever followed. She, who had never been a friend
to women, felt suddenly and sharply for her own

kind, knew with terrible certainty what she had begun. Without her, Charles would simply find another obsession, some other red-haired pet to torment. Elisabeth murmured a prayer for her successor, let the thought of her slide away, closed her eyes, waited for the sea, slipped at last into the oblivion she had craved for days. Waited for the tide and never felt it.

A body was only a body, the man on the quay thought again. Since that woman had died, and then punished him by coming back, he had acquired twins and his wife was pregnant again. It was only because he so loved his own woman that he felt guilt for that other husband. The guilt was wasted, had he known. As the sea had swept over the slumbering form of Elisabeth Tysall, her husband Charles lay on a couch in their extravagant London home, reading his favourite poet, Browning, remembering his wife in the days when she was perfectly pure, obedient and good,

> . . . Happy and proud; at last I knew
> Porphyria worshipped me: surprise
> Made my heart swell, and still it grew . . .

I love you, my Porphyria, he had told himself. Did you not know? Come back, before I find another.

One death alters nothing and everything. As Elisabeth Tysall's hair floated out beneath the water, the erstwhile landlord of her holiday cottage felt the first intimations of mortality. In a large house half a mile beyond the end of the quay in the opposite direction from the public beach, Mr Henry Pardoe, entrepreneur, self-made man of frugal habits and large pretensions, played Scrabble with his timid little wife and found, to his amazement, he enjoyed it. She let him win, of course, something he half realized but blocked the full knowledge. He rubbed his chest where the faint, but nagging pain was a constant re-

minder to him to make a will sooner rather than later,
although he did not seriously believe in death as a
concept and was damned if he'd pay that old rogue
Ernest Matthewson his London rates the way he had
always done in the past. Daylight robbery. Mouse
would help him draft a will. He looked at her faded
prettiness with affection.

Life went on as the hungry tide came back through
the channels and covered the earth. The coastline
shifted with the seasons, flooded at high tide, drained
by the low. Which meant that everything was the
same, no matter who lived and died.

The men on the quay broke ranks. They made la-
conic farewells, drifted indoors for the innocent pleasure of the Sunday meal.

CHAPTER ONE

Malcolm Cook, advocate for the Crown, legal if cynical vigilante against injustice, was dark, lean, thirty-five. The only weight he carried was a surfeit of knowledge. He knew more about man's inhumanity to man, and rather less about domestic harmony, than he liked. While his work was merely the reflection of human perfidy, his own reflection was something he tried to avoid. An aversion to mirrors often sent him out of doors wearing odd socks.

This morning he could not ignore his own image as he shaved, and as usual, felt himself flinching. A mirror was a cruel object. The contrast between himself as he had been before, a grossly fat clown of a man, and the thing he was now, streamlined by his own efforts into the shape of a marathon runner, was a sight which occasionally amused him. He would shake his head, smiling, expecting the old self to return, knowing the new one was merely a figment which did not fit the description of handsome, however often it was applied. These days, the contrast he saw in his own expression was more immediate. He looked old and worried, like his adoptive father in the throes of illness. The comparison between this and the person who sang through his morning ablutions was one which wounded him. He was losing something, and with it, all his fragile self-esteem. It felt like losing his teeth.

'Get down, you silly girl,' he muttered without

taking his eyes away from the mirror. At least the
dog, with her constant need to be close, never wavered in her affections, followed him from bedroom
to bathroom like a silky, red shadow, so grateful for
the sight of him she could not stay away. It did not
do to make comparisons between this affectionate
creature and Sarah, or to hope the gratitude of the
one would inspire the same devotion in the other, but
he made the comparison all the same with rueful
humour and a slap to his own wrist. After all, he had
saved them both. A pair of red-haired beauties, both
in need of a champion.

Who looks after me? Malcolm thought with a sudden wave of self-pity, which he suppressed only
when he saw to his horror how his eyes filled with
tears in the privacy of the bathroom. Quite right to
avoid mirrors: he had always been too emotional for
a man, even a fat man. His father, Ernest Matthewson, had said so. Ernest had exercised the right to
speak his mind since the day he had married Malcolm's mother and become the benign but tyrannical
influence he was. Strange how roles altered themselves when no-one was looking. Who looked after
whom these days was a moot point. Ernest Matthewson, senior partner, a man of old-fashioned principles
and terrifying, irrational loyalty to clients of the firm,
no matter how frightful they were, was also the indulgent employer of Malcolm's Sarah, but his pow-
ers had waned into frail irascibility in the last twelve
months. Anyone serving a client like Charles Tysall
deserved to be ill.

Malcolm snorted, waving his hand at the mirror.
There was nothing to envy about his father's career.
Ernest had the sumptuous office and the salary to
match, but Malcolm felt he had a certain moral ad-
vantage. It was not one which could ever make him
oblivious to Ernest's good opinion. Malcolm loved
Ernest, Ernest loved Malcolm; they were stuck with

it, even if they rowed like enemies to hide an attachment they simply could not avoid.

He might despise my relative poverty, Malcolm thought, but at least I am licensed to tell the truth. And at least I can sneak my dog into my office without anyone worrying about the furnishings.

Nor did he have to care today about the fact that it was too late and getting later, and he did not give a damn. The dog's lead evaded detection. Must be in Sarah's flat, that's where it was; she had been the last to walk the beast. Malcolm stroked the spaniel's silky head, felt the warmth behind the ears, the thump of her tail. At least there was some consistency in his life.

They walked downstairs from his spacious attic in the huge Victorian terrace on the side of the park, round to the front door, inside with the key and up one floor to another door where a small brass plate announced 'Sarah Fortune'. Somehow in the intervening year, they had lived between the two places, tending more towards his, especially in the early days. That was during the time when her flat was being cleared up, to put it mildly. The contrast between then and now hit him again as he opened the door. There was a new mirror, winking at the end of the hall, new carpet on the floor, a mushroom colour in a hall lined with pictures, all slightly dusty. He could never forget what had happened here, even on a fine morning like this when the sunlight sanitized the memory.

The trust of the dog was infinite. She never growled on crossing the threshold: it was Malcolm who did that. She should have murmured at least, he thought resentfully; she was badly hurt in here, but then she has nothing of which to be ashamed. She does not suppress memory; she simply forgets everything but the next meal. It was a knack Sarah should learn too.

There were a few new marks on the clean paint by the kitchen door. Spilt coffee, tribute to Sarah's domestic carelessness, at odds with her flair for making things beautiful, translating junk into elegance. Coffee stains, or wine, not blood. Malcolm was beginning to understand that he might be stuck with the memory of the blood, however much he encouraged it to fade. Each time he came here he felt as if he was retracing his own fleeting steps, following the dog up to this apartment where she had led him twelve months ago, inspired by her mischievous curiosity. Disobedient dog, running amok at the end of a late-night run, cannoning into the insecure front door, up the stairs, leaving him no choice but to follow, cursing her.

No, don't remember it. Memories were for old men. Past accidents, old horrors, should be recognized, of course, put into the scheme of things so that life could continue as soon as possible. Too much analysis only increased the weight of the baggage and both he and Sarah carried plenty of that already. Malcolm sighed, resigned to a mental ritual. OK, run through the facts on record, including those which embarrassed him personally, as if explaining them briefly to a stranger, then put them back on the shelf where they belonged. It was his way of dealing with it. So. Charles Tysall, Dad's super-rich handsome bastard of a client, got involved with Sarah, whom he met through Dad's firm. No, correction, not involved, obsessed. Had this fixation, see, with red hair. Sarah gives him the cold-shoulder, so he breaks in here one night, waits for her. There is a fight in which a large mirror is broken. Sarah falls on the glass, has lots of nasty little injuries all over, though not on her face, God knows how. Led by his daft dog, he, Malcolm, had intervened and pursued the attacker out into the park, and this was the bit he most loathed to recall. Bringing the man down like a Rottweiler after cattle, hitting him far too hard and too long for the purpose, and, oddly, enjoying it. Malcolm hated violence, had never known he was so capable of it.

It had been a cruel way to bring Sarah into his life, he would concede for the record, but since he loved her with every ounce of his sinewy frame, the means of this savage introduction were less important than the ends.

The dog's lead was in the kitchen. Malcolm found it and then took a quick tour of the rooms, guilty again, looking for the negative, for some signs that she was not packing up and leaving. She could not do that now, not with all the exclusive knowledge which bound them together. Knowledge of Charles Tysall, not only as that rich and privileged business man-thief, whom Malcolm had pursued with all the futility of the law long before it was made apparent to Sarah what else he was. Bugger the past. It was the future Malcolm wanted.

The dog froze at Malcolm's flank, leaning against him. Red hairs from her long coat already decorated the trousers of his suit. Footsteps, upstairs in the flat above, harmless, unhurried. They both relaxed. The dog shook herself; he felt inclined to copy. Dog lived in the present; so should they all. Charles Tysall was dead. He might have mutilated his own wife and driven her to suicide, then turned his attentions to Sarah, but now he was dead. Dead as an old potato chip.

That was all right, then. Perhaps all himself and Sarah needed was a holiday. Brisk sea air, that sort of thing.

I am only an ordinary man, Malcolm told himself. An ordinary man who tries to be decent and honourable. I should not have memories like this, complications like this. I only want to love and be loved.

Back outside in the sunshine of summer, crossing the park to the road, he made himself think of sea air, but his thoughts only shifted back. That was the problem with reliving memory, even in the tidy way he did: it infected everything, like rancid oil in cooking. He could not think of sun, sea and sand without thinking back to Charles. How the man who was the closest thing to evil he had ever encountered went on being so, even in death. Only Charles Tysall, moving unit of harm, could choose to despoil some innocent seaside resort by committing suicide in it, just as his wife had done. Had the man never heard of preservation?

Life, Malcolm thought to himself, is a bitch. If he could ever have thought of Sarah as a bitch, it would be easier.

Watching the dog lolloping away, he began to laugh. The laughter was the result of suddenly seeing himself introducing Sarah to others. This is my wife Sarah. We met in the hall, beneath the mirror, through an extraordinary set of coincidences you would find impossible to believe and so do I.

The word 'wife' stuck in his throat. He wanted to be a husband; take this wonderful creature and make an honest woman of her. Laughter ceased. Oh yes, he told himself, you can lead a dream to water, but you cannot make it drink.

Sarah Fortune had been taught by her mother never to complain. She had also been warned that there was an element of indecency in her nature; that her energy was a nuisance and that a woman's lot was not happy. Parental ambition had amounted to a kind of Calvinism, a constant push in the direction of career over frivolity which dictated that Sarah keep her nose to the grindstone and her red hair in ugly plaits until she was qualified to earn a living. With the double standard of a mother, Sarah's had still wanted her daughters wed, the sooner the better; wanted them free but still suppressed, clever but stupid, independent but biddable. By damning with faint praise, she nurtured in Sarah a profound sense of worthlessness which secured obedience to all expectations. The girl passed examinations, became a lawyer, acquired another as a husband and everything seemed well, until the point when he died behind the wheel of his car, distracted by recent sex, not with Miss Fortune but her sister. He was a lazy opportunist who went for the nearest. In one fell swoop, red-haired Sarah lost trust, a spouse, a sibling and all her mother's values, as well as the foetus she carried at the time.

After a period of recovery in which she remained, as always, a reluctant but efficient professional, she set about shedding the work ethic as easily as she shed her clothes, an exercise she could complete with incredible speed and efficiency. Miss Fortune recognized no moral principles other than thou shalt be kind, few instincts which were not positive and no incontrovertible fact other than that men always leave in the end.

She retained that bitter sense of worthlessness, saw all the accidents of her life as a reflection of it. Sarah could no more believe that someone truly loved her than she could have flown over the moon. She saw sex as an enjoyable necessity, love as a variety of claustrophobia, a fine deceit, a trap. She was warm as fire, generous to a fault, occasionally as cold as ice. She took nothing for granted.

Miss Fortune, at thirty-three, was contemplating the dreaded moment of saying goodbye to Malcolm Cook for a number of reasons which made eminent sense in the middle of the night, rather less in the bright sunlight of a July morning. He had loved her from afar for two years, at closer quarters for one, saved her life and continued to offer the kind of single-minded devotion he himself received from his dog. He was fuller of natural goodness than a bowl of cornflakes and it drove Sarah beyond distraction. For one, she knew she wasn't worthy of that; for two, she did not want to receive what she knew she could not give; for three, he would be better off without her; fourthly, she was already too far involved with his family; fifth, she felt like a prisoner and was not the stuff of a good wife.

These were the reasons she counted on her fingers as she reversed her car into the wall and heard the back wing crunch against concrete. Each reason had an element of truth. Malcolm would demolish them like a row of ninepins, argue with the full force of his finer feelings and his enlightened compassion. Finally, he might threaten her with ownership of the dog. Sarah was feeling sufficiently liberated by the satisfying sound of mashed metal to recover her sense of humour. Perhaps that was all she wanted in the first place, not a lover who lived in the same building, whose father was her employer, but a dog.

The car was easily the flashiest of Sarah's possessions, a misguided bonus from the firm to keep her happy. The engine leapt into willing life at the merest touch, rather like Malcolm. From the outside it looked as if things had fallen into her lap. Which they had in the last year, with such crushing weight she reminded herself of a shopping trolley and it made the same sense as giving the world tour to a small, red squirrel.

Ernest Matthewson, close to retirement, inhabited a huge office decorated by his wife, which was why he could not get rid of all the humming birds climbing up the blinds and fluttering amongst the fabric of the chairs which were intended to make him feel thoroughly comfortable, a reminder of how he lived at home. Cushioned, catered for, resplendent, like a pasha on a throne, with a loving woman who bashed the heart and the ulcer by alternate feeding and starving of same. He considered the dreams of slender youth, currently advanced to closeted luxury, weight control, client accounts, computers, goodwill, diplomacy and language. Sarah Fortune had been his choice: he had interviewed her years since, when she was freshly widowed, but he couldn't pretend she was partnership material, not in today's grey world. She was also the girl his wife favoured as daughter-in-law.

'I disagree,' he said aloud, banging the desk, wincing. 'All right, ALL RIGHT! I still disagree!'

So: Sarah may well have turned his fat and isolated stepson into some semblance of a human being and brought him back into the fold, but one look at the child was enough to show the liaison would be a disaster. Women envied, youths simpered, clients salivated at the sight of Sarah, and although Ernest, out of respect to his age and his fragile health, did not follow suit, he considered his protégée as a jewel beyond price who belonged, for safety's sake, locked inside a watch. He also loved her dearly in a manner which made him feel only slightly treacherous for hoping she would go away, even though a morning when her feet went by his office without pausing was a bleak day indeed. Having made his announcements to an empty room, Ernest listened.

She usually fell at the bottom step opposite his door, where the bad carpet curled against the good leading away from where important clients trod in quality shoes. The worn patch caught the headlong rush of her steps whenever she was blinded by the armful of flowers for her room and the minuscule briefcase containing some pretence of overnight work. As she tripped, she swore loudly. The sound of absent-minded obscenities made Ernest curl with laughter. He did not like to think what they did for his errant son.

'Oh shit a fucking brick. Not again.' She spoke it
in her low, musical voice, like a person reciting poetry. Ernest flung open his door, pretending to be
angry, terrified in case she should be gone.

'What's wrong with you, woman? You do that every time and you always swear. I don't know. What's
the matter with your vocabulary?'

'What's wrong with your carpet, more to the
point? Does this too, every time. I've just put a dent
in the company car, nobody else's motor involved,
you understand. Just some fucking concrete pillar.'
She was standing there, grinning like a recently fed
cat with half-clean paws, every inch of her unsuitable
for the office of a solicitor of the supreme court,
more like a bouncer at the Hippodrome if only she
wasn't so tiny and so highly coloured. The colour
came from the freckled skin and the brilliant red hair.
No-one could say she dressed like a siren, in a perfect camel-brown dress, but there was something
about that great, wide belt of soft, tan leather which
made her look as edible as the bacon sandwich she
proffered in his direction, shrouded in greasy paper,
the whole gift presented with a grin.

'Yours,' she said. 'Oh, yes, and the racing pages.
How's things?'

Ernest relaxed. His large stomach growled and
sagged like a parachute landing. Sarah always made
a man mindful of his girth, first to suck it in, then to
let it out in glorious relaxation.

'Terrible,' he said. 'Awful, really. Come in. I've
got a case for you. Should take you out of London
for the summer. Come in.' The words came out of
his mouth before he could stop them and he turned
away abruptly, winded by the devilish inspiration
which had been incubating for many days and only
now came into words. It was like delivering a baby
with a knife. He was saddened too, at this instinctive
combination of wanting her out of the way while

knowing he would miss her. There was something about the effect she had had on their late client, Charles Tysall, to say nothing of his stepson, her ability to make strong men putty, along with something else which smacked of love and a profound suspicion.

'Only if you want,' he added hurriedly, sitting to hide his confusion, lunging towards the bacon sandwich. Monday was always one of Mrs Matthewson's sensible days, Fridays were better.

'I'm only suggesting you leave for a while to save me from this,' Ernest mumbled with his mouth full, feeling the decadent bacon grease creep down his chin. 'You're not good for my insides.'

'The bread's wholemeal,' said Sarah, tranquilly, as if that made all the difference. 'Full of fibre.' She never had believed in diet, ate anything which was not moving. Looked at him with that complete acceptance she granted the human race. What she thought behind those great big eyes, he never questioned for fear of being told. Looking at his fidgeting, she thought how it was just as well that she and Malcolm and Malcolm's lovely mother had conspired to subvert Ernest's post bag and save him from the worst demands, as well as the hateful revelations, of his clients. Also, how she and Malcolm had managed to excuse her absence last year by saying she had suffered an accident. She was a gifted liar. Making him ooh! and aghh! about the effects of a broken windscreen had been far better for his explosive ulcer and fragile heart than telling him the truth about a client. Charles Tysall had done enough damage, most of it still unmended. Some people needed the truth. Others needed saving from their own beliefs that all clients were good chaps. Ernest was one of the latter. He might not have been once, but now his health made him so.

'Tell me about this case, then. I need amusement.'

'Very important client,' Ernest mumbled again.

'It can't be, or you wouldn't be sending me.'

Ernest sighed. 'Important by my standards, not by those of the partnership. Clients I've had for a long time.' He meant clients not eligible for the seduction of his junior partners, who rubbed grey-suited shoulders with bankers and accountants, captains of industry and Government officials, drinking mineral water at lunch-time, for God's sake, not a human being among them. Ernest was well aware of being slightly redundant in the new generation, retained for the weight of his age and the number of nasty facts he knew about others, but Sarah had no chance. She was tolerated in the attics of the low-earning litigation department because someone had to do the odds and ends. The someone was preferably a woman without ambition. No partner would miss her for the summer. None of them guessed how valuable she was.

'Well, if these clients are important to you, I'll make them important to me. Why out of town? When do I go? And what nasty thing do you want me to do?'

Ernest nearly fell out of his chair. For an idea with such a difficult, if spontaneous conception, this was all growing suspiciously fast. Not that she was usually unamenable to suggestion; the passivity hid the obstinacy of a mule, just like her smile hid depths of despair and a strange knowledge beyond her years, touching the parts other women did not reach. Too late, Ernest remembered Charles Tysall and where he had died.

'A family estate,' he began, 'needs sorting out. By the sea. You're always saying you like the sea.'

'I know nothing about probate. Or the sea.'

'What's that got to do with anything? Look, we're only talking about a family who need their heads knocking together. Just stick around, work out what they want, get a draft agreement on who should have what . . . the boffins and the Court of Protection can do the rest.'

Sarah dusted crumbs off her skirt. Ernest so admired the way she ate, like a delicate wolf.

'I haven't got the faintest idea what you're talking about. You'd better explain,' she said. He took a deep breath, prepared to mix fact with fiction in order to make the prospect more appealing.

'Large house in the country, right? No, not an ancestral mansion, but plenty of land, and . . . no, I'm not going to tell you why the estate is as big as it is. You can let that titillate the imagination and find out for yourself. It needs an entirely fresh mind, so the less you know the better. Family consists of two sons, one daughter, eighteen to thirty-four, I think, all of them at war. Why? Dad died two years ago, left the whole caboodle to his wife for life, and then,' he rummaged on the desk, flicked the pages of a grease-stained photocopy, '. . . I quote, "to all my children in whatever shares my wife should decide". Perfectly poisonous will; he should have asked me to draft it, ungrateful sod. I did everything else. He must have been out of his mind.'

'And was he?'

'Probably, but not provably. The point is, his wife is. Off her rocker, barmy, barking, out of her tree.' He liked to mix metaphors. 'She's never going to be in a position to make a valid will. If she dies intestate, disaster. Terrible tax implications. The children aren't exactly carving each other up, I think they have straws between their teeth, or would it be sand? Needs an outside mind to construct an acceptable arrangement, working out who'll get what and when. Then they can run their lives peacefully until the old lady pops her clogs and even then, the transition will be easy.'

Sarah rose gracefully. 'You need an estate planner, not me,' she said.

'I need a litigation expert who knows how to make people avoid litigation. I think you've got to be on the spot, hopeless otherwise. They'll put you up, always a spare cottage, they rent them out, saves expenses.' He was full of admiration for himself: everything dovetailed so neatly without him thinking at all. In fact, he rarely indulged deep thought.

She was standing over his desk, reached forward and pinched his cheek.

'Wake up, Ernest, will you? This is me, Sarah. You must detest these clients, or you wouldn't consider foisting me on them simply because you would like me to be a hundred miles away from Malcolm.'

'Sarah, nothing was further . . .' He was blushing like a schoolboy caught smoking in the lavatory, and she was smiling like an indulgent teacher who was going to forgive him.

'Nothing was closer to your mind, Ernest dear. Don't worry about it, please, but don't treat me like a fool. I may not deserve much, but I deserve better than that. Of course you're right to think I'm all wrong for Malcolm in the long run. I know that; he doesn't. Yet. It may take him some time. Now, do we understand one another?'

He could have wept. She sat down again.

'Don't fret, Uncle Ernest, please don't. Worry's infinitely worse for the ulcer than a bacon sandwich.' She looked at the grease-stained photocopy of a badly typed will. 'But is sending me to this particular part of East Anglia a clause in the master plan? Same village, I see, where Charles Tysall walked off and drowned, mimicking the actions of his wife the year before. You want to punish me or something?'

'No, no, I promise you . . . Sarah, I swear!'

'You've just told me not to do that. I believe you, but if you'll excuse the pun, I thought you might have wanted me to lay the odd ghost.'

* * *

Malcolm Cook did not have his stepfather's shrewd business acumen, nor did he think his life was ruined by the omission. He considered that less pay for more enlightenment was a good bargain. As for the rest of his limitless kindness, he had learned his compassion as well as his tolerance on the sharp learning curve of his own loneliness. The metamorphosis from laughable clown to thin athlete also made him an incurable optimist, most of the time, although not on this particular evening. 'You don't know anything about women,' Ernest had warned him, a truism liberally applied to the whole male sex, but one which was, in his case, less accurate than usual. Malcolm's former fatness had only preserved a habit of celibacy, not innocence, making him a confidant rather than a practitioner, without rendering him naïve. So had childhood illness. Even a once-fat man, helplessly in love and struggling to disguise it, knows when he is being abandoned.

There was no point in going back over old ground trying to work out where one or the other had failed, no point arguing; no purpose in analysing performance and saying 'if only'. He knew you cannot make a person stay if they want to go any more than you can make a tiger a truly tame beast, and with Sarah the analogy was sound since she had that sleekness, with none of the ability to maul or scratch. Nothing had been said, neither in her flat (where she hid her shopping from him), nor in his, where he had nursed her more than a little following the ministrations of obsessive Charles Tysall. They had survived a hot summer of healing wounds, a companionable winter of hot toddies, laughter and warm blankets and he had thought she was his for ever.

He should have known how no man is allowed to assume anything. In the spring, he could feel her straining the leash, like the dog guided away from the daffodils. He could feel that numbness of loss from the moment of realization when he began vainly arming himself. He must not carp, he must not complain, he must not. He could never go back to what he was before and if he loved her, he must let her go with grace, make himself run into the distance without complaint.

'Where the hell have you been?' he said peevishly as she let herself in at eight o'clock. So much for grace. Grace is a virtue, virtue is a grace, Grace is a dirty girl who will not wash her face.

'Your father sent us some wine,' she said, humbly. 'He and I went out for a drink.'

There was a pause when both of them turned to the task in hand, she to taking off her jacket and making a fuss of the dog whose greetings took precedence over all other formalities, he to watching rice boil, while both privately, desperately considered whether they could get away with another evening of pretending nothing was happening. Ready to eat and fill the air with smells and brittle conversation, drink to cure emotional indigestion, pray that neither would say anything real. She came into the kitchen, followed by dog.

'Your father has a job for me. Norfolk, somewhere.' She was ultra casual, foraging for food. 'So I'll be away.' She shrugged her shoulders as if she had no choice. 'Don't know how long.' Malcolm stirred the rice unnecessarily, hiding his face in the steam.

'That'll suit you fine, won't it? You must have persuaded him. No-one litigates in Norfolk. What does he want you to do, go and dig up Charles Tysall? Pay your last respects?'

'Charles was buried in London. Your father gave me the client's address. You know how vague he is on that subject. I honestly don't think he even registered it was anywhere near ... Old client, he says.'

He turned on her, his face hot, his throat choking and his eyes full of salt and water.

'My own father, who professes to love me, enters the conspiracy! Well, well, well. As if you needed help to escape. You've been detaching yourself from me for three months, only you don't know how to say. Am I right?' He tried to keep his voice light.

'Right.'

'Don't say sorry, will you?' He poured a glass of wine with a shaking hand, then stuck a piece of kitchen roll near his eyes as if it was the heat which troubled him. The day had been long and hot; he was hungry.

'I would say sorry since I mean it, but not if you'd prefer I didn't. Listen, Malcolm, it's nothing you've done or haven't done: I love you and I owe you, but I can't breathe.'

He was an articulate man, a large, kind man who liked to cook, a patron of defenceless animals, a natural lover, and all he wanted to do was hit her. He caught that look of mute terror in her eyes and heard the warning growl of the dog before he knew that one arm was bunching the front of her dress in his fist, while the other arm was raised, ready to inflict the futile blow which would never connect.

Malcolm slumped, let his arms drop to his sides.

'I love you, Sarah,' he said. 'I love you to pieces. I'd never hurt you.'

'I'd better go,' she said, the terror still in her eyes.

'Yes, you'd better. Just go.'

She went with door closing softly behind her, the dog pawing against a panel already ruined with her claws. Malcolm's appetite for anything went with her. The dog slunk back and pressed her wet nose into his groin, waiting for him to be pleased. Instead he pushed her away with his hand so tightly around her muzzle she began to protest and he stroked her instead. Couldn't hit a dog, could have hit a woman, and the mere temptation to violence was a kind of death in anything in which he believed.

It was finished. She had left him ashamed.

Mrs Ernest Matthewson dumped a tray on the table in front of her husband and watched fondly as he struggled from the depths of the plump sofa to stare at it.

'What's this?' he barked.

'Poached cod. With samphire.'

'Samphire? Seaweed?'

'Full of iron, dear. Better than spinach.'

'It looks disgusting. Do I get potato?'

She wagged a finger, roguishly.

'Not today. You've been drinking. Eat it up and I'll get you pudding.'

'And what might that be?'

'Low-fat yoghurt.' He groaned, shot her a murderous look which turned into a smile.

'You remember the Pardoes?' he asked, looking at the seaweed.

'Oh yes. Awful great house on the coast somewhere. A long drive from here. We used to go and see them quite a lot, didn't we? In the days when we had to do that kind of thing.' Mrs Matthewson shuddered. She left home as rarely as possible, did not rue the days when loyalty dictated dreadful social visits to clients.

'Didn't he make his fortune out of socks, or something? Tried to become a country gentleman, didn't know how? All sorts of fads and all sorts of mistresses? Bought half the village he lived in? Vulgar taste?'

Ernest nodded, holding her eyes and taking a long slug of her wine. He did not underestimate his everloving wife, but there were times when she was easier to distract than divert. Reminiscence was the cue.

'I saw that, Ernest. Don't think I didn't. You know,
I can't work out why Jennifer Pardoe put up with all
her husband's playing around.' She glared at him, as
if infidelity was infectious. 'Such tolerance that
woman had, such marvellous, I don't know what,
qualities. Serene, somehow. She was called Mouse,
wasn't she, because she was like one, small and
brownish, pretty, ineffectual little thing, you had to
like her. Sympathize, I mean. No-one took any notice
of her.'

Ernest shuffled and coughed. His wife's memory
always amazed him.

'One son came out good, daughter a bit of a dope,
nice girl, other son, well he was a nasty little thing,
always playing nasty practical jokes. Luck of the
draw. You told me it all came all right in the end,
with Mouse and her husband, didn't you? He had
that gold hair I'm so fond of. He seemed to fall for
her all over again. Then he died. By God, you lot
take it out on us. We damn well earn our pound of
flesh.' She patted her stomach, comfortably.

Ernest cleared his throat, waved his hand and
grasped her glass like a man in need. She did not
protest. He tried to swig with nonchalance, couldn't
quite manage it.

'I'm sending Sarah there. Mouse—was Jennifer
her real name?—well, she's gone mad. Got to get the
estate sorted before she dies too. Sarah's the right
woman to do it.'

Mrs Matthewson lowered the second glass she had
poured while this information was passed with a
vague hesitation, incapable of fooling her for a minute.

'What are you planning, Ernest? Why on earth
send Sarah away from our Malcolm? Someone else
could have gone. You could have sorted it all out
from here. Who'll cook his meals?'

'Good God, woman, you don't think Sarah cooks

his meals, do you?' he roared, putting into his voice all his own guilt and his dislike of the fish.

'She does other things, then,' said Mrs Matthewson defensively. Ernest sniggered.

'I'll bet she does.'

'That's enough, Ernest.' His bark was worse than hers, but not as bad as her bite. She threw back her wine as if it was water, allowing the silence of her disapproval to sink in. After a pause, she went on.

'You don't know anything about Sarah and Malcolm. You know much less than me. Mind you, he always tells me everything's fine. Such a liar, that boy. I suppose he takes after you. Send her away? You must be out of your mind—'

'Sarah will sort out the Pardoes,' Ernest interrupted more firmly, recognizing a mutual capacity to lie. 'She's a catalyst, she analyses dreams. And,' Ernest continued as if his wife had never spoken, 'she'll never marry our boy, you know. Never in a million years. No grandchildren there.' This was a cunning move.

'How do you know?' she wailed. 'She led him out of the wilderness and she loves him too, in her own way. You just can't bear the fact she knows too much about you. And the wretched clients. Oh Ernest, what have you done? What have you done?'

'I've done nothing!' he shouted. 'She wanted to go! She wants the sea!'

She hesitated for a full minute.

'Charles Tysall's dead, isn't he?'

He lost his rag and his skin went red.

'Of course he is! Dead for a year! Wife dead for two, though it took them a year to find her. What more do you want, woman? Sarah Fortune's as strong as an ox.'

She held her peace.

* * *

Sarah had long since bought the new mirror for the hall of her flat. Like the old, it caught the reflection of herself as she entered, greeted her at the end of the corridor on to which the door opened, revealed her with the cunning of an old enemy. The replacement of the mirror was supposed to be therapy, a positive step towards putting things back the way they were before the former mirror was broken. A gesture to prove it was not all her own fault, as everything else was. Sarah Fortune knew she was beyond redemption. Leaning out of the window with her arms on the wrought-iron balcony, staring into the night, imagining the sound of the sea and the wind in the trees, waiting for thunder, tears and some sensation of liberation, she was feeling nothing, apart from a desire to run back up to his flat, demand entry and say, I didn't mean that, can we just go on as before? An impulse so overpowering she had found herself halfway there, twice. Then crept back, regretting as much as anything the failure to explain, the sheer cowardice. But if she had said, It isn't as if I don't love you, as well as revere everything about you, he would have laughed and said, How can you love and leave at the same time? And she would say, Because I cannot be what you want me to be and in the end you would hate me for that.

He did not imprison; he was too kind. At least not with stone walls or shackles, only with constancy; the terrible patience of waiting for her to arrive and the unspoken denial of what she had been and what she was. She saw him come out of the big front door at midnight, dressed in a track suit, the dog alongside. Jogging away across the park, running for company, his nightly ritual. One lover, the best and most honest of them all, padding across the brown grass, back into his world. And she to hers.

Only if she put her hands very firmly over her

own ears, could she conjure up the remembrance of dreams, the instincts of courage, and the sound of the sea.

CHAPTER TWO

There was no fence to separate the small figure of Stonewall Jones from the scrubby garden into which he stared, or from the greenish, mud-coloured land which stretched from behind his thin back into the distant strip of gold which meant the sea. From his small height, he could see everything he wanted. When he was as still as now, he merged with any landscape, a colourless little boy, whose pale orange hair corresponded with the freckles all over his skin and the eyes which seemed merely to reflect, without any shade of their own. Stonewall suited his nickname. Others were called Jack or John and came to fit a more aggressive mould even at eleven years old, but Stonewall blended effortlessly into ageless scenery as a born observer. No-one noticed him at home any more either. He had once been the apple of his mother's eye, but that was when he was a baby. She had new babies now and there was no room. He was good for nothing but hanging round in school holidays, coming up here with the bait he dug twice weekly for Edward Pardoe and which he had just delivered to the kitchen at the back.

'Baah,' he breathed. 'Kchoo, coo, coo.'

Stonewall desperately wanted to be loved, even though his own habits of silence discouraged affection. There was no way to express his own love for the sheep in the garden except by making a sound like a pigeon. Birds he could magic from the skies,

31

lugworms from the sea, but none of it helped a boy who was looking for a dog. Sal had never behaved; she had been a russet-coloured flirt, skittish as a sand piper, which was why she could have been spirited away so easily by a thief. Stonewall was quietly craving possession of this placid sheep for something which would love him unreservedly and mutually. He also liked the house, simply because it was more than half a mile from all other houses and looked as if the inside was big enough to swing several cats.

Not that he would have dreamt of such barbaric methods of measuring space since animals of all kinds, not only dogs, had the effect of melting his bones. His own dog had been given to him to act as a constant companion, keep him safe in his wanderings and make him more forthcoming. The failure of the latter purpose, and the presence of baby twins gave some explanation as to why he had not been encouraged to weep for her loss in that small, cramped and shrill-voiced cottage where a dog had been a luxury and everyone encouraged him to get lost. It was not as though they did not care, he simply felt he took up too much space. He supposed they would let him have another, but he couldn't think of that, yet. A sheep with twisted horns would be less of an obvious substitute for a walk through town. Stonewall smiled widely at the very idea. It could graze on the ever-present washing in the back yard. He could get it a lead.

'You're a silly thing,' he murmured, then shook himself and sighed. Sheep always seemed so content. The breeze made his hair stand on end. He was not bored on an idle day like this, since that was a condition he could not understand when left to himself, but he was a trifle restless. Rick would not play this morning: no-one wanted to go looking for ghosts. They all talked about a white-haired ghost who stole bits and pieces from the dustbins, but no-one, not even Rick, was going to believe his sightings. It was a mistake, Stonewall reflected gravely, to be known for both silence indoors and exaggeration elsewhere.

He turned for one last look at the house. From an upstairs window, an indistinct figure in bright clothes was waving at him. For a moment he was startled, then waved back, putting energy into his arm, twirling and dancing for her benefit, watching her double over in laughter.

That was no ghost. It was mad Mrs Pardoe, always ready for a game. Funny the way she noticed everything, even himself. He thought of cantering across the lawn, telling her he'd left the sodding bait wrapped in newspaper by the back door, and would Edward please pay him some time? Or shouting, Have you seen my dog? He did neither.

On the way home for the sort of dinner he despised (shepherds pie and peas), Stonewall formed the conviction, on slender circumstantial evidence, that the ghost had got his dog, only because it was better than believing she was dead.

He slouched the half mile back into what he thought of as a town.

A fly buzzed at the window. The room was full of half-read books, usually less than half. Edward Pardoe pretended he had read them all, so that he could quote the odd bit of poetry or drama and dazzle the hayseeds with whom his superior artistic tendencies were forced to slum. At his feet was a painting of Joanna. Edward read from his pocket book of Browning.

That's my last Duchess painted on the wall,
Looking as if she were alive . . .

She didn't. His sister's face looked flat and dead, a bad piece of chocolate-box art. Edward threw the book away, kicked the painting under the bed and turned to the doll's house.

'Enter the dreamers,' he murmured, and they obeyed. Inside the stage set on which they performed, each tiny wooden figure could only bend and gesture in strict response to his own fingers. They could sit on chairs with legs crossed, lounge on beds, raise their arms, look as if they were running for their lives. He often played with the doll's house he had made. Other grown-up boys of twenty-two played with steam trains or computer games, depending upon the early taste of their fathers, but Edward was different. He was like the God of Eden who could never quite leave his creatures alone.

'Oh Mummee, Mummee,' he whined, as a little figure held in his hand sat in a sulk with her ballerina skirt sticking straight to expose a wooden crotch and miniature sexless limbs. 'Oh Mummee, I've got a headache and my dress is RUINED!'

'Shut up,' Edward replied. The little figure lay down on her back, knees apart. 'You be careful, Jo,' Edward murmured again.

Crouched over the doll's house, he concentrated on the mummy puppet on a sofa, decked out with ribbons and looking like a dead tin general ready for a funeral. At the dining table, sat the tiny figure of Julian, coated in a little tweed suit. Joanna had made that in the days when she humoured him more. Real men don't sew, she had told him. They may create houses, but they don't sew. Edward had always wondered why not.

'Oh God!' The genuine Joanna, too tall, too broad and shockingly blonde, exploded into the room. 'What are you doing, Ed? It's too hot to be in here.'

'Go away, Jo. Leave me alone.'

'You should have locked the door if you wanted peace.'

He stood with his back to the doll's house, his

wiry frame too small to hide his preoccupation, his
face unable to disguise his pleasure in seeing her.

'Playing!' Joanna said, contemptuous but nervous.
'Playing happy families, I suppose. You'd be better
off painting. Why don't you grow up?'

That was Edward's problem. He refused to grow
up. Wanted to be king of the castle without doing
anything to earn the crown, his father had said scornfully. Joanna always felt slightly guilty about the dis-
parity between their father's treatment of his second
son and only daughter. Edward could never do anything right. She could do nothing wrong.

'What?' he jeered. 'Grow up like you? Progress to
the amusement arcade? Very sophisticated. Completely mature.'

Joanna was not in the mood to take offence.
Edward's teasing lacked any real force, unlike his el-
der brother Julian, who could make her weep with a
mere glance. She flung herself on the bed, began
chewing a length of her blond hair, twitchy and insecure as ever.

'Oh big brother, I'm so miserable. Do you know,
I could feel him trembling when he held my hand?
Now he avoids me. Weeks, not a word. What did I
do? Am I too fat? I want to die.'

'Of course it isn't anything to do with the way you
look. I've told you why, how many times?'

They both knew the subject of Joanna's religious
fervour. The conversation was stale, but it was the
only one which would have tempted her into his
room. Edward shook his head. The room was full of
sighing. He moved to the window through which the
sun streamed, leaned on the sill, looked at the view
he had examined a million times before. The front
garden led down to the narrow road; beyond that, flat
land spread out in a brown plain until the sun caught
a yellow spit of sand. To the left was the village and
beyond that he could just see the ground sloping up

into gentle, pine-clad dunes. On the stillest of nights, the sea was audible; by day, never more than a ribbon flecked with white. The view swam before his eyes in the shimmering heat. In his mind's eye, he planted exotic shrubs into the flatness, ripened the sea lavender which would change the dun colours into purple during August, included a bit of yellow corn and a few dappled deer, added alien palm trees. An artistic eye could always create such an improvement.

It was so much easier to amend the landscape than it was to acquire the skill to portray it in paint. He had tried to learn, but like everything he did, the discipline defeated him. He blamed the teachers. Blaming others for his own laziness was Edward's first and last resort. Silly old farts.

'What gives?' said Joanna, peevishly, changing the subject in deference to his indifference, still chewing her hair like a little girl. He liked her like that.

'You're home early. Don't tell me you've got the sack again.'

Another sigh. Edward had turned back to his doll's house, about to replace the dolls, but the gust of his impatient breathing knocked over the sofa on which Mother sat and sent her tumbling to the floor. She lay with her head in the fireplace.

'No, not yet. I didn't have much to do today, honestly.' He shuddered and Joanna shrugged in sympathy.

'All right, don't sound so defensive. You know what I think? I think the idea of you being an estate agent is ridiculous. There, I've said it and that's all I'll say. Anyway, since you're here, I could do with a bit of help.' She was lying on the bed with her arms folded behind her head, her bare feet leaving dirty marks on the coverlet. It was this last detail, along with her bitten nails, which reminded him that the languid attitude was not one of a willing courtesan in a painting, but the artless, unselfconscious sprawl of a teenager. 'I need help,' she continued, 'because of this awful solicitor woman coming to stay in the cottage. Do you think you could clear up some of your fishing tackle? It does get in the way in the kitchen. And the hall, and the dining room. I suppose supper ought to be better than usual.'

'It's always good,' Edward said gently. 'And often marvellous.'

She flushed, the pleasure quickly hidden by a flick of the hand across her pink face.

'Oh, pooh. Not what Julian says. He says if you really want to cook, go away and learn how. Why does he want us both to go away?'

'You know perfectly well,' Edward said gently. 'Neither of us can, can we? Julian wants to grab everything and shove Ma in some horrible home the day after we leave. How many times must I tell you?' He lightened the sombre tone which always caught her attention. 'Anyway the cooking does a lot for me. You could even make me fat.' Jo grinned at him, threw a cushion from the bed towards his head. He caught it, threw it back, growling; she seized it again and hurled it harder. Edward let it drop, then went into his King Kong mode, lurching towards her with legs splayed and arms raised with the elbows above his shoulders, fingers twitching. Jo behaved like a maiden waiting for a dragon, wringing her hands and shrieking. 'OH! Oh! oh!' until he came closer and there was a hint of real fear in her laughter. Edward dropped the pose.

'You don't take me seriously,' he said. 'No-one does. Oh dearie, dearie me. I'll never get to eat a virgin.'

'Sturgeon, maybe,' said his sister, leaping off the bed noisily, shaking out her skirt. The waistband was loose round her small waist, the skirt itself extra voluminous, old-fashioned, flounced and girlish to hide the wide hips she detested. If only, Edward thought, I were larger all over . . .

Joanna also detested her white skin, her cheeks currently blooming into pink as they always did in response to the slightest emotion or exertion. Edward frightened her sometimes. He always took a joke too far.

'And of course I take you seriously,' she added carelessly, retreating. 'Though maybe not as a maiden-snatcher. Oh, I wish someone would snatch me. Listen, do you think Julian will lay on wine for dinner? In deference to the Law amongst us?' Julian, tyrant, despot, unfair critic and spoiler of everything.

'I expect so,' Edward murmured, suddenly depressed. 'Provided we undertake to keep it away from Ma.'

'Oh yes. Easier said than done.' Both lapsed into silence. Edward moved back to the doll's house, where he replaced the little figure he had blown off the sofa. He felt Jo bending beside him to look into the room with the same old fascination she found so easy to scorn and he so quick to rekindle. At moments like these, they could have been the same childish age instead of he four years her senior. He wanted to pull her closer. The effort to restrain himself was almost too much: he could feel her breath, the babyish talcum powder smell of her and it made him want to faint. His fingers itched to feel the warm patch at the back of her neck.

There was a sound from the road which separated the summer garden from the channels beyond. It was a tinkling parody of Big Ben chimes on the hour, Da dah, dah da, dah da, da dah, garish and eerie. The ice-cream van, calling to Joanna like the music of the spheres.

'Oh no!' she wailed. 'It's him! And I look so awful!'

Edward clenched his fists. The door slammed, the

room shuddered and everything in the doll's house
fell over. Edward peered inside and took the ballerina
figure and the small doll dressed like an artist with a
smock and placed them with their arms around each
other on the master bed of the biggest room upstairs.
Then he threw a cloth across the whole construction
as if he was silencing a parrot in a cage and took up
a station behind the window, out of sight.

The ice-cream van drove down the drive, where
weeds had almost overtaken the remnants of gravel
and the lawn, where a sheep grazed, somehow ex-
panded into the grassy flower-beds. Mist was beginning to roll in from the sea, warm and wet,
promising oblivion. He watched as the ice-cream van
stopped below, still tinkling, shut his eyes, tried to
imagine the sound of the distant waves, failed. Please
don't run, Jo, please don't. He could not abide to
witness her humiliation or watch her bitten nails
pushing through the blond hair; could not bear to see
her preen the way she never had for him. He
clenched his fist. 'Why is it I never get what I want?'
he murmured petulantly. 'Things will change, Dad,
just you wait and see.'

As the van drew to a halt, with its monstrous bells
still ringing to the faithful, a figure emerged from the
front door of the house with a joyful scream. Edward
closed his eyes again in the instant he recognized
that high-pitched shrieking and the jumble of excited
words which followed so harsh on his ears. He
looked, without amusement, as a plump figure
banged on the side of the van, yelling, 'Hallo, hallo
oh, goodbye, darling thing, are you being good today?' The van stopped, lurched forwards a few
yards, part of an act. The bright little figure ran after
it, whooping with laughter. Edward relaxed. At least
this little fool wasn't Joanna. Only his own darling
mother, sweetly dotty and harmlessly senile. He
looked down at her with more indifference than con-

tempt. As soon as he could manage it, she was going
to live in a zoo. If not a zoo, at least behind bars, and
a grave would be best of all.

Joanna, money, this house to pull down and this
landscape to alter. If only. He wanted never to work,
and to go on as he had so far, in the careful cultiva-
tion of an image of himself as a cunning player of
games and a deeply interesting, deeply unpleasant
young man. Oh, yes, and maybe a better fisherman
than his father. Nothing else mattered.

Everyone mattered too much.

'Nice evening in store, Doctor?'

'No,' said Julian Pardoe, writing the prescription
as he spoke. 'I very much doubt it.'

'Why's that, then? Lovely big house, yours. So
I'm told. People says.'

'Ah, the word of authority. People says. Lovely
house. You should try living in it. You should try
coping with leaks and delinquents of all ages. You
should try . . .' He stopped, not embarrassed, but
ashamed for listening to his own voice rising into a
petulant yell. Miss Gloomer, obdurate spinster, eighty
years old, chronically and courageously ill, sat across
the desk in his surgery, knowing her manners, while
he forgot his. Her face was a map of pain, patience
and fortitude. She managed to sit in her chair without
trembling only because of the stick with the ornamental duck's head she clasped with both hands
pressed into the top while the ferrule was digging a
hole in his carpet, absorbing the constant trembling
of her limbs. I'd be so much better, Julian thought, if
I talked to them more, the way I used to, but I can't
bear it. Women of virtue like this are the worst, so
patient and kind they take a piece of you. I've nothing to give them, even when I like them as much as
this, I can't be patient. He turned the bark into a

laugh and finished the prescription. 'Mustn't complain, mustn't complain,' he said, testily.

'Why not?' she said surprisingly. 'It's allowed. We all got problems. Perhaps you should try living alone. You've been the same since your father passed away. There was a time when you had a kind word for everyone. I suppose they call it stress.' Snatching the prescription quickly to avoid more than a split-second release of the stick, she was on her way to the door. Oh Lord, he thought, I should be helping her, instead of sitting here like an inconsiderate dummy. In his own confusion and her rumbling movements, he still recognized something horribly astute.

'I appreciate it's very hard living alone, Miss Gloomer ...' he began to say, trying to make amends with a particle of conversation. She stopped dead and cackled.

'Don't you believe it. Only thing I ever got right. Even if it is frightening, sometimes.'

'I'll probably see you later.'

'No need. Only if it suits you.'

This time his smile was right from the eyes. He heard the stick guide her down the corridor and waited before pressing the bell. Living alone seemed like a vision of heaven and he would appreciate it now if the next patient was a hooligan tourist deserving of rudeness. 'Next!' he yelled, when the bell brought no response. Nurse popped into the room, smiling, her endless cheerfulness like sand in a graze.

'You've been through them all like a dose of salts today, Doctor. Reckon that's the lot and you can go home.'

'Oh. Dr Freeman finished too, has he? Or would he like me to take one of his?'

She shifted uncomfortably. 'Well no, I don't think

so. He's got a couple waiting, but they're his regulars, if you see what I mean.'

Dr Freeman was far more popular than Dr Pardoe. Nor did nice-natured women freeze him in his tracks. Once upon a time it had been the other way round.

Julian did not know if fury or relief was uppermost in his mind as he strode to his car. Relief to be out of the ugly modern medical centre with its compassionate efficiency, or fury with himself for skimping time with the patients and shying away from the opposite sex as if they could sting him. If only he could emulate the charm of Dr Freeman; give each one his undivided attention, instead of champing at the bit, brooding, hating himself, moving from one captivity to the next, taking no comfort. The interior of his car was overpoweringly hot. It had been cleaned that morning in readiness for house calls to patients who would tell him about ghosts, as if he did not have enough of his own. Freeman's car was carelessly filthy and parked beneath a tree. Julian wondered what had happened to his comfortable dreams and the endless sympathy he had once commanded, felt faintly savage, ashamed of himself for his own dogged misery.

There was a smart red car with a dent, parked next to his own in the space marked 'doctors only'. The sight of an inconsiderate outsider only increased his irritation.

Sarah Fortune felt a stranger, off territory and slightly confused. She was not due to reach the Pardoes until early evening and it was only early afternoon. She had several motives for reaching the village sooner than expected, but was unsure which to take first, so she dawdled in the high street, trying to orientate herself. In briefing her for this task, Ernest Matthewson had been deliberately economical with the background information he had given her, which consisted of an Ordnance Survey map, directions and little else. She was left to glean what she could of the family who were paying her fees and giving her a place to stay while she earned them. Which was why, on a whim, in a state of indecision and not relishing the next task, she found herself in the hairdresser's. Hairdressers knew things and it was a place to sit.

'On holiday, are you? You've been in here before, haven't you? I'm sure I know you from somewhere.'

'No,' said Sarah, smiling her disarming smile. 'No to both. I'm working. For the Pardoes. Do you know them?'

The woman towelling her wet head of hair did not pause for a moment, but chuckled.

'Course. Everyone does. I got no worries I pay my rent. How do you find Mrs Pardoe? Comes in Monday mornings, all the clobber. Mad as a hatter, but still independent, you know. I suppose they'll have to get someone to look after her soon. Poor little Mouse.'

'I haven't met her yet. I'm not due up there until this evening. Thought I'd have a look around first.'

'And get your hair done? Good idea.' They eyed each other in the mirror. 'Blow dry, or set?' Sarah looked at the row of four ancient hairdryers, beneath which sat a selection of dozing women with hair tortured into rollers, their hands crossed on ample stomachs, a comfortable sight, along with the smells. In the ample bosom of Sylvie, conversation and coiffure would be more rewarding.

'What kind of work are you doing for the Pardoes?' The curiosity was mild, so innocuous it demanded an answer. Sarah never saw the virtue of being entirely honest when a vague evasion would serve the same purpose and, besides, she wasn't entirely sure. Ernest had been infuriatingly vague. You need an unsullied mind, he had said.

'Oh, something to do with their house.' The woman nodded, understandingly.

'Oh yes? I've heard they could do with a bit of decoration. Mr Pardoe was always adding bits on. He was a dreamer. Never finishing anything off.'

Perhaps Sarah's clothes, smart in comparison to what she had seen outside, suggested interior decorator rather than woman of letters. She smiled again as her hair was brushed with rough efficiency.

'That bad, is it?'

'Well, old Mrs Pardoe isn't up to doing much, poor soul, is she? Daughter does her best and all that, the doctor's too busy, I expect, and that Edward's no more use than a sick headache, spiteful, lazy little sod. If only his sister would see it, but she won't, worships the ground he walks on. Funny things, families. Mary!' she half turned to yell at her girl assistant. 'Turn Mrs Smith off, will you? Otherwise she'll melt.'

It was pleasant to be spoken to as if she knew them all.

'Poor Mr Pardoe,' she said solicitously. 'How long is it since he died?'

'Fell off his roof with his heart attack, you mean? About a year, I suppose. Mind,' she lowered her voice and switched off the dryer, 'there's other things he could have died of, only I think he'd given that up.'

'Such as?' Sarah ventured. The blow-drying started again.

'Falling off a big woman!' Sylvie yelled, breaking into raucous laughter, then subsiding into the confidentiality of a stage whisper audible from a hundred yards. 'He did a lot of that in his time. All right, Mrs Jones? You waiting for me? Please yourself.' She coughed impatiently.

'That Mrs Pardoe was wise, though,' she continued shouting. 'Never complained. She just pretended she didn't notice, waited for him to stop his nonsense. They all come back in the end, don't they?'

Sarah nodded, slightly unsure of what kind of worldly wisdom it was she was endorsing. It never seemed to her worthwhile to wait for anyone to come back. Her head was hot, her hair floating away from the brush.

'Lovely colour,' Sylvie yelled. 'Natural, I can tell. Used to have a customer with hair exactly like this. What was her name, now? Oh, hallo. Look what the cat's brought in.'

The door of the shop had opened, the bell clattering. On the threshold stood a large young man, twenty-one or so, Sarah guessed. For all his astounding good looks, he had an air of shy uncertainty. Next to him, standing proudly in his shadow, was a boy the colour of sand. Sarah, her back to the door, screened by Sylvie, watched them through the mirror.

'What do you want, Rick?' said Sylvie, snapping as if scolding, but patently pleased to see them both.

'Boy needs a hair cut. He got chewing-gum in it.'

'Get your arse out of here, the two of you, and send him back in half an hour, all right? Can't you see I'm busy? You want spray?' Sylvie bellowed to Sarah all in one breath.

Sarah Fortune, with her cloud of clean hair and her small sum of knowledge, walked out beyond the town, away from the people and away from the sea. *En route*, she bought provisions for the cottage the Pardoes would provide and left them in the car, except for the flowers, which she took with her. This last action made her define the real purpose of being early, not merely to explore—something else far more important. She had craved the sea for the last few days but once in view, found herself afflicted with a strange reluctance to look at the creeks, the

channels and the quay which existed at the bottom of
the street and ducked into the town instead. She was
suddenly an alien, far from the metropolis which was
home, and if not afraid, at least wary.

Tomorrow she would crave the sea again: the mere
thought of it made her excited. So often she had
dreamed her ignorant dream of living in an unpreten-
tious place like this, inside a cottage with roses
round the door. The dream had become a habit of familiar escape. Similar visions of privacy and non-
accountability prevailed as her greatest ambition, the
tawdry golden thread of her adult life. Somehow she
had come to imagine Elisabeth Tysall may have felt
the same.

On the edge of the village-cum-town, stood the
church. According to the Ordnance Survey map, the
only church, bearing bravely the signs of neglect as
evidence of the dwindling faithful who needed no
more than the burgeoning graveyard and the occasional blessing of a half-remembered God. Elisabeth
Tysall, twice-buried, once beneath a sand bank and,
later, here, had needed both. It was her consecrated
grave which was the purpose of Sarah's pilgrimage.
The newer graves spilled into a field, less attractive
than the mossy stones surrounding the church at
crooked angles, like drunken friends on the way
home, the names obscured, the grass growing between. The interments of the last two years were less
cheerful for being still remembered, harassed in
equal terms by grief and dead flowers. Some had already begun to sink into the unkempt; others bore
vestiges of fresh planting. A temporary wooden
marker bore the legend of Elisabeth's name. No-one
had requisitioned a stone, but then Charles had died,
had he not, so soon after she was identified. The
grass grew round it freely. On either side, the close-
packed graves bore bright, white stones, the soil

packed with pansies to the left, a bunch of tired flowers in a plastic container to the right.

Elisabeth, who had chosen the wrong one to love. Sarah wanted to weep for her.

'I'm sorry,' she was saying. 'I'm so sorry. I should have come sooner. Maybe you know how it is. I should have come to your funeral, but I didn't know the full story. Still don't. Did anyone come to your funeral?'

She found she was raising her voice to the level of one commonsensical woman talking to a friend on equal terms, a person who was businesslike, ashamed of sentiment, but always prone to it. Sarah parted the grass to lay down the flowers, wishing she had bought something grander; there was no impulse of which she was ashamed, except meanness. Buried beneath was a suicidal woman of youth and beauty, unmourned, unnoticed, and that was an abomination. Sarah began to tidy, until her fingers struck razor points and she withdrew sharply. Blood appeared on her knuckles; she sucked her fist, squatting back on her haunches to look again. Covered by grass, there were thistles lurking, dead, massed into a bunch beneath another bouquet of fat, desiccated roses, purple with indeterminate age, which crumbled at her touch. Sarah parted more grass and laid her own daises, level with the feet, not the heart. The silence of the place was extraordinary.

There was a posse of black crows congregating at the bottom of the field. Two years before, Elisabeth Tysall, wife of Charles Tysall, had walked out at low tide across the creeks. She had been presumed the victim of an accident. Sarah could hear the cultivated voice of Charles telling her of the need for punishment and knew the version was not true. His Porphyria had lain down amongst the lavender and waited for the sea to take her. She may have covered her own elegant limbs with sand, the better to remain buried for a whole year before the tide broke the bank and released her.

'Why?' Sarah asked her. 'You let him win. I do wish I'd known you.' A redhead you were, like me. A beauty, since Charles would have wedded nothing less. You should have been mourned, whatever you were. Not only by Charles, who loved you in his own, perverted way, followed you into the sea to find your resting place, drowned in the same, aberrant flood.

Sarah looked again at the grave, the dead roses and the scornful thistles. Who loved you? Who cared for you then? Where did you go? You and I, we could have been friends. Instead, you were merely the catalyst in a story and another source of my endless guilt.

The silence struck again, like a blow to the ears, making her long for a voice in return. The intensity of it, the dearth of birdsong, made her look round, notice for the first time the mist of the now late afternoon, obscuring the sun, hiding the wicket gate to the church. She stood and looked down at the daisies.

A headstone for Elisabeth Tysall, something to mark her life, someone must. Something grand and beautiful for a woman who had wanted to live as much as the woman who stared at the flowers now.

Sarah walked back to the landward side of the village where she had left her car and took a wrong turn out of the town, looking for the coast road. The red car with the dented wing crawled through the lanes, following instructions, driving like the locals in second gear. To call this a town was a misnomer: it was a village. She imagined the populace from the hinterland trucking in on Saturday nights, like cowboys from the desert, in search of liquor 'n' entertainment. A fish-and-chip frontage and a Victorian behind, was how Ernest had described it; a sort of harbour

flanked with an amusement arcade and signs saying
don't park the car on the front, or the tide may take
it. Drive along the quay, Ernest had said, ignore a
bend. Go straight on, he had said, off the main road,
keep the sea on your left until the track runs out. The
house is there, half a mile at most. You can't miss it.

She did miss it, because she detoured round the
town out of curiosity and found herself stuck in a
narrow lane against a wall lined with hollyhocks and
someone waiting patiently behind. She went back to
the quay, found it swathed in mist and wondered
what Ernest meant about keeping the ocean on the
left when she could not see a glimmer of water. The
receding tide moved in a dirty little channel out beyond brown banks towards the invisible sea. The garish lights of an amusement arcade hit her back and
the din was raucous. People sat on a wall which separated quay from road, eating fish and chips; the air
smelt of salt, vinegar, petrol. It was all so messy and
so normal, shabby holiday life, nothing sinister in the
pedestrian litter. The mist was puzzling rather than
frightening; it spread round her like a warm blanket,
bringing with it a premature darkness and making
her realize at long last that she was very, very late
for the Pardoes.

There was a cake on the kitchen table, a lopsided
travesty of a confection which looked more like Plas-
ticine. Two slabs of solid matter, wedged together
with a gluey icing made with flour in mistake for
sugar. One of Mother's better efforts at occupational
therapy, Julian thought. The kitchen looked like a
bomb site after her efforts. At the best of times it was
a good enough kitchen, despite Edward's fishing
mess; the oldest part of a patchwork house. There
was a big pine table, large, heavy chairs which did
not match and an old-fashioned Rayburn stove which
Joanna loved for all the trouble of tending it and all

the unreliability of the oven. A heavy kettle stood on top, simmering endlessly. The room was always warm. The pantry beyond the ancient fridge was cool by contrast, a large, walk-in store with stone-flagged floor, netted windows and pale shelves crammed with stores. On the floor in there, at all times, were two or three bundles of Edward's always superfluous fishing bait, worms, inelegantly wrapped in newspaper, an unlikely source of protein for the inmates of the house. The cake, Mother announced in one of her very rare, comprehensible sentences, was for the guest. Joanna looked at it in horror. If only Mother wouldn't.

'She's late, this rotten old bitch of a lawyer, thank God she's late, the cow, nothing's ready.' Joanna's temper was running high; Julian's likewise.

'Don't flap. It doesn't suit you. What do you want me to do? Worry about impressing her? I doubt if she's a cow or a bitch, it's physically impossible to be both, she's only a sort of hired help.'

'We should have a lot in common then,' Joanna hissed. 'Only I'm not paid.'

'No, but it's patently obvious you're well fed,' said Julian. This marked the end of the shouting. The row had caused the delay and rendered a light cheese sauce inedible. Joanna had started again, which was why she was not going to cry now. The poached halibut required no extra salt.

Impatiently, Julian stacked two fishing rods against the wall. Edward's fishing tackle seemed to penetrate every room in the house except his own. Wherever he went, he seemed to fall over Edward's deliberate attempts to impress as well as dominate. Fishing and Edward did not really go together. He only did it to be manly, like his father.

'Did you check her room?' Joanna snapped. 'You know, the cottage? I suppose you managed that?' It

was a poor attempt at sarcasm, her voice too shrill
for impact.

'Yes, but I don't see why you didn't ask Ed first,
he's far more time than me. It's fine. Could have
done with some flowers, though.'

'She's only the hired help,' Joanna hissed, pleased
with herself. The pleasure faded quickly. No-one
should have mentioned flowers, or even thought
about them. Mother could sense a word from a mile
away, also a row and the way to make it worse. She
had the uncanny instinct of appearing on cue, in the
wrong role and always the wrong costume like now
as she stood in the kitchen doorway, holding an enormous bunch of dandelions in one hand, a clutch of
nasturtiums in the other. She had a full bottle of wine
poking out of the pocket of her coat. An evening
gown swayed round her ankles beneath a mackintosh
and there were three ostrich feathers in her hair. Julian took away the wine and placed it on the table in
a swift manoeuvre, well practised if devoid of humanity. Mother's eyes filled with tears. She had always been so infuriatingly defenceless, he thought.
Earned her nickname of Mouse for always weeping
like her daughter, neither able to stand their own
ground.

'Why did you do that, darling? Oh, I'm hungry.'
She moved unsteadily towards a small pile of grated
cheese on the chopping board.

'No you don't,' Joanna said. 'Leave it alone, will
you? What do you want?'

'Something to eat, I think. Just a little something.
Don't you like my cake?' She stood centre stage,
smiling at them both through bright, watery eyes.

'Are you going to change for dinner?' Julian asked
ironically.

'Should I? It's only a bitch or a cow, you were
saying. I was just going to put flowers in its room—'

'No!' Joanna shouted. 'No you won't. Not after I've swept, hoovered, put out towels, no you don't.'

Mother's upper lip trembled. She looked at both her hands, the one holding garden weeds, the other, *pissenlit*.

'Yes, I will,' she murmured. 'I'm sure the cow will like them.'

She scuttled sideways, swifter than a crab, towards the front door, just as the bell rang. With the row and all, no-one had heard the sound of an engine, usually discernible from a hundred yards. Each knew the sound of their various old cars, parked outside like a row of sentinels. Edward was feigning deafness in his watchtower, pretending to paint his rubbishy daubs and reading poetry, defying the necessity to earn a living, while his sister suspended life through cooking and pretending that was enough. Julian surveyed them all with despair. Mother was agile. She reached the door first, could not work out a way to open it with her hands full, stood back, grinning like a cat. Edward bounded downstairs, straightening a big floppy cravat; Joanna stood back and Julian hesitated. They were not used to guests.

Another knock. None of them could answer the door. She would have to open it herself.

A figure stepped into the gloom of the hall. Mother staggered forward, still grinning, dropping the flowers at Sarah Fortune's feet.

'Oh,' said the guest without a hint of discomposure. 'How lovely. You shouldn't.' She stopped to pick dandelions from the floor, carefully and swiftly, like a person used to gathering weeds with great respect. They watched, fascinated. She had straightened up with the flowers in a neat bunch by the time Julian switched on the cruel hall light. Dressed in khaki, she was, a princess in her brown freckled skin with her red hair kinking over her shoulders and a tan belt round her waist and small hips, clothed in nothing which was not utterly neutral while remaining a mass of colours all the same. A humourous face, a square jaw and a smile which embraced the giver of the dandelions. Not beautiful, but stunning.

Mother picked up the last, ceremoniously. Sarah bowed and stuck it down the front of her dress. Mother beamed.

'Would you mind coming straight on in? Supper's ready. No time for washing and all that stuff.' Joanna spoke roughly.

Sarah nodded. 'Of course. I'm really sorry I'm so late. I wouldn't have been but I'm such a silly cow, I got lost.'

'Cow!' Mother collapsed in giggles. Sarah took her extended hand.

'What fabulous feathers,' she said. 'I wish I was allowed to wear those.'

CHAPTER THREE

They all stared aghast. It was love at first sight. Before grace, before dinner. Before the second batch of burnt cheese sauce and before anyone heard the sound of the distant, ghostly tinkling of the ice-cream-van bell. There was a full second of silence until the sound died. Mother clapped her hands.

'What the hell's he doing here?' Edward snarled. Sarah turned her gaze on him. He wilted.

'I'm afraid that's my fault. I stopped at a, what do you call them, amusement arcade, to ask directions, and this man volunteered to lead me here. I thought it was charming. I've never had such an escort.' Joanna was brick red. She no longer cared if dinner was edible. Instant love turned to instant hate and then to love again as she fled to the kitchen. Edward looked amused. This was only a woman, not the gimlet-eyed professional he had slightly dreaded; she was too attractive to be a threat. Julian led her inside. His manner was barely less than brusque; he was shaking slightly and he did not seem able to take his eyes off her hair.

Outside, Hettie the sheep bleated. Mother had placed a bow round her neck. Only a youth called Rick noticed and remembered fondly as he drove back to work.

Stonewall hung about the amusement arcade as long as he could and as late as he dared, sick with anxiety and knowing that, sooner or later, he'd be shooed away. There had been twenty minutes of sheer bliss, when he'd been left in charge when Rick came in from a quick stroll on the quay, talking to someone, said he'd be off for five, would he, Stonewall, take charge? The arcade belonged to Rick's dad, who was a sort of uncle, like everyone round here, but not Stonewall's favourite by any manner of means. Especially not when he came in drunk and found Stonewall in charge of the till. There'd be trouble when Rick got back, which was why Stonewall hung around, because someone had to protect Rick from his dad.

It was no good. Even with his new, short haircut, to which his fingers flew all the time with nervous pride, Stonewall didn't have the power and it made him want to shout. Hit me instead, he wanted to say to Rick's dad, as if Rick would ever have let it happen. Instead, that surly man went out for another drink or two, came back and took Stonewall by his newly exposed ear and pushed him in the direction of home. Rick didn't prevent him.

'Go on with you,' he said gently. 'See you tomorrow.' Stonewall felt the urge to kick shins and scream. Rick's dad didn't like witnesses.

'Go away,' Julian muttered in his sleep. 'Physician, heal thyself.'

He was dreaming of a girl with red hair who had run on the beach. The background of the dream was the strident, fairground sound which emerged from the arcade, as if such sound could travel the half mile to where Julian Pardoe attempted to sleep and cursed himself for his own insomnia. There was no excuse, no cause for alarm. The meal had been easier than anticipated, the guest, whose expertise could lighten his own burdens, had been the soul of charm to disguise, rather than hide, those over-intelligent eyes and that blatant talent for perception he somehow knew she possessed. Julian felt she could read his soul and all the shame printed on it, dismissed his imaginings as the kind of nonsense induced by red wine and over-ambitious food.

Besides, he had no soul to reveal. By day he was an automaton about his business, by night a heap of restless limbs, made fanciful only because he had embarrassed himself staring at her so much, read too much into those blue eyes, felt again that sickening guilt and despair. Take your time, he had told Miss Fortune, formal beyond the point of rudeness, wondering even then how soon he could phone Ernest Matthewson and get this paragon recalled to the safety of her own city.

Instead he found himself saying, Come into the surgery tomorrow and I'll tell you a bit about the estate, have the rest of the weekend to think about it. Don't feel you have to take meals with us. Don't feel you have to stay.

Edward was acting out the role of serious, unconventional younger brother, quoting poetry and describing the land. He made it sound as if he owned it all, puffed himself up to look like a small man with a big career, like his father, instead of a boy who failed at everything he tried. The guest listened intently. Mother put half-eaten food on the stranger's plate while Julian's own abruptness shocked his sister and nothing fazed the guest. He had wanted everything settled, his father's family safe, but not like this. Not with the aid of a woman with hair like that, and those calm, amused eyes.

They had taken her over to the cottage, followed by the sheep with the crumpled horn which lived in the garden and was fed by Mother. Miss Fortune didn't seem to mind that either. There was nothing to surprise her frightful composure.

Julian turned restlessly, hearing again the creaking on the stair he had heard before and never wished to investigate. Could be his mother prowling, Edward going out fishing, he did not want to know, could not watch them all the time or even half of it. As long as it was not Edward going into Joanna's room, something as yet unprecedented, but hanging over his household like the threat of thunder. How immoral to wish away his sister's virginity on the first unrelated youth who tried to take it, but that was what Julian wished. If only she would leave before some accident of desire should upset her life . . . better if Edward went out fishing, even if it was to foul the sea shore as he did, leaving lines and hooks for seals, just as he littered the house with equipment and the pantry floor with buckets of soft-shelled crabs and lugworms for whiting.

The silence of the night increased the rattling in his mind. Julian felt responsibility without strength or confidence. He had killed his own self-respect, found himself left with nothing but impotent knowledge.

From a great distance, he thought he heard a scream.

Worms beneath this mud: good for bait.

'You don't know nothing, boy. Nothing. You don't know your arse from your elbow, or where to put that big dick of yours, or even where you want to put it. Dirt all over the van. You want to put dirt up her fanny? That what you want? I bet you bloody do.'

The sound which followed was a soft grunt, the noise of the boot into the ribs almost inaudible in itself, except for the air dispelled in the effort and the boy's biting back of pain. Both of them were covered in mud. The boy curled away on the bank, his left shoulder embedded in mud. Black mud bubbled where his elbow sank below the surface. There was blood inside his mouth, tasting of iron, salt and slime. Rick thought of the ragworms below the surface, imagined something slithering down his throat, struggled to sit, spat, coughed.

'I could have killed you, Dad.'

He was spitting out weary words, fielding another blow to his ribs, thanking heaven for his father's boots being so heavy with mud he could scarcely lift them. It could have been worse, had often been much worse. No blow had connected with his groin; he had turned on his back, wishing he had learned the trick when younger, before the damage was done and before he had realized the whole ritual of violence was far quicker if he did not resist. Lie there, let the boot go in, never mind about the shame.

'Kill me, you little fucker? Kill me! You could scarce kill a fly. You let that little runt look after the till while you're out running after that tart? You need to be towing the line. With a hook. I'd stick it through your mouth. Or up your bum.'

The boy allowed himself to be lifted out of the mud, shaken like a rat, dropped back. He could have taken his father then, knocked the old man's teeth through the back of his head, but he lay like a puppet and listened to the breath in his chest. Out of the corner of his eye, lights from the outside of the closed arcade shimmered on the water, blurred by mist. He could hear the tide running swift and deep through his head and his skin, vibrating through each portion of his body. Dad raised his wet face and sniffed like a dog.

'Best move,' he muttered. 'Water's coming on.' He was suddenly cold, shivery, adrenalin gone, replaced by a sensation which was the nearest he could get to shame. No more punching, rolling and snarling at the east end of the quay. The boy was right. He was strong. He could take his old dad any time, better watch it.

'Come on home, boy,' said his father, almost humbly, the way he was when it was far too late. 'You'll catch your death.'

'Bugger you. I got my own place.'

'You could do with a wash. You and me both.'

'I could do with a new set of balls after what you've done to me over the years. That's enough, Dad, do you hear me?'

Weird, to be speaking like a pair of blokes who had gone for a drunken stroll to look at the stars. They struggled up the bank. Past midnight, everything as silent as the grave. The apologies, oblique and humble, were the feature of Dad's drunken violence which Rick found worst.

'I thought you were taking that bit of Pardoe stuff out. You mustn't touch her. You know what that poxy little bastard told you, leave his sister alone. Otherwise no job, no arcade, no nothing. We're doing all right, boy. Don't rock the boat.'

Rick adjusted his trousers, tried to manage a laugh.

'Dad, I do leave her alone, but for my own reasons. I might have gone to the boat by myself, when I could still walk straight.'

'Don't give me that. Leave her alone? You've been up that house twice today, bashing the van over that track. I saw you, I heard. Kids might be robbing the till and off you go.'

Rick took a deep breath, which hurt to the degree where he knew he would live.

'Dad, I goes the first time because Mrs Pardoe likes ice-cream, poor old bat. I goes the second time because this bird came in the arcade and asks directions, doesn't she? Said she was working up there. Christ, what a looker. A bit old, but a looker.'

Dad grunted. Sometimes he knew the truth when he heard it, not always.

'What do you mean, old?'

'Thirty. Something like that. Said she was a lawyer. A cracker.'

His father gave a great shout of laughter, flung his great thick arm round the boy's shoulder. Rick flinched. He might act for now as if there were a reconciliation but he had done it once too often. All he wanted was a clean body and sleep. And a dream. Running the arcade all by himself. Swimming in the sea with Jo Pardoe. Lying with her in the hot sand . . .

'Old! Thirty! So you lead some lady lawyer up there in the bloody ice-cream van! Doesn't that beat all!'

Rick could see him, telling the story in the Globe, the Ark Royal or the Golden Fleece, any of them would have done. The wet and weighty arm descended back to his shoulder and Rick let it rest. He felt for his groin. No soreness this time. His clothes were soaking and stinking, the body beneath weary beyond relief.

What a life. Work hard to keep your body in one piece, let alone the dreams. Not many of those left. Not a body worth a prayer, either. Not a thing to take to Joanna Pardoe.

The sheep had surprised Sarah. It had wanted to come indoors to this strange little cottage, last in a row of three, standing in grand isolation, thirty yards to the left of the house. I suppose this was once a farm, Joanna had volunteered, chatty and shy, a nice, nervy child. Workers would have lived here, years ago. Dad wanted a farm once; he wanted to do everything once. I'm sorry you haven't got the best one, but we had a fire in it a few weeks ago, still don't know why. Might have been the village ghost, we've got a new one this summer. Good night, sleep tight, sweet dreams.

The cottage was a shoebox of a house, living room-cum-kitchen, stairs to a bedroom, bathroom and tiny room under the eaves, explored in half a minute. Any sounds were the mere echo of her own activity. In her bedroom she faced a storm-proof window, open for airing, with a breeze moving pretty chintz curtains. Someone had made sporadic efforts, leaving the place less spartan, with an ancient hot-water cistern, older lavatory, clattering pipes, the kind of thin cord carpet which chilled the feet; two hangers in the wardrobe with a loose door, an over-soft bed.

She was absurdly disappointed that she could not hear the sea, let the lawyer in her take over to quell the disappointment. What did she know about the Pardoes and whatever was she supposed to do for them? She had a glimmer of their personalities, none of their supposed riches. Julian, the doctor, sandy-haired blond, churlish, driven and tired; Edward, a young, cunning braggart, self-consciously keeping himself the rebel and the subject of his sister's devotion. The girl, bright with gilded innocence and the friendliness of a puppy, watching her mother as if someone was going to take her away, while Mother herself overplayed to the gallery the loud rituals of her madness, comic and irritating by turns. Find out the dreams, Ernest had said without giving her a single clue. Find out, then work out how to finance them fairly: that's what lawyers should be for. Instead, Sarah thought of Elisabeth Tysall's punctuated dreams, the colour she might choose for a headstone, and the right shrub to plant.

The air from the window was like a drug, closing her eyes although the bed was cold. Not damp cold, but lonely cold, intensified by the quiet. No distant music, shouting, footsteps, no humming city life where neither silence nor darkness was ever quite complete. There crept into the chilly vacuum of her bed the panic of separation and the muck sweat of fear.

Her fingers touched her face: there were lines forming round her eyes; she could take great clumps of skin and pull them off, could lift her scalp away from the bone, feel the scars on her shoulders and her arms, force herself to think of the healing sea which would cure it all. Perspiration trickled down her back before she slept. It was not the countryside of which she had dreamed.

The day bore no relation to the night: from burial in the terrible silence, she was suddenly elevated into the delightful cacophony of dawn. Birdsong first, little fatty thrushes squabbling for attention and clattering on the roof; then the soft cooing of a pigeon, stupidly repetitious, two high notes, one low, no variation but long pauses, and at last, a wholly manmade sound, cutting across the natural like a knife. The mournful wailing of a distant siren, swelling into a full-bellied moan, fading, rising again to a steady wail, diminishing, howling, three, four times. It sounded like a crowd in anguish, an animal in pain, a prayer for the dead, a muezzin calling from the turret of a mosque and she listened spellbound. Minutes later she was out of doors.

There was nothing but clear sky and a view without ending. The village, with a long bank of land curving away from it seaward like a question mark, lay on her left, half a mile away. In front of her, opposite the house which stood the width of its garden from the cottages, a vast expanse of land amounting to nothing. She watched idly as she walked, until the nothing began to move as the light caught the surface, showing random, glimmering channels full of chuckling water. Sarah in plimsolls

jogged towards town. The channels became wider
with each fifty yards, the deceptive flat land gave
way to channels of water no longer lapping but guz-
zling louder and louder in the ten minutes it took
her to reach the quay. From the evening gulley of
mud and sand, it had become part of the ocean upon
which it fed. The sea lapped high against the harbour wall; boats which had been invisible the night
before now rode proud and level with her eyes,
bobbing and straining with lazy ease. Remnants of
tufty land which she had glimpsed standing high
and dry in the mist, poked above the surface of the
water, like the uncertain remains of hair on a
smooth, bald head.

Early. Salty, fish-smelling. Two men throwing
open boxes out of a boat, slamming them on to the
stone. The boxes were full of wet, heaving fish. Another man sluiced the deck of the boat from which
they unloaded. Blood, mixed with water, ran down
the sides. Sarah tried to hide her nausea.

'Excuse me . . . What was the siren I heard?'

'Siren? Oh, that. Lifeboat.' They did not waste
words, not unfriendly, but busy.

'Do you fish with hooks?' she asked stupidly, eyeing the watery blood.

'Hooks are for fun. You only catch one at a time
with hooks. Nets, we use.'

The fish smell defeated her, she was ashamed to
be asking the obvious, risking their mild contempt.
The village lay glistening. There were swans in the
harbour, carried along by the tide with comical,
dignified speed. The amusement arcade was em-
phatically closed at an hour still too early for the
postman. A youth was hosing down the pavement
outside, oblivious to bold seagulls whooping over
waste-paper bins in search of yesterday's chips.
The same uncertain but gentle giant who had appeared in the hairdresser's with his charge, and,

later, escorted her beyond the boundaries on her regal progress, recognizable even when the pale sunlight illuminated the fresh bruises on his face. He seemed too lethargic to resent interruption, leant on his broom and watched her cross over from sea to land side of the road, trying to smile in mutual recognition.

'Hallo,' she said. 'Look, thanks for showing me the way last night. I told them up there,' she nodded in the direction from which she had walked, 'that I felt like the Queen. It was very kind of you.' This time his grin managed to emerge, splitting the face into dimples and making her remember what a star he had looked, in his tight-fitting jeans and brilliant white shirt, among the lights of the arcade with bingo going on in the corner, how politely he had listened to her above the din. A contrast to his dull-haired misery of the morning, no longer a king but a servant.

'That's all right then,' he said. 'My name's Rick.'

'What did you do to your face?' The question would be asked two dozen times during the day and for others he would invent a story, make them laugh, but the hour was too early for concoction.

'Nothing. Had a fight with my dad for taking the van out.' There didn't seem much she could say about that, except what she did say.

'I'm sorry. I'd rather have stayed lost than got you into trouble.'

'What makes you think you're that important?' he flashed back, jeering. 'Doesn't take a reason for Dad to hit me. Fact is, he thought it was funny, me taking you out there. Didn't like me leaving this place, though. Might have missed taking money or something.' Rick was suddenly uncomfortable, talking so much, but she didn't waste his time being shocked or anything. She looked fresh out of bed and besides he hurt all over and wanted someone to know.

'Do you look after all those machines?' she asked, pointing to the arcade.

'Yeah,' he muttered. 'All those crappy machines, all that row. And I do the ice-cream-van round. Smashing.'

'Do you? What a marvellous place to live.' She knew as she spoke that the question and the observation were fatuous. He spat into the gutter.

'You've got to be joking,' Then he spat in the road, to emphasize the point again. She was mildly irritated, not much.

'OK. OK,' she said. 'But you're far too good-looking to let anyone cover it in bruises. Why don't you dump your dad on a boat and tell him to sail? You're big enough, unless he's bigger.'

He let out a great shout of laughter, then clutched his waist because laughter hurt.

'For Christ's sake,' she said. 'Give me the damn brush and sit down.'

'I can't. My dad—'

'Give it me.' He did, slowly crossed to the wall opposite and lit a cigarette, then sat there watching, waiting to be amused. Sarah swept the pavement in front of the arcade like a furious housewife with only moments to spare, picking up fish paper, hamburger remnants, shoving everything into the plastic sack with which he had come equipped. Then seized a wash leather out of his bucket and cleaned the windows with the deft movements of a person who hated housework, endeavoured to complete it in the shortest possible time with all the refinements of sheer impatience. She scoured door knobs and scuffed panels of paint, covered every inch in ten hyperactive minutes. The emotions of the last few days had driven her to scour her flat from end to end with the same relentless energy in a practice made so perfect her swipe of the last windowpane called for a slow hand clap. Rick ambled back across the road.

'Are we quits?' she asked.

'How much do you charge an hour?' he asked, still trying to jeer, the smile less painful, strength coming back into his limbs. She was a looker all right, a lovely bum when she bent.

'Oh, I couldn't possibly tell you. It depends what for.'

'You really a lawyer, like you said? I knew the Pardoes were expecting one. Mrs P. told me. Said it would be some old cow.'

'That was a perfectly accurate expectation. Here I am.' They were both grinning broadly now.

'I don't know anything about them,' she added cunningly. 'Why would people say, for instance, that Edward was a shit? Someone said so, in the hairdresser's.'

'Because he is. Because when he goes fishing up yonder,' he gestured beyond the far distance, 'he won't even stop if he sees a seal. Leaves hooks and line for other things to swallow. He likes nasty practical jokes, Edward. And that ain't all.' Yes, she was a looker. Not old at all, with her jeans and the smut on her nose. Then his mind went into overdrive, remembering Pardoes in general, discretion in particular, wounded pride and his dad.

'Come out for a drink tonight, I'll tell you.'

She'd laugh, of course, a woman like this, find an excuse. He picked up the bucket and hurled the dirty water into the road, swirling the last slops towards her feet, playfully, watching to see if she would scream or move, half hoping she wouldn't, a challenge.

'Yes,' she said, ignoring the water. 'Where?'

'Meet me here? My night off,' he said, thinking of Dad with inexplicable triumph.

'See you then.'

She began to walk back. The quay was suddenly busy. A small boy, the colour of sand, stopped at a corner and stared at her. The stare was similar to a public undressing, all the more intense for the childish lack of inhibition in the dropped wide mouth and the lack of preening which went with it. The stare followed her as she passed and remained lodged somewhere at the back of her neck. A clock on the wall of the harbour stated the time of high tide and low, and next to it was a record of the highest the water had ever risen. Sarah liked that, wondering what else it was could rule these lives.

Here it was Charles Tysall had died and his wife before him. Charles, who had chosen her as his next obsession. Punished her as he had punished his wife, and then walked out to seek the spot where the wife had died. Charles, whose love destroyed what it touched. She felt her arms, suddenly cold. There were the ghosts of spoiled dreams, shimmering above the water.

Mrs Jennifer Pardoe, always known as Mouse, had a fondness for things which glittered. She took her wardrobe seriously and the morning selection occupied an hour. For this hot summer, evening dress was *de rigueur*. Ball gowns, and her several euphemistically called cocktail frocks, were ideal for late July. When worn for their proper functions in wedding marquees, stuffy dinners in draughty old houses, charity dos in barns, openings of horrid little galleries in picturesque villages, any frocks which were chiffony, *décolleté*, short sleeved, were always too cold for comfort. No wonder a girl needed a fur coat: a girl was usually well advised never to take the damn thing off. Mrs Pardoe had once described the sailing club dance as an acre of gooseflesh sprayed with starch, not a remark, even whispered as it was, designed to win either friends or the plaudits of her spouse, who was, in those days of his social climbing, ashamed of her.

Today, she thought she might wear the silver lamé shift, *circa* 1973. Her stylistic roots were with Marilyn Monroe, while her figure, small and plump like a trim-waisted frigate, dictated a preference for the loose fold rather than the tight twist. Joanna inherited the same curves and one day the child would learn it did not matter.

Mouse uttered a brief, emphatic, 'Huh!' when her wavering concentration lit upon a vision of her deceased husband scolding her for filling cupboards with frocks for occasions she had never wanted to attend in the first place, but did anyway because she simply did not know how to disagree. Then the whole concentration went into the moment. Which one? The mid-calf, gold fabric shift without sleeves or back would do fine for the simple reason it was going to be hot. Big, glittering ear-rings, a golden bangle shaped like a snake with little green eyes and a pink stone in the tail; perfect. Nights of agony in crippling high heels came to mind wistfully as she selected what she had always secretly yearned to wear then, a pair of pink training shoes. Thus attired, she went down for breakfast with her coat on top.

Champagne cocktail for preference. Brandy in the bottom and sugar round the top, cornflakes on the side.

It was a big, ugly house, Sarah observed as she approached on her way back, seeing it clearly for the first time and realizing with something of a shock how the Pardoe mansion was no jewel in a simple setting. Had it been reached via a long curving drive, it would have been a huge disappointment and even as it was the monument grew straight out of the sky with every step nearer revealing another, discordant detail. East Wind House was a marriage of additions. The tiles were a new and vicious orange, ill-suited to the mellower brick of the walls and making the whole edifice resemble a person wearing the wrong hat for the occasion. The bright blue of the eaves and the guttering added extra disharmony along with the extension at the back in the wrong stone at the wrong height; windows had been replaced with modern replicas of originals. All in all the house looked like a woman dressed in a fit of indecision with more money than taste, a vision of half-executed dreams, absent-mindedly amended and finally worn for a careless fit like an old cardigan.

The massive front door, made of oak and curved to a point at the top, belonged to a church and only added to the impression of a folly. Sarah ignored this entrance and strolled round the back, her feet wet in grass which swayed to the knees. There were remnants here of a vast kitchen garden dominated by rampant rhubarb and a smell of unculled vegetables. A row of ornamental cabbages thrilled the eye with purple splendour. The sheep with the twisted horn hanging drunkenly over its wall eyes, munched and burped next to a pot of uncontrolled nasturtiums flanking the back door.

What the hell game was Ernest playing? There may have been an element of expensive eccentricity, the sense of money spent unwisely, but there was nothing in this establishment which had the perfume of riches, a scent Sarah Fortune found easy to detect in a client and often easier to despise. Charles Tysall had the odour of an arrogant minority, but there was nothing yet discernible here to attract the hourly rates of Ernest's London partnership. Not even the row going on in the kitchen, to which she listened without shame.

'Where's Mrs Tysall? Doesn't she eat breakfast? She looked very thin.'

'Shut up, Mother. Just shut up . . . And will you go and change out of that horrible dress? She's not Mrs Tysall, she's a lawyer from London and she's going to think you're even madder than you are, dressed like that.'

'Mrs Tysall and I would like champagne.'

'Oh, for Christ's sake, Julian, get her some lemonade, will you?'

'I don't want—'

'Yes you do. You just said you did. Drink your tea, you look like a—'

'Don't hit me,' Mummy was whining until Julian's voice rose, deceptively calm, with a hint of weariness.

'Don't be so silly. No-one's going to hit you, never have, never will. Why did you let her wear that dress, Jo?'

'Oh, here we go again. Let her! Have you ever tried stopping her? She does what she wants. How do you suppose I'd stop her? I've got enough to do—'

'Sitting on your bottom all day? Playing house? Leaving dirt everywhere and the garden a mess? Pretending to cook? I don't know where you get the energy.'

Sarah remembered the elaborate meal of the night before, the polish on the furniture, the semi-tidiness, her own clean sheets, and reflected that Julian was being less than fair. Joanna's voice now had a hint of tears.

'Oh what's the point? I do nothing while you play God with the sick. Bet they're all queuing up now, praying for the chance to see another doctor. You look like those dead cod off one of the boats.'

'At least I work. One of us has to.' His voice was dangerous. There was a pause, a clatter of cutlery, then a crash.

'Oh, what a pity!' Mother's voice rose to a giggle. 'No champagne for Mrs Tysall!' Julian ignored the interruption.

'I'd have more to offer the sick if I wasn't surrounded by idiots at home. A brother who can't work and can't get a job unless I get it for him, a sister who thinks she deserves to be kept.'

'OK,' she howled, 'give us some money and we'll go. Isn't this what the lawyer's for?'

'Mrs Tysall, please,' Mother chanted.

'Money?' Julian taunted. 'Other people start their lives without.'

'I'll go,' Joanna shouted, 'and you can keep Mother. But you wouldn't, would you? Would you?' Her fist was pounding the table, her voice rising in hysteria, then sinking. Mouse began humming tunelessly; there was the sound of a chair scraping back on a stone floor. Julian's voice again, dismissive and distant.

'Tell Miss Fortune, when she deigns to appear, that I'll be in the surgery at twelve, and do remember what else I told you. Don't forget to give her directions. Don't offer to feed her either, not tonight, not any night. She supports herself as long as she's here and I don't think it will be long.'

Sarah waited. There was the remote sound of a door banging somewhere inside the house, silence but movement inside the kitchen, a sensation of relief. Sarah knocked on the open door and stepped inside.

Joanna leapt to her feet and turned back to look busy at the vast Rayburn with its large simmering kettle, rubbing her eyes with a tea towel, while Mrs Pardoe's mouth formed into a startled OOOh of something like pleasure. She looked as welcoming as a placid baby with exactly the same span of concentration. There was a stale-looking edifice of chocolate cake in the centre of the table.

'Good morning, Mrs Pardoe,' said Sarah. 'It's a lovely day.' The sleeveless gold lamé dress was only as shocking as the enormous ear-rings which hung down to bare shoulders, tinkling as Mrs Pardoe finished chewing her toast and dabbed at her mouth with the corner of the tablecloth, leaving small traces of marmalade.

'Good morning to you, Mrs Tysall. How nice to see you.'

Sarah felt cold as Joanna, flushed and uncertain, came back to the table with a pot of coffee.

'I do so hope you enjoy your stay, I made you a cake. I'm always making cakes and things, but no-one eats them.' Mother was continuing in the same, fluting tone of a hotel receptionist fresh from a training course.

'Oh Mother,' said Joanna uneasily, embarrassed, but all fight gone.

'And I do wish,' said Mother, rising from the table and affording Sarah a glimpse of her pink trainers, 'that you young things would wear frocks. Trousers, my dear, are made for men.' With this she swept from the room in a cloud of perfume, a bright smile and fluttering of fingers to indicate her blessing. Joanna looked at Sarah across the table and tried to smile. Tears still lurked, not as well controlled after a quick appraisal of Sarah's appearance in the light of Mother's remarks. Joanna did not notice the dirt on the jeans, only their immaculate fit and the vibrant silk shirt ending across slim hips, and the fact that Miss Fortune's appearance in trousers bore no resemblance to her own.

'Did you hear us having a row?' she asked abruptly.

'Think I caught the tail-end. Sorry.'

'That's all right then. You must have missed the worst bit, when Edward was in on it too. He stormed

out a while ago. A morning ritual. I should stay in
the cottage if I were you, until after eight-thirty on
weekdays. After that, it's only me and Mother. Have
some coffee? Toast?'

'Please. Coffee.'

'By the way, you've to meet Julian at his surgery,
about twelve, he said. I'll take you, but I'm under
strict orders not to discuss business beforehand, not
that I know much, not about the estate, whatever you
call it, and all that.' The words were rushing out in
a fit of apology.

'That's fine. I wouldn't expect you to disobey orders.' They smiled at each other conspiratorially, two
women mourning the dominion of men. 'But can you
answer me two things? First, why does this family
need a lawyer to sort out who should inherit what?
Why can't you do it for yourselves?'

Joanna waved vaguely round the mess of the
kitchen, the tea spilt on the wooden table, rubbish
stacked at one end, two fishing rods next to the
Rayburn, the smashed glass on the floor. 'You can
see why, can't you? We're not exactly good at the art
of communication. Bloody Julian gives the orders
and buggers up our lives, Ed looks after me. He and
Julian never speak, that sort of thing. What was the
other question?'

'Why on earth,' Sarah asked casually, 'does your
mother call me Mrs Tysall?'

'Search me ... Oh, I remember, Edward said
something about it when she started this morning.
There was a couple called Tysall had a holiday cottage down here, a few years ago, he said. Mrs
Tysall had red hair, like yours, she sometimes came
here by herself. Then she had some kind of accident and drowned. Ma used to talk to her in the
hairdresser's. Well, everyone talked about her, I
gather. It was a bit of a scandal at the time, because

the body got stuck somewhere, wasn't found for a
year, after a high tide. Must have been horrible.
Lots of red hair.'

'What about her husband?'

Joanna thought hard. 'I dunno the details. More
scandal, but you'd have to ask Julian about that.
He dealt with the bodies: it suits him, he's better
off with dead people.' She laughed at her own wit.
'Oh, yes, once this Charles was told where his wife
was found, he thought she'd run away, or something, you see, he must have walked out to see and
got caught by the tide. He got washed up in
Holkham the next day. Must have been love. Romantic, isn't it?'

Joanna was pouring more coffee, enjoying herself
with ghoulish tales which did not touch her own life
and mattered less than her eighteen-year-old concerns with love and spots. Or so Sarah guessed. The
passions of the over thirties were obscene mysteries
to teenagers.

'Charles Tysall was a client of ours,' she volunteered without quite the right kind of indifference. 'I
knew him.'

'Did you? I never did,' said Joanna, wondering
how a person managed to acquire a figure like Sarah's and the jeans to fit it. It must be a combination
of smoking instead of eating breakfast, and living in
the sinful paradise of London which she did not
crave.

'Well, knew him slightly.' She sipped her coffee,
black. 'What an action-packed place this is,' Sarah
added lightly. 'Family fights, suicides, sirens, death
and all other adventures. Even a ghost, you were saying last night. Everything happens here.'

Joanna shot her a pitying glance of incredulous
impatience.

'What on earth are you talking about?' she wailed.

'We own most of the village,' she added mournfully, 'and absolutely nothing happens here. Nothing at all.'

CHAPTER FOUR

The medical centre could have been anywhere. There was nothing rural about it and the clean, hygienic smell, still reminiscent of sickness, made it somehow a fitting place to discuss a will.

'. . . the residue of my estate, whatsoever and wheresoever, to my wife Jennifer absolutely. For her to dispose of between my children entirely in such shares as she sees fit.'

'Look,' Julian was saying from the opposite side of a depressing metal desk, oblivious to her curiosity, cutting short niceties and looking at any point in the bare room which did not include Sarah's presence, 'I can't pretend I like this because I don't. I don't like any of this business and I regret the necessity for your presence here. Ernest Matthewson was my father's lawyer for half a lifetime, but I don't always see the sense in his ideas.'

'I thought it was your idea,' she interrupted. Julian looked blank. A brief, forced smile touched his features like a magic wand, to reveal a glimpse of humanity on a face carved from stone, distressed by chronic pain which may or may not have been his own.

'My idea? Ernest simply told me you were coming. Never mind. You ARE here, for better or worse. You've looked at the will, but not the list of assets which form my mother's property as it is now.'

She waited for signs of smugness, saw none as he

handed her three typed pages, headed with the name
of a local estate agent. A glance at the list showed a
longish list of houses, business premises and shops.
Sarah wondered fleetingly if there was anything freehold left in the village belonging to anyone else.

'About two thirds of it,' Julian said, guessing her
thoughts. 'Took him twenty years. My father,' he
continued, 'believed passionately in bricks and
mortar, exchanged the proceeds of his manufacturing concerns for nothing else. Hence it was apposite
for him to be on a roof when having a heart attack,
because, at the age of seventy, he chose to clean
leaves from the gulley. He always was an over-
achiever and a lousy delegator. Since his death, my
mother has been as you see her; it appears to be a
permanent malady. She can no longer read or cook,
has no sense of property or propriety, no sense of
time, no sense of fear, absolutely no insight into her
own condition and no perception of ours. She's difficult, irritating, demanding, vulnerable and quite
incapable of dealing with her own affairs since she
doesn't even know what she owns. Neither do I, entirely. I believe Edward does. He works at the estate
agent's who manage things.'

He sighed as if bored by the whole subject. 'Father
was copping out, you see.' Julian went on with the
same suppressed irritation. 'For such an astute and
materialistic man, he was very indecisive. He left it
all to Mother to sort it for him. Amazing. I thought
he loved and trusted me. Obviously not.' Sarah
watched him flinch.

'For the last couple of years, he and Mother
seemed to rediscover each other. They behaved like
lovers, told each other jokes instead of him simply
issuing orders. Father even gave up social climbing,
she hated it anyway. He perfected his skill at fishing.
Talked about raising rare breeds of sheep. There's
one left, in the garden.'

Sarah wanted everything. She wanted to know where Mrs Pardoe had worn her gold dress for the first time and what Mr Pardoe had been like. She wanted family portraits, anecdotes, signs of grief, instead of this unnerving formality. All she could see from here was that husband and wife between them had created a good-looking tribe, disparate in appearance, Edward, dark and slight, Joanna fair and rounded, and the eldest, sitting opposite, stocky and attractive with a jutting chin, red-gold curls, the blazing eyes of a fever and no inclination to wander from the point. Sarah supposed she had better act as she had always done with clients and pretend that she had more to offer than educated common sense. The pretence often became real.

'Look,' she began, 'it's a perfectly valid will.'

'Yes, I know that,' he said rudely. 'And it leaves me, as the eldest, to administer an estate over which I have no power. Mother can't make a power of attorney in my favour, because she'd have to understand what it was. I've tried and failed. I manage to collect rents, pay cheques and run things only because the bank manager's a patient, but I've got responsibility without authority. I also know, before you deign to tell me, that if she dies, Edward, Joanna and I would inherit in equal shares. Meantime, we're all stuck. We've got assets without a huge income. Enough, but not generous. Mother could last for thirty years.' He made the last statement fondly, a glimmer of admiration in his voice. Sarah caught him smiling, smiled back and watched his face harden, a man coarsened by bitterness and a loneliness beyond his own curing. Sarah was watching the fleeting betrayals of a condition which was second nature to herself, saw a man who had passed harsh judgements on himself.

'So,' she said briskly, 'this is what we do. Itemize the estate, then value it. Decide on how it should be

managed, whether in or outside the family. Then go
to Court of Protection with our plans. They can write
a will for your mother.'

'Simple,' said Julian ironically, the smile coming
back.

'No. Not simple, but possible. It'll cost you the
price of a house on a Monopoly board, but I don't
suppose that matters, you seem to have plenty of
houses. The object of this planning is to make sure
your mother is safe, happy and well provided for.
That's the primary aim. Then, to free up enough cap-
ital for you, Edward and Jo to spread your wings and
fulfil your dreams sooner rather than later.'

Julian laughed, surprising himself. There was irony
in the laugh, but at least it was laughter.

'What dreams? What dreams could a simple coun
try doctor have?'

'Everyone has dreams,' Sarah protested. 'Your father must have had dreams to acquire as he did. Jo
tells me that Edward has dreams of being an artist.
She may dream of being a cook. Money's for refur-
bishing dreams. Why else work for it?'

'Some of us don't.'

Surely she could not believe Edward had honest
dreams. So much for her wisdom. Edward dreaming
of being an artist only meant the same Edward who
blamed all his failures on being bored, growing from
spiteful boy into lazy man, drifting through one job
after another until his father had got him a sinecure
in the local estate agent's office. His ability to con-
centrate was pathetic, his lack of convention a sham.
Julian looked at Sarah and decided her neutral expression was a clever sham too. She might repeat
what she was told, but only believe what she chose.

He sat back. This time the smile did not retreat
into the gauntness of his face.

'Miss Fortune, I believe you may be a witch. I was
waiting for you to accuse me of cupidity and you

talk about dreams. I suppose you also exorcise demons?'

Sarah shook her head, smiling. 'I find it easier to
pay them off. Gremlins, demons, goblins, regrets.
They're the symptoms of life after thirty.'

Julian allowed himself another bark of laughter,
which stopped abruptly to coincide with a knock on
his door and the entry of a buxom nurse who bustled
toward the pile of notes in a wire basket on the edge
of the desk, smiling her professional smile. Then she
stopped, face to face with Sarah, ceased smiling,
grabbed the notes and scuttled away without apology.
The door clicked shut angrily behind her. Sarah pretended to study the list of Pardoe assets Julian had
given her. 'Amusement arcade, East Quay,' was a description which sprang from the page. The room was
suddenly hot.

'Is that enough to keep you going?' Julian asked,
back into the persona of a doctor asking if the med-
ication would last the week. She wanted to slap him,
but rose gracefully, tucking the papers under her arm.

'I wonder if your nurse thought I was a malin-
gerer? Asking for a sick note to sit in the sun, or
something of the kind? She seems . . . a little possessive.' She felt unreasonably angry, looked down at
the pristine slacks which had replaced the dirtier
jeans, too smart for a village surgery, noticed that
Julian's skin resembled the colour of chalk.

'I'm sorry. You must have given her a shock. Actually, you gave me a shock when I first saw you.
You happen to be the graven image of a patient of
ours, oh, two years ago, but she was . . . well, difficult to forget.'

'Mrs Tysall,' said Sarah flatly. 'Your mother calls
me Mrs Tysall. Someone in the hairdresser's said I
was like an old client. It's extremely disconcerting, a
person could get sick of comparisons, but I suppose
you all mean Elisabeth Tysall who resides in the

graveyard, without even a headstone on her grave. Wife of Charles.'

He had risen from his seat, still pale, twisting a pencil in his large hands.

'Your sister says you dealt with both bodies, Elisabeth and her husband,' Sarah went on artlessly, driven by the same flat anger. 'She was your patient, you say. I always wanted to meet someone who knew her. Was she very lovely?'

The pencil snapped.

'Get out of here. You're right. Comparisons are odious. You don't resemble Elisabeth at all. No-one does.'

Sarah stopped, watched his rage crumble into a thinly disguised distress, the veneer of control exerting itself slowly.

'Demons and gremlins,' she murmured. 'I didn't mean to touch a nerve. Was she a friend of yours? She certainly needed one.'

He shook his head, reverting abruptly to the original state of officious rudeness.

'Please go, Miss Fortune. I doubt if you're at all suitable to help us. Spend the weekend in the cottage, as our guest. Then we'll reconsider.'

'As you please.'

Stonewall Jones ran from the amusement arcade, left down the quay, left again and then cut through a crooked alley leading to the main street. On the way, he could nod in several directions to houses where various relatives lived, first his mother, out at work at the moment, her carefully made sandwiches mashed in his pocket, his baby brothers three doors up with Aunty Mary, Uncle Jack round the corner in the police station. The place was a mine of people who were good for a fifty-pence touch, and those who would, in various scolding ways, let him in had he asked, but not one compared with Cousin Rick.

Rick had his drawbacks, but as a hero he was
faultless, while as a spy, Stonewall was the soul of
discretion, with the added talent of being able to lie
convincingly, although truth was his natural inclination. He also had a memory as long as his fleeting
stride and a fine eye for detail. Which was why he
was now so excited. The redhead.

The memory was visual rather than verbal. Stonewall talked all the time to Rick, sometimes to his
mates at school, while anyone else got short shrift.
The redhead girl came back before his eyes from a
time when he had been smaller, but not such a baby
he'd fail to remember a woman with her face full of
stitches, coming out of the medical centre, crying.
That was two years and a whole lifetime ago; but he
never quite forgot because he had not had the
chance. First he had found her credit cards and stuff
with her photo on it hidden in the creeks. Then he
and his stepdad found the body, exactly one year after.

Dad had been terribly sick, which Stonewall had
not considered a good example. Tutored by illicit,
adult videos, seen in the house of a mate, he wasn't
that shocked himself. The redhead looked like a real
dead dog, not a person, the impression accentuated
by the long hair like red spaniel ears covered in
muddy sand, floppy, silken, gritty and wet. She was
a thing, not to be confused with anything live.

The man they had found a month later, well he
was different. This time it had been him and Rick,
the rovers of the creeks in their idle hours last summer, looking for flotsam, only Stonewall secretly
hoping they'd find another corpse, because of all the
fuss people made of him last time. Being famous
gave him a wonderful, fleeting insight into being noticed.

They'd been so brave, they could still make themselves shudder at the memory. The second body, a

man, had only been in and out of the sea for two days and was so nearly alive they couldn't look at him. A man with his face in the rictus of a smile, another gob full of sand as he lay on a bank, sluiced with mud, his good trousers dragged off his ankles and his bottom a little white mountain. Turned him over and his goolies fell out. Hung like a donkey, Rick said. They had sniggered while trembling, called Uncle Jack who panicked and talked about sending for the lifeboat. More sniggering, hugging themselves, as if anything more than a rowboat could get near at low water, he'd have to go by land. Seen one, seen 'em all, said Rick. They had stood in the tideless channel and rocked with mirth until the doctor came and seemed to know who it was. Then it was harder to laugh. In the end, it was he who carried the corpse away with their help, brought his car as far as he could, using a piece of Rick's dripping sail to lug the thing over two creeks and into the boot; it was all anyone could do with the tide rising all the time.

Mostly, though, it was left to the doc. Everyone else turned away; so had Rick and he, but not before they had both seen what they had seen: the doctor, kicking the corpse as if it had been a football. Just a couple of kicks, but hard. Stonewall could still hear the sound of a shoe going into a waterlogged chest, could not quite recall the sight of it, since even he had turned his head, but he could always recall the sound. Schluck, schluck, schluck, the thudding of mad hatred. Funny at the time. Everything with Rick was funny, but they never, ever discussed that bit again. Stonewall had felt sorry for the drowned man, later. He reckoned that if he drowned, he would be taken away and buried somewhere like the man was. His mum and dad wouldn't come to the funeral either. They'd be too busy.

Stonewall pounded on the door of Swamp Cottage,

then opened it. There was a lock which was never used, nothing to steal; burglary was not a problem in the village, except recently, when it could be called the work of tourists or the ghost. The door led straight into a tiny scullery where only two dishes lurked in the sink and a fly buzzed at the window, down a step into a living room where a TV blared. Rick sat in an old sofa, his finger easing stuffing out a split in the arm as he gazed at the screen. The sight of the haversack on the floor and the bruises round the eyes threw Stonewall into a panic.

'You're not going, Rick? You're not going away, are you? Your dad'll kill you.' His voice was high with anxiety.

'He already tried,' Rick grunted. He got up, towering in the gloomy room, his head inches away from the ceiling as he ruffled the boy's hair. 'Don't fret, boy, it wasn't so bad. Only I might go on the boat tonight. Then again, I might not.'

'Can I come too?'

'Nope. Only in the mornings. Your mum'd miss you. God knows why.' Stonewall relaxed. If Rick was teasing, he must be all right. The boy took up occupation of the sofa and began to play with the stuffing, rolling flax between his fingers. He was utterly relieved to find Rick so normal, had news to impart which made him as full to bursting as three rounds of chips followed by chocolate.

'Tell you what, Rick, I just seen a ghost just now. I did, honest. A woman.'

'Oh yeah?'

'I saw this woman, see? Same one as I used to see, long time ago, when my dad started taking me out in the boat—'

'And you were scared to death of the water. Oh I remember that. You'd cry like some mating cat in heat, you would.' Rick taunted without malice. 'Wait a minute,' he added, still teasing, 'you mean you saw one whole woman ugly enough to be a ghost? Just the one? There's dozens out there!' His laugh hit the rafters.

'It's the same one,' said the boy stubbornly, 'that came up out of the sand. She went down the creeks, drunk, her face mashed up. I was with Dad, he ticked me off for laughing at her. Course, that was MY body, the one I found with Dad, not the one I found with you. I'd never have remembered her if it wasn't for her stuff, with her picture in. Anyway, this one I just seen got the same red hair. Lots. Got to be a ghost. Or a twin?' He wilted under Rick's glare.

Stonewall could not resist the importance of being present at the finding of two bodies, made reference to it whenever he could. He'd been a cosseted celebrity in school twice over. Rick, on the other hand, had only ever found the one. A few dogs and cats down the creeks, a couple of swans poisoned by lead weights, a seal killed by massive fishing hooks, but only one corpse. It was the only feature of Stonewall's little life which gave him any superiority. He milked it.

'Red hair? You saw a ghost with red hair this morning, did you?' Rick jeered. Stonewall was deflated.

'Saw her this morning, when I went out looking for you. Saw her again, walking into town, with your girlfriend,' he said cunningly, but Rick only shrugged.

'That weren't no ghost, baby. That's a lawyer, so she says. Belongs out with those Pardoes. They could do with a gardener, never mind a lawyer. And Jo isn't my girlfriend.'

'Oh no? Not what I heard,' said Stonewall, looking so much the little man. Rick wanted to laugh at him but hadn't the heart.

'Anyway, I follows them both. That's how I come to reckon the red one was a ghost. Your Joanna went in the grocer's; the ghost went in the doctor's. Just like that other one with the hair used to do, all the time. My Aunty Mary used to say it was shocking.'

Stonewall loved to be the purveyor of adult gossip, which lost none of its sparkle in his eleven-year-old eyes for the obscurity of its implications. He simply liked the tone of it, knew they were talking about sex when they lowered their voices and went into corners. In his own home with two babies, he was not a powerful person, always last in line, listening. Brilliant, Rick would say, sometimes in genuine amazement at what this child, so silent indoors and so loquacious out, could collect as second-hand knowledge. Stonewall sensed attention was beginning to wander.

'Going to get your girlfriend on the boat?' he asked, to rekindle interest.

'She ain't my girlfriend, I tell you. You deaf?'

'She thinks she is,' Stonewall muttered.

Rich swaggered. 'Her and who else?' he said, then caught sight of his face in the cracked mirror propped over the mantelpiece, let his mouth drop in a leer. 'Her and Granny Pardoe, at this rate, any woman draws a short straw with me,' he muttered. 'Fancy an ice-cream down on the beach?'

The boy hid his enthusiasm by shrugging, nodded, followed with a little skip and a sigh of pleasure which somehow got out before he could stop it.

'And there's another thing,' he began as they went out into the alley.

'Oh yes, another ghost, I suppose. The one with white hair? Tall bloke? Come on, everyone says they've seen that.'

'Maybe ghosts come out at the same time.'

'Well, I don't know,' said Rick admiringly, cuffing him round the ear. 'I think you need glasses, boy. Dark ones, with wipers, stop you seeing so much.'

'That ghost got my dog,' said Stonewall stub-

bornly, horribly ashamed of the way his eyes filled
with tears. 'He did. I saw him, and then Sal ran
away.'

Rick was thinking of his evening date, half wishing he hadn't made it. Thought of Jo and tried to put
her out of his mind.

When Sarah got back to the homestead, wondering
whether it was better simply to pack up her bags
and leave before she was sacked, two sights met her
eyes as she went, like an old familiar, to the back
door. The first was Mrs Pardoe, sunbathing in the
cabbage patch. She looked like a religious emblem,
lying in the pose of a crucifixion with her legs dis-
creetly crossed, the dress hoiked up and the arms
spreadeagled. A little dirt didn't seem to matter.
Sarah approached with caution until her shadow fell
over the body. It was very hot; her own longing for
the sea was intense.

'Hallo.'

'You're taking my sunlight,' said Mrs Pardoe,
shifting in irritation. 'Give me back my rays.'

'Can I get you anything?' The body laid out on the
earth still had very good legs, the face resembled a
pixie, oddly ageless.

'Ice-cream,' said the lady, dreamily, then closed
her eyes.

The second sight was Joanna crying in the kitchen,
with none of her mother's aplomb, but again, there
was a sense of absent beauty.

'Sorry,' said Joanna, beyond embarrassment.
'Sorry. I can't help it.'

'Is it your mother?'

'Oh no, I'm used to her. She's fine, honestly. Absolutely fine. You sort of adjust, you know?'

Sarah didn't know, but nodded.

'I mean, she's quite safe by herself and everything,
and she doesn't ask for much, never did. I mean, I

could go out this evening, even though Ed and Julian are always out on Fridays. I mean, I think Ma quite likes a bit of time to herself and anyway, she goes to bed ludicrously early, so that's fine, she doesn't need a babysitter; but I can't go anywhere, can I? I mean, not even round to Caroline's, can I? Even though she's asked me twice and I said I would ...'

Sarah continued nodding.

'Because I'm different, and Caroline's very together, you see. And she knows I was going out with Rick who is, let's face it, the best looking boy around, but he won't talk to me now. Julian warned him off. And she'll have her friends there, and I've got to pretend I just don't care, you know, have a glass of wine and make a joke of it. Which I just about could, just about, even if it isn't true and it's only a small party, but not like this. Not when I've got nothing to wear ...'

Sarah nodded. An obscure dilemma, one she remembered well. King Richard offered his kingdom for a horse. A love-sick teenager would offer hers for the right suit of clothes. Twice seen, Joanna was remarkably badly, almost childishly, dressed. Sarah settled into an uncomfortable wooden chair and kissed goodbye to her dreams of a distant beach for the afternoon, pulled out her cigarettes, lit one, did not offer the rest. The child was a smoke-free zone.

'What sort of clothes,' she asked gently, 'do you think you need?'

'Classics,' said Jo, fervently. 'I read it in a magazine ... Caroline reads it too. Stuff that makes you look sophisticated. You know, older, thinner, all that stuff. Expensive stuff. Julian says I can get them if I want, but Edward says don't, it's bad to grow up too soon. I always laugh, tell him it doesn't matter, but it does.'

Sarah felt a recurrence of spontaneous dislike for Edward Pardoe.

'Classics. A bit of nice jewellery? Just a bit?' said Sarah thoughtfully.

'Exactly. Edward would murder me. I can't afford it anyway, I promised him a new fishing rod for his birthday, they cost a bomb—'

'Stand up.'

Joanna stood, much taller than Sarah.

'I've got some lovely shirts, fit anyone. Leggings for the bottom? Come with me.'

'Oh, I couldn't, Miss Fortune, honestly. I'm really sorry, blubbing all over you, scarcely know . . . Oh, it's so awful . . .'

'Sisters under the skin,' said Sarah lightly. Clothes could be the stuff of dreams or the staff of confidence. 'I wouldn't listen to Edward,' she added kindly. 'Men are no good on these things. A nice, bold colour, no patterns, is what you need.'

'Black,' said Jo fervently. 'Then I could cope.'

There was darkness and privacy in the pine woods which covered the dunes and led to the beach, but when the man with snow-white hair came to the brow of the last ridge, the wind took away his breath into a vast, galloping sky, leaving him shocked. Memory played such tricks, even since yesterday. He had forced himself to walk this far with his military steps; the sea should have been closer, instead of that distant, mocking promise. The tide was a fickle woman who never obeyed orders. The man saw only the horizon, noticed no details, felt no pain and counted nothing but the minutes.

The sand was soft, his ill-fitting shoes suddenly struggling for a sinking foothold as he thrashed the air with his arms, overbalanced, fell with his jacket flapping, rolling over and over, sand in his hair and his mouth, landing on his back on the beach. There was an initial sense of fury, then exhilaration in letting go like a child, falling into a blissful, uninhibited waving of limbs without any sense of danger. He wanted to do it again. The sky was blinding blue when he opened his eyes and laughed. A face came into focus above his own.

'That wasn't very graceful,' said Edward Pardoe.

The man grunted, sat up, stroking his luxuriant white hair which curled into the back of his neck. His clothes were the ill-assorted garments of a tramp, too heavy for summer, but he folded his long, thin body about itself and clasped his hands to his knees with a kind of elegance. Strange, how wearing the clothes of a person of no importance could turn one into exactly that. He was beginning to perceive how disguise became habit. The transition had frightened him once, not now.

Edward considered that the face beneath the stubble of beard had been handsome once, possibly exceptional. They sat and said nothing for a while.

'I'd like to reorganize this shoreline,' Edward remarked, frowning. 'It's so . . . imperfect.'

'But it's here,' said the man.

'Yes, I know, but the sea should be lapping at my feet. The trees should be more exotic than these drab pines. A few extraordinary shrubs. Flowers in winter. I could do it. I shall do it.'

'After art, nature,' the man murmured. 'These kinds of dreams are expensive.'

They were silent again. The sea stayed the same distance, the man staring at it as if mesmerized.

'Have you been seen?' Edward asked as if it did not matter.

'What do you think? From sea or land? I suppose so. A beastly little boy and his dog. The dog ran after me. I loathe dogs. I move about, beach hut, boat, occasional empty cottage where people obligingly leave me their soap. The village is crowded with holiday-makers, ignorant pigs. They don't notice anyone who looks so venerable.' He touched his white locks. 'People don't notice me now.'

'They may have done once, when you were younger,' said Edward nastily.

'I am a person of no fixed abode,' said the man quietly. 'That is my choice, not my destiny. It does not mean I am a person of no consequence.' Even as he said it he wondered very briefly if it were true, looked down at his hands. Of course he could still remember how to pare his nails.

'What did you do about the dog?'

It was disturbing the way the man exerted superiority so easily with his patrician voice and his air of sheer indifference. He looked like an outcast and behaved as if he were a prince.

'The dog? Buried it. It was only a dog.'

Edward swallowed.

'You aren't invisible,' he said sharply. 'I've been hearing local rumours about a ghost with white hair committing minor burglaries. You're obviously perfecting this talent of yours.'

'Mrs Tysall was good at picking locks,' the man volunteered irrelevantly. 'She was never fond of keys, but she could always get in, or out.'

'I never knew Mrs Tysall,' said Edward, profoundly irritated. 'It was my wonderful brother who knew her, as I told you in some detail.' Both were staring seaward, their eyes never meeting.

'I have to be sure,' the man said.

'How to get into the surgery,' Edward continued, 'is something you must work out for yourself. As I said yesterday, you'll need the keys to his desk.'

He dropped a ring of keys on the sand in between them. The man never took his eyes off the horizon as he felt for them with long, lazy fingers.

'By the way, don't stay in any of the cottages nearest the house again, will you? We have a visitor in the end one. My mother calls her a cow, but she seems quite observant.'

'Aah, your lovely sister.'

'Leave her alone, she's mine,' said Edward sharply.

'Of course I shall. I didn't doubt it for a moment. Ah, the love of a sister. How could you be ashamed?

' "Say that we had one father, say one womb
Are we not therefore each to the other bound
So much the more by nature? by the links
Of blood and reason? One soul, one flesh,
One love, one heart, one all?" '

Silence again.

'Who wrote that?' Edward asked softly. 'I like it.'

' *'Tis Pity She's a Whore.'*

Edward clenched his fists.

'John Ford. A play. I'm not being personal.'

Edward relaxed.

'Here,' he said roughly. 'Be grateful for the love of a sister. She made these sandwiches for me. She does every day. Pity you can't fish for food. I could give you a rod.'

The man took the sandwiches without thanks, opened and ate them with the voracity of a dog before the daily bowl, swallowing rather than chewing. His teeth were brown. The silence was punctuated only by the sound of his jaws, the soft slushing of the trees behind them and the distant shouting of games. Edward could imagine the thin man eating carrion, crumbling bones and all, and shuddered slightly.

'Food,' the man announced, 'is a matter of complete indifference. I detest the vulgar business of eating. I suppose it would be useful if I had learned to fish. Can you fish?'

'Not well. I go out at night to learn,' said Edward, miserably. 'When no-one's watching. My father fished,' he added inconsequentially. 'He said it made a man of you.' The silence stretched again, unbearably.

'However did I come to meet someone like you?' Edward asked facetiously, simply to interrupt it. 'You've quite enlivened my summer.'

'Dreams,' the man said abruptly. 'We are all entangled in dreams.' From his mouth, the word sounded oddly obscene.

'Oh yes?'

'You met me,' the man said evenly, 'when you found me trespassing in that cottage of yours. It seemed to amuse you. You said you wouldn't turn me out immediately, would even show me another empty place to stay, provided I was good enough to set a little fire inside it, enough to stop it being used. It wasn't much to ask of a man on holiday.'

'We seem to have gone on from there,' Edward murmured.

'Into the dreams. You dream of changing the landscape. For which you need your brother destroyed and your mother dead.'

Edward would never have put it so baldly. He felt the prickling of his scalp, a terrible tingling in his limbs of dreadful excitement.

'And you?'

'On my master's behalf? I dream of the proof of wickedness and adultery. I dream of revenge and the satisfaction of honour. "Death, thou art a guest long looked for; I embrace thee and thy wounds." ' Edward scrambled to his feet, lightheaded. Enough was enough.

'Don't tell me what my dreams are. I'll see you here, same time, tomorrow or Sunday.'

The man nodded, the breeze lifting his long white hair off the once spectacular face, his eyes still staring towards the sea.

* * *

Sarah Fortune had packed a case for all eventualities except the extremes of country life, being ignorant of what it was; black could be provided. A sueded silk overshirt with the elbow-length sleeves she always wore, slightly padded shoulders, cool and elegant over leggings, completed by a deep cerise belt and a discreet but heavy silver necklace and ear-rings. The child looked ten years older, transformed into a sleek, black cat with a whole decade of confidence.

'Shirt needs an iron. Where is it?'

'Oh, in that cupboard. Oh, Sarah! This shirt is positively divine!'

A lawyer dressing a client for a night on the town. If these were the worst eccentricities of country life, Sarah thought she could take to it. In the course of this long foraging through her suitcase, she had heard plenty of family history since Joanna talked non-stop. Such as, Father being a lovable tyrant, they'd all wept buckets; Julian a despicable one. Such as Mother never getting her own way about anything when Father was alive, poor thing. About Edward being marvellous, but constantly misjudged, and about how all Joanna Pardoe wanted to do with her life was to learn to cook properly, get married and have a lot of babies.

Sarah had agreed that feminism was overrated, no, a career was not always a route to happiness, and that yes, family life was a perfectly honest ambition, if you had the temperament for it. Then she heard all about Rick and how wonderful he was and how he didn't love Joanna any more. Julian had told him to fuck off.

'I suppose,' Joanna finished wistfully, putting on the freshly pressed shirt, which looked easily as expensive as its price, 'that's a better reason for being rejected than being too fat. Heavens, look at the time.'

'Fat? Who's fat?' said Sarah. She had dragged a

mirror from the bedroom. Joanna pirouetted in front of it, giggling, half convinced, but better than that, being sure she could convince others of profound sophistication.

'What did you do to my hair?' It was twisted above her head: it would fall throughout the evening, gracefully. Blond tendrils escaped round her ears. 'Look, are you sure I can wear this?'

'You can be sick on it if you like. I wouldn't have ironed it otherwise, would I? Eat your heart out, Caroline what'sit. You look a million dollars. I'd kill for hair like yours,' Sarah added fervently.

'But yours is so lovely.'

'No, not always,' said Sarah.

Mrs Pardoe had removed her station to the upstairs window where she often waited throughout the late afternoon, in case the ice-cream van came, not every day, but often enough to warrant her vigil.

She watched her daughter, crossing from the cottages where she had seen her go earlier with the old cow. When she saw Joanna striding back like a modern princess, head held high, face enlivened by a rosy glow of hope, she sat back and sighed with profound pleasure.

Ernest Matthewson was an old friend, one to be trusted. He had such good ideas.

Ernest made her think of food: ice-cream, chocolate cake, steak and champagne. And all those years of being called Mouse.

CHAPTER FIVE

Malcolm Cook sat with his stepfather and his mother over the evening meal they shared once a fortnight, sometimes under sufferance, although never when Sarah had been included. There were no apologies for absences; the food was elaborate since it never took long for plump Mrs Matthewson to recover from a period of dietetic austerity. Ernest was spared the low-fat yoghurt in the interests of feeding Malcolm, a son who was far too thin in his mother's estimation. She did her best by hiding cream in the soup, serving hot garlic bread ostensibly made with low-calorie spread. Her husband ate heartily while Malcolm failed to be fooled, played the game back, complimenting everything, eating only what he needed.

'Want some more, Malcolm dear? Another potato?'

Everything calm so far, just like a normal Friday dinner, as long as she was careful not to leave them alone for too long. So they all sat with their coffee, their spines sunk into the feathers and the humming birds of the chairs and behaved as if nothing had happened, until the phone rang in the hall and Mrs Matthewson thought it was safe to leave them.

'Father,' said Malcolm, 'why did you send Sarah away?'

'I didn't,' Ernest responded indignantly. 'It was her choice, she volunteered. Couldn't wait to go. She wanted the sea, didn't mind where it was. She's always talking about living in the country, by the sea. Good chance to experiment. Nothing to do with you.'

Malcolm felt in the cigar box on his left, set on an ornate table decorated with more birds. He withdrew one of his father's best, tucked it into the open pocket of his shirt, then lit one of his own cigarettes which Father despised. Ernest winced at the subtlety of these gestures of insolence.

'You must think my stupidity is entirely comprehensive,' Malcolm continued in the smooth, authoritative tones of the advocate he was. 'But sometimes it lapses into an aberration called intelligence. You may have been right about Sarah and I, I doubt it, but did you have to be so cruel to her?'

'Cruel?' Ernest blustered. 'Who said anything about cruel? All right, I thought it was time both of you did a bit of thinking and it seemed like a good opportunity. I must admit to not quite realizing where it was I was sending her. She said it didn't matter. There was something she wanted to do in that part of the world. Someone to see.'

'Of course you knew. You were once friends of the Pardoe family. You sent her to sort out an estate which could be sorted out better by someone else in a matter of hours, to the place where Charles Tysall's wife committed suicide, and he followed suit.' He kept his voice calm. Ernest was at his least reliable when alarmed. All he could do at the moment was grunt.

'What happened to the Tysall business empire, Father?'

Ernest snorted in disgust. 'The estate will take years to resolve. What do you know or care about business? You like it down where you are, prosecuting grubby criminals—'

'And what else was Charles? The soul of probity?

Eton educated he may have been, good family, yes, but he founded his companies on stolen ideas, drove people to ruin, brutalized his wife—'

'There's no proof about that,' Ernest muttered. 'He may have told me things, but he may have fantasized. Don't speak ill of the dead.'

The Persian cat sprang from its cushion as Malcolm leaned over his father. There was a little hiss from Ernest of post-prandial sleep, only possibly feigned. Malcolm, ever aware of the shame of violence which was subsumed in himself by the habit of running twenty miles a week, was far too humane to strike someone already unconscious, although the temptation was certainly there. If only this old man were not so Machiavellian; if only they had talked more, instead of just enough; if only they had really exchanged information about what had happened to Sarah immediately before Malcolm found her. If only the son and the mother, in the interests of Ernest's health, had not sought to protect him from information which could shock and alarm, and if only it was not too late now.

'I'm thinking about Sarah, not your bloody clients,' Malcolm muttered, more to himself. 'Because she taught me about loving, Dad. That's what she did. That's what she does. I don't mean just sex; I mean loving.'

Ernest jolted out of a dream, rubbing his belly.

'Tart. That's the problem. A bit of a tart,' he muttered.

'What did you say?' Malcolm asked. 'I was talking about Sarah.'

'So was I, but what I meant was that I shouldn't have eaten that pie. Too tart,' Ernest grumbled, still stroking his paunch. He looked at his stepson pleadingly.

'Do you know your loyalty to your clients is ludicrous?' said Malcolm. 'You take the code to

extremes. I thought you'd have been cured. Would
you tell me, for instance, if Tysall was alive?'

'No,' said Ernest. 'He isn't, but I wouldn't. Not
for you to do what you were trying to do before.
Prosecute him for fraud when all he ever did was
steal other people's ideas. Perfectly good capitalistic
practice. I couldn't let that happen to a client of
mine. Not even a dead one.'

Again, that terrible temptation twitched in
Malcolm's fingers, made him ball his hands into fists
and keep them by his sides. The ample figure of
Malcolm's mother stood frozen in the doorway, the
whole of her suddenly forlorn. After all the work she
and Sarah had done, there they were, father and
adopted son, back at loggerheads, with love, that
dangerous and volatile commodity, as elusive as ever.

'You see? I love it, see?' Rick yelled above the din.
'I mean I just do. Could be all I know and that's for
why, but I love it. Can't help it.'

'Can I try?'

'Course you can. Pity Stonewall isn't here. He's
the expert. Which one do you want? Try this one,
this one's really good.'

Sarah wasn't confused by choice, only the row.
There was a background and foreground of thunder, of
bleep, bleep, bleep, explosions, machine-gun fire, electronic voices issuing commands, the muffled explosions of a dozen bombs, the sound of falling cash. In
the corner of the large room, separated from the rest
by age, the older generation sat to play bingo in a serious, dedicated row of grey heads with handbags on
laps, listening with all the earnestness of a congregation in church to a voice echoing sonorously through
a microphone. 'Number eleven, go to heaven, take a
dive, number five . . . on its own, number one . . .'
Above them hung the tawdry prizes for which they
concentrated as though their lives would be altered by

lime green furry bears, brilliant pink dolls, plastic skeletons, jigsaw puzzles and on the top tier only, dusty under the unforgiving light, glass and brass table lamps with heavily frilled nylon shades, brilliant vases, sets of cheap tumblers, bigger teddy bears with bows, grinning pottery cats with glittery eyes, none of it worth the price of three tickets for a game or the yearning it inspired.

Sarah sat on a pedestal as comfortable as the seat of a bicycle, inserted fifty pence and watched a man with a mask run up the street on the screen in front of her. Windows opened each side of him; the enemy dropped bombs on his head, emerged from doors and windows with the sole purpose of assassination. Pressing a button and pulling a lever in an unnatural feat of co-ordination would shoot the killers into the sky and save the refugee from the gang of thousands. She failed dismally: he was dead within seconds, gone in a big boom, noisier than all the rest. Game over, said the screen.

'You know what you are,' Rick yelled in her ear. 'Useless! Another?'

To her left, a boy stood, his body braced, his hands moving so fast they were blurred, his eyes transfixed by green monsters which bathed his hair in the same colour, his screen emitting the rat-tat-tat of a rifle and the muted sounds of artificial, bloodless agony.

'No thanks. Where do you go to draw breath?'

'Why?' he shouted.

'Is this all there is?'

He grinned. 'Isn't it enough?'

He liked the noise, but heard the message, led her to the back of the arcade where a voice still had to be raised to make sense, although not as much. She was temporarily deaf and blind. The light was eerie here, the carpet ran out into a couple of ante rooms, one containing a table, chair, sink, kettle, cardboard boxes and signs of disuse, the other, more machines, untidy, unlit, strangely lifeless, lurching towards one another. They reminded her of the graveyard.

'Dead ones,' said Rick. 'I don't like to see them really. Some broken. Mostly gone out of fashion. They change all the time. Nothing lasts long. The kids master them, want something else. Don't want to see the dead ones. I stay out front. There's nothing else out here, only a back yard.' He opened a door beyond the silent machines. The remnant of fast-fading, natural daylight on the cusp between late evening and summer night, was faintly shocking after the dazzle of the screens. In that light, Rick looked exhausted. The bruises had merged into the lights of the arcade; out here, they formed extra shadows to his handsome face. An attractive boy, ten years her junior. His face should not have held the merest line. The world should be his for the asking; he should be full of dreams.

After an hour in a pub called the Globe, he had volunteered to show her the arcade, or was it because she had asked? He couldn't remember, forgot as well how he had worried about this rash offer of a drink in the pain of near dawn when she had done his housework, just liked being where he was, with her, half hoping everyone he knew, except Jo, of course, would see. Which they did, good bit of gossip tomorrow and a lot of explaining to do to poor old Stonewall. Then, looking up into the stars visible from the back yard of the arcade, he felt suddenly sad, bereft, lonely, wanting to spill his guts, tell her stuff he never told. Also sleepy, the bruised ribs and early rising taking a toll. Must be the beer, the unaccustomed silence, the perfume. He slid down the wall and stayed at the bottom. She squatted beside him.

'Sorry,' he said. 'Things catch up, you know?'

'You've gone all pale, Rick.'

Without thinking, he felt for her hand. Must be drunk.

'You're nice, you know? Why'd you say you'd come out for a drink? You said you fancied a walk by the sea, but I'm a wreck, look at me.'

'A nice wreck. Place is full of your friends.'

He struggled to his feet. 'Think that's good enough reason to go out the back way. Cup of coffee's what I need. I live round the corner. Goo'night. Sorry.'

'I like coffee too.'

There was a shame in it, sneaking through the alley from the back yard of the arcade on his night off, back up the road to Swamp Cottage, letting her in with him to see the place where he lived. Tidy, scruffy, but clean; he was good at cleaning, good at nothing else. Strange the way she took over without being bossy, just as she had this morning. Made toasted cheese sandwiches without asking where anything was, terrific. You'd think she'd been here dozens of times, it was like being with Stonewall only not like that at all. It was food he needed, food he had forgotten all day. A whole day with nostrils full of hamburger onions or ice-cream with a chocolate flake stuck on top; a man forgot to eat, he explained. The room came back into focus, leaking sofa and all, he was still proud of it. He loved the way she ate, long fingers, nibbling mouth, and he still wanted to spill his guts. Wasn't much good for a bargain, was he? She'd wanted to have a look at the sea, talk about the Pardoes and he'd never mentioned anyone but himself. And Jo. Oddly, it hadn't felt like a betrayal, talking about Jo. It felt nice when she'd told him about Jo dressing up earlier to go out with the girls. Not with some other bloke. That was the point when the room refocused with shocking clarity. He'd been talking about Jo for twenty minutes.

'Why did Edward warn me off?' he asked out loud.

'Edward? It was Julian. You told her.'

That was what it was like, being with a woman who listened. You didn't have to explain anything, all your disjointed, drunken, exhausted thoughts were assembled for you.

'No. I met her once. Told her how her brother told me to fuck off. I meant Edward, of course. Julian's all right. He wouldn't do that. He wouldn't threaten you if you were behind with the rent, no more than his dad would have done. Edward told me to fuck off or get evicted. Not that there was any need. I love Jo, you know? We've played together since kids. I fancy her rotten, but what's the use? I'm not much use to a gorgeous bird like that, am I? Even if I love her. Even if I want her so much I think about her all the time.'

'Why?'

It was the only piece of his evening's rambling conversation which she did not seem to follow, she who seemed to piece together what he said even while he said it, she should have known this last bit, but how? Christ, she'd had half the story of his life, the arcade, his dreams, all but the greatest. She'd been more than perfect, she'd raised his stock with the multitudes, including his dad, sitting in the corner of the bar with his mouth open, serve him right, and she still didn't know nothing. About him being a virgin, at his age, the only one never quite able, out of fear of failure, and even after fumbling efforts, to do anything but grope.

'Why aren't you any good for Jo?' the woman was reminding him gently.

'I got too many kickings from Dad!' he yelled, loud enough to be heard over a thousand screens filled with computerized deaths and loud heroes. 'He did for me, Dad did. I think.' He was holding her hand again, didn't know why, there didn't seem too many minutes since he first had, sliding down the wall of the yard, and then here, a moment or two before the focus on his own room came back, still holding. He could smell her, wanted to smell her. Cheese, toast, perfume. Long sleeves of stuff he liked to touch, felt like suede. Here was this fancy bird, watching him crying like a kid. Just like Stonewall had on the beach this afternoon, when he'd found his dog's collar come in with the tide, as if he'd needed any confirmation that the bitch was dead.

Still holding hands, him and this other bird, sitting on his couch, in tune with all that old corrosive despair and shame. Her doing something else, touching something else, saying not much, putting her chin on his chin, tiny as she was, no doubt so she could look into his eyes and laugh herself sick. Only she wasn't. Smiling but not laughing, she was doing something else. She seemed to have lost her shirt. There were pretty little marks on her arms, like a series of meaningless tattoos.

'Kicking,' she was saying from a distance, 'doesn't do an ounce of harm, never did. Big man like you.'

He thought of the big man he and Stonewall had found, hung like a donkey, skin so white, dead like his attributes. It had mattered more to him than any imprint from Dad's boot, and he also knew he'd seen the last of those. The last, the last, the very last, of both sensations of disgust.

He would wonder later how it was he lost either his fear or his virginity on his sinking, third-hand couch with the stuffing hanging out. He would have liked to remember the details, recall them for inspection.

Rick woke, admiring himself for what he knew he had done for the first time in his twenty-one years. Fucked someone, slowly, beautifully. Someone who left him with a blanket up to his chin, his feet out of shoes, his head steady, a waft of perfume and a sense of pride which owed nobody.

Edward lay after dark and slept. He could have gone fishing, but he didn't. Fishing to prove he could do something, or to please a dead father, or simply to gain power over the fish, he didn't know which. It was an addiction. The old silk coverlet was twisted, the space next to his own body empty and cold. Ever since little Joanna had crept into his bed to tickle him awake in an orgy of innocence each morning, a practice she had suspended long since of her own accord, Edward woke with the expectation of finding her there. She had crept into bed at a dangerous age for a boy teased at school, tormented by his hormones and scolded at home for laziness. He had simply let her remain etched on his mind and imprinted on his skin as the only desirable girl in the world, rehearsed in wet day-dreams his own part of her deflowering, envisaged her whimpering joy and the slavish passion to follow. He saw them both, she blonde and round, he dark and slight, copulating in the sand of the dunes, riding each other, and then racing naked into their own private stretch of sea. The result was simply himself, getting up fastidiously, to change the sheet.

The light was gone. The doll's house in the room was covered. Edward now stood with his easel facing the window. A piece of watered paper was stretched on a frame, showing under the light a portion of Ordnance Survey map copied on a larger scale. Instead of the marked paths and the symbols, he had drawn depictions of the things themselves. The pine woods along the coast formed a forest of tiny, dark green trees. The footpaths were bordered by bramble bushes, hung with miniature fruit. There were untruthful innovations on his version of the map, such as the village church being Mediterranean white, the fields corn coloured, the gardens full of palms. He had moved the graveyard nearer the coast, depicted highly coloured half-human figures like his mother, dancing and digging their own graves; made the high street houses Georgian dwellings of immaculate proportions to replace the crooked, uncontrolled and irregular cottages. All this gave Edward a sense of power. The village and the coast became an elegant habitation under his rule. All of it slipping away, like his rod when he cast, like the fish he always failed to land, however savagely he tried with whatever expensive equipment. Like Jo.

Perhaps it was a vision he was simply too lazy to shift. Such devotion. Sandwiches every day, whether he needed them or not, a hot bottle in his bed at night, his shirts ironed, his paint brushes clean, even his fishing bait kept under her eye, a child seeking his approval in everything. But that was the other Joanna. Not the one flaunting herself this evening, not the girl who once let him choose her childish clothes but was now immune to his criticism and who looked as if she could stop a party by simply standing in the door. In whose clothes? With whose expertise? Sarah Fortune's. The hired help Joanna had previously referred to as the cow, suddenly friend, confidante and creator of glamour, all in one destructive day.

Edward had abandoned all thought of fishing. He had glared at his giggling mother with murderous eyes as she waved Jo goodbye. Knowing how capable he was of striking her, Mother giggled more, withdrew to the kitchen, then to bed, while he went to his own room to brood until after dark, which was now, when hunger struck.

The normal Joanna would not have left the house without leaving him something for supper. For him and him alone. Not his brother.

* * *

They collided in the kitchen doorway, both of them looking for the light switch, each recoiling from the other.

'Sorry, Julian. Didn't know you were in.'

'Sorry, Ed.'

Each wanted food, but rarely the company of each other which they avoided as often as possible, except breakfast, dinner and the more than occasional late-night snack which could be necessary after one of Jo's more experimental meals. Their habits made her claim she could never keep stocks, never quite knew what there was.

Julian was looking at the newspaper on the floor of the pantry. Edward's bait for fishing, given pride of place because they were Edward's; fish hooks in the drawers of the kitchen table, reels and bits all over the place. Julian could not look at the bait without imagining the lugworms lying so docile on the inside. Lugworm, harbour ragworm, white ragworm: they could live for a fews days in newspaper, but Edward was always over supplied as if it increased his own chances to acquire them and let them die. Julian could never pass the supplies on the cool pantry floor without wondering why it was so many of the civilized men he knew could bear to pick up a worm and spear it so bloodily on to a hook, simply in order to fish for the dabs they could easily buy.

'I wish you wouldn't keep these in here, Ed,' he said, keeping the irritation out of his voice.

'They can't get out, you know. I'll put them somewhere else, if you like.'

Edward was being conciliatory, even jovial.

'Want a drink, boss?'

'Yes,' said Julian, surprised into acceptance simply because he wanted what Edward offered, a single slug of indifferent-quality whiskey which made his mouth pucker. Julian did not keep the stuff near him:

it had been dangerous in the past, cured no ills, turned insomnia into nightmare.

'Where's Jo? And Ma?' he asked, not because he needed to know, simply for something to say.

'Ma's in the land of nod. Jo went out earlier. I saw her as I was coming in, wanted to have a word with you about Jo. And about our learned lady solicitor.' Edward practically spat the last words.

'Oh.' Julian was wary, always in the habit of mistrusting everything Edward said, especially if he was serious. He could always give Edward his seventy-seventh chance, but since childhood the boy had never departed from being liar and cheat, features Jo simply refused to see, while he saw them all the time, that and the idleness. Be fair, he told himself. Mother had always spoiled the boy, while Father had seemed to dislike him from the moment he could walk. He could resist the opportunity to be fooled yet again, but not the chance of discussing Miss Fortune, however obliquely. The very same unsettling creature he had seen, minutes before, as he passed the arcade, sitting on a pedestal seat like one of the kids, playing a game with enthusiasm while under the wing of some unidentifiable lad. The sight had given him the same terrible jolt of recognition as last night when she stood in the doorway. So much for his original estimation: the woman was a lightweight, a silly cow . . . The violence of his own unspoken descriptions appalled him in their patent unfairness. He was simply looking for excuses.

'Look, Julian,' Edward was saying, 'I just don't like that woman. She's far too charming to be anything other than a bad influence.'

'What? On you?' Julian joked.

'No. On Jo.' Julian waited for explanations, warmed to his brother's seriously concerned face, thinking. Perhaps I misjudge him, I must not be so hard.

'Listen, when I came back home this evening, I met our sis going out, highly pleased with herself, showing off to Mother. Dressed in that solicitor's clothes, I ask you. Done up in black, like some high-class call-girl. That isn't Jo. That's somebody else. She's still a child at heart.'

Which is what you want to keep her, Julian thought wryly, somehow pleased. How often had he urged Jo to dress like a young woman instead of a juvenile? He dismissed the thoughts easily, knowing they would return, willing to suspend criticism of Edward's suspicious resentment in his own willful search for an excuse to get rid of their visitor, simply because he found her disturbing. Edward's eyes shone with the sheen of sincere dishonesty, the guile of his own strange corruption; Julian chose to ignore it all. He rubbed his hand over his forehead.

'Sorry, been a long, long day. I just went to Miss Gloomer's. She's been burgled, poor soul. Some bastard holiday-maker. A loaf of bread and her stick, pathetic. She said it was a ghost, but I think she's just picked up on gossip. A man with white hair: she saw him going away, couldn't move. Wouldn't have a sedative, so I prescribed sherry, it made me hungry. Anyway, you were saying, Sarah Fortune?'

Edward was blushing slightly, swallowing fast, never hesitant for long.

'I think, since we need a lawyer, we should get someone else. This one's too . . . subversive. Impertinent, over familiar. She makes Mother hysterical with excitement and Jo bolshie.'

They looked at each other in a moment of rare complicity. Julian nodded.

'I agree. We'll tell her tomorrow.'

'Fine.' Edward moved to leave.

'Ed? Talk to me more, will you? For what it's worth, I know you think you've had a rough deal, and I'm sorry. It's not been an easy year.'

'No,' said Edward, horribly surprised and touched.
'No, it hasn't.'

The ghost with the white hair and the all too human
face moved no further away than the garden immediately beyond Miss Gloomer's tiny patch. This allowed him to watch the doctor come and go, wait for
the fuss to die down, sit on the still warm ground and
eat the bread in great gulps, three slices at a time,
rolling it into a doughy ball, swallowing it whole. He
would have killed for the services of a dentist on his
back teeth. He supposed it was vaguely dangerous to
stay where he was; there were other things to do, the
beach hut he had chosen for the night's lodging was
a long walk. In a year, he had not driven a car, eaten
a decent meal, entered a shop or looked any living
person in the eye. His own worm ate him, kept him
alive in the process of consumption.

A year which had sped, or rather eclipsed, since
the day he had been caught by the tide. Made himself
float on the cold water under the warming sun which
saved him, surprised that it was time to die until he
became indignant. Acted cunning with the tide, moving minimally to save his strength to make a burst
for the shore five miles from where he had begun.
The nakedness of his state, the liberation of it, had
made him run for cover, hide in a half-derelict
church while putting up two fingers at God, revelling
in the sheer pride of outwitting even the ocean. He
felt omnipotent and free, intensely alive, at one with
the flat wilderness of the coast, wandering through it
like a king surveying his country.

The newspaper, bought with stolen money, since
stealing was always easy, told him he was dead. It
amused him that some stranger had apparently died
in his place; increased the feeling of power to do
whatever he liked. It was as if he had been able to
commandeer that other man's death. Any investiga-

tions into his own life would presumably die with the
same speed. It had suddenly seemed an excellent
idea to remain dead. He could do what he had to do
undisturbed, then reveal himself and resume his
place, like a phoenix from the ashes, horrify them all.
The man had told Edward he was on holiday, but
time slipped and slithered in this limbo world, while
he tried to get a fix on time, circling round the coast
and hinterland, slipping from village to town, sleeping through the better part of a winter. Each day
seemed like a minute. In the spring, Merton called.
He had been idle: there was work to do. Memories
had altered focus too, all except one.

Who buried her? Who touched, who buried her?
And there, in the light coming out of Miss Gloomer's
door, was the enemy. A fond enemy, speaking softly
with evident affection for the occupant inside, but
still the enemy; while in his own pockets, out of the
surgery desk, was the proof.

After an hour, he removed himself with the casu-
alness of an invited guest who has suddenly remembered the time, slipped out into the high street, back
down an alley and into the yard behind the arcade.
The back door yielded easily: there was no attraction
in a patch of mossy stone, warm rooms containing silent machines which stood like sentinels. He felt
sick, burped in the darkness. He dreamed of himself,
being hunted across the dunes and out into the sea;
the sea closing over his head and no boat coming. He
dreamed of the pack being led out to hunt him by the
boy with the dog which had followed him, stayed
with him, eaten some of his precious food with the
surreptitious speed with which he ate himself. A red
dog; the outrage had sprung into his fingertips, round
the animal's neck, holding her whimpering and trying to kiss while he slit the throat with a piece of
broken bottle off the beach, untying the collar first
because it stopped him getting a hold. How foolish to

exercise his own strength in this way, but he had needed the reminder for himself, in case the strength should slip away. Like a woman with red hair, slithering out of his grip and onto the ground, still breathing. He thought of gravestones, coloured red, chestnut trees spreading tentacles beneath a buried body, wished all these colours would emigrate from his mind, but he never once doubted his reason.

'. . . all and each
Would draw from her alike the approving speech,
Or blush, at least. She thanked men—good! but thanked
Somehow—I know not how—as if she ranked
My gift of a nine-hundred-years-old name
With anybody's gift.'

His Porphyria, Browning's last duchess, they all became confused.

The air was fresh and warm; Sarah was beginning to learn the sound when the tide was changing, the musical clanging of the halberds of boats in distant channels, the night-time mewing of gulls, the fact that there was no such thing as total silence, only the subdued noises of intense life. She was growing used to walking, choosing not to use her car, but in what seemed a year rather than a day, she had still not seen the uncontained sea. Only these mysterious inroads, lying quiet by running deep in the quay, gurgling in secret, incoming streams across the land, intriguing, pretty, mysterious yet inadequate to suffice the craving for some vast blue sky, a wilderness edged with powerful water.

The Norfolk coast was full of such according to her map. Tomorrow, the Pardoes could wait, if they had not already told her to go; for tonight, she was faintly exhilarated. The tide was out but coming back; she could feel it. She could breathe, she was fully herself. Behind her, a boy was thoroughly asleep; sweet dreams, young man, and more to follow.

Here it was safe in the dead of night. Outside her cottage, where the roses trailed round the door a trifle sadly, bitten by the wind from the sea which she had not yet felt in the heatwave, Sarah looked at the isolated terrace as she might a home. That crazy sheep stood ready to greet her, making her laugh, butting her in the side as she opened the door and felt for the switch. Another thing she knew by now: there was no such thing as total darkness.

The electric light was brutal. On the floor of the kitchenette there were a dozen large worms, oozing flesh, lying inert on a double sheet of newspaper. They were lazily twined with one another, like the head of a Medusa. One moved, very slightly; the rest were patently alive, confused into inertia or dying.

They were meant to make her scream, but they brought into her throat a bile which prevented her scream, made her choke instead, and then the sheep saved her. Hettie blundered through the narrow entrance behind her, blocked her retreat, sniffed at the wet mass of corrugated, underground flesh with every sign of complete indifference and belched loudly. Sarah's heartbeat, remaining abnormally loud in her own ears, became slower and slower. Her skin was hot; life flowed back, and with it, the remembrance of the wellbeing which had walked home with her and a faint sense of the ludicrous. She had not come so far or lived so long to be frightened by worms. She had wanted country life and now she had it.

Eyes averted, teeth clenched to prevent the nausea, she found a plastic bucket, picked up the corners of the damp paper, put the whole collection inside. Holding the pail in one hand she stepped out and over the road, flung the whole container as far as she could. There was a bouncing thump and splash; she was absurdly pleased. Then she doused the kitchen floor with bleach. Only then did she find room for anger.

There was a light on over at the house, across the other side of the lawn. One light at the front door, directly opposite hers, another, glowing from the back. There were two cars: Jo was home then, so she should have been at two in the morning. The anger drove Sarah over the wet grass; the sensation against her bare legs, dragging at her skirt, oddly inhibiting, slowing her steps. By the time she reached the back kitchen window, she was hesitant and stealthy.

They were a household which went to bed and stayed inside with their cars parked like guardians. Not all of them. Through the kitchen window, Sarah saw Mouse Pardoe sitting at the table. Without ballgown, *pissenlit*, jewellery or anything else but a dressing-gown and a pair of glasses, looking like the Queen Mother without hat and the same soul of concentrated sanity. She was eating a delicate sandwich which she had clearly made herself, reading the *Guardian* with easy concentration. There was none of the theatricality, the divine display, the endless smiling.

Mrs Pardoe turned a page and refolded the paper with effortless co-ordination and long practice, sipping a glass of wine with decorum. She turned to put the big heavy kettle on the Rayburn, rubbed her hands, went on reading.

As a woman, Sarah did not understand caution. As Ms Fortune the lawyer, she did. She went back to her cottage.

CHAPTER SIX

Joanna was as jumpy as a cricket. She swooped by Edward's seat at the kitchen table without pecking his cheek, moved on.

'You were late last night,' he said with surly accusation.

'Was I? Not particularly. Oh isn't it nice it's Saturday?'

'What's good about Saturday?'

'The clouds lift, Caroline says, but that's because she's got a job. Maybe I should get a job. Caroline says she could get me a job. Takes your mind off things, she says. Anyway, I've left your sandwiches in case you were going to go fishing or something. Only I'm going shopping, all day ...' She turned away, breath running out.

'I thought you might come with me. Look, I'm sorry if I laughed at your grand clothes yesterday.'

'S'all right. Perfectly all right. Got to go, I'm busy.'

Something of this new, unprecedented independence, its blustering bravery, words spoken with bold resolution, breakneck speed and underlying nervousness in case he should mind, touched him like the breath of an icy wind.

'Ed,' she was saying, 'what were you eating in here last night? There's nothing left.'

'Worms,' he said grimly. He hated being called Ed.

115

'Grilled or fried?'

The worms were bothering him, bothered him more as he sat in the kitchen and watched the sun stream through the door. Taking the bait from the pantry floor on a malicious impulse was something he slightly regretted like one drink too many. Everything, including sleep, conspired against him and the only thing which was right was Stonewall Jones delivering more lugworms first thing this morning. Edward wanted to grumble out loud. He had detested his mother and Julian for as long as he remembered, was accustomed to receiving dislike ever since he had played his first childish trick, not dissimilar to the one played on the guest, but he did not feel easy. The man with the white hair should not have taken Miss Gloomer's stick; Jo should not put herself first; Julian should not have laid a hand on his arm and said he was sorry. Any minute now, Mother would float downstairs and blow him a kiss and the whole fabric of comfortable hatred would begin to fray.

'Here,' said Jo, thrusting a bag on to his lap. 'Do us a favour, will you? Take these back to Sarah, I mean Miss Fortune, don't look so vacant. Tell her thanks a million, and let me know if she wants to eat with us tonight, will you?'

'Julian made it quite clear not,' he said sternly.

'I like Sarah and I live here too.'

It was something, if a slightly uncomfortable thing, to do. Crossing the lawn, Edward hoped Miss Fortune had already packed her bags and gone, since if that was the result of his handiwork, he wouldn't feel again this strange compulsion to apologize.

Halfway across the lawn, he could see her car was missing. He persisted, looked through the windows of the cottage which someone seemed to have cleaned. The room inside looked different. There was a bunch of flowers in the sink; beyond the kitchen areas, he could see a shawl thrown over the nasty settee. Hettie the sheep was guarding the door, bleating loudly. Edward kicked her, felt his foot sink in the woolly fleece as she sprang away, adept at such manoeuvres and used to his casual attempts at brutality. He left the parcel of clothes balanced against the door and hoped the daft brute would eat it.

He could go fishing all day with the sandwiches he so often left in bins. Should he go and see the man on the beach this morning, progress the plan to rid himself of all his family restrictions? Make him a present? No, too late already. Let him wait. By tomorrow or the day after, the bitch from the cottage would be gone and everything would be clearer.

Sarah was looking at a display of cakes. There were buns and flapjacks, scones, enormous sponge slabs stiff with butter and all with the lopsided look of the honestly homemade. The cakes were under glass in the high street café where a plump girl struggled with solid wedges of white bread sandwiches for a dozen customers and their equally lumpy dogs. Over the road was a shop window full of knitting wool, a wry reminder of what an honest woman might expect to do with her long, winter evenings.

Sarah was not an honest woman by any but her own standards, had rarely baked a cake and knew she was a freak. Baking had never been part of her obligations with any of the men she had ever known and the thought filled her with wry amusement.

'Have some more,' a woman was urging a man. 'It's good for you.' Sarah ducked her head, light-framed and light-hearted. Would Julian sack her for lack of tact, and did she mind? Yes, she did. She had been examining with care the exhaustive list of the Pardoes' assets. They owned this café, a boat or two, the freehold of a pub, the hairdresser's, the amusement arcade, half the shops, over a dozen houses. They owned, in fact, the lifeblood of the town. They

could strangle this mini seaside empire, set like a
semi-precious stone among the dun-coloured, waterlogged land.

Sarah sat and considered dreams, thought in the
same loop about Ernest eating cake laced with
worms and hoped it choked him. Thought of
Malcolm refusing to eat cake and missed him with a
poignancy she had so far managed to avoid; pictured
him here with his lack of prejudice, the dog sniffing
in gutters with selective enthusiasm, a thoroughly
streamlined beast, that dog, compared to these. Last
night, in the conversation which had preceded his
second pint, Rick had told her about Stonewall and
his dog. And about how Stonewall earned pocket
money, digging up lugworms for other men's bait.
She had been glad of that knowledge, later—it had
defused the effect of the worms on the floor.

The coffee arrived, weak and insipid, served with
triumph, not the stuff of dreams, but Sarah's sense of
taste was blunted by indifference and she had no
dreams left, save the lingering vision of innocent and
self-sufficient country life. With her eyes still on the
impressive list, she felt a hot, non-apologetic stab of
envy when she considered the dilemma of the Pardoe
family and their unquiet expectation of riches. No-
one should be allowed to inherit so much and then
spend their lives sulking. Once upon a time, Sarah
had regarded wealth as an end in itself, the means to
change things and forge a link with freedom. She sat
back in her uncomfortable Bentwood chair, watching the eating of sandwiches and wishing she was
hungry. Dreams were food, like riches, to be vicari-
ously consumed by simply looking at the other con-
sumers. If she herself could no longer define her own
ambitions, let alone fulfil them, had neither the stamina to earn millions nor the compunction to steal, she
could still advise others on the subject of wealth.

How to use it, enjoy it, or if that was the best thing to do, give it away.

A man in the corner roared with laughter. He wore cheap clothes, fed his red face on ice-cream in a state of uproarious contentment. He was not rich. The Pardoe children should be happier than him, looking at the world as a cake for nibbling, not moping about with their private disorders, listless, lovelorn, bitter. Their money was a privilege, their behaviour an abuse and some time during the day, the brothers would foregather and tell her to leave.

A shadow fell over her table, the girl with the coffee, twittering. Rick stood towering, bruises fading, grinning widely.

'Not stopping,' he said. 'Only I wanted to show Stonewall here, that you weren't a ghost.'

'I have no illusions about that,' she said primly, the dimples of a big smile forming in her face.

'No,' he said. 'Neither do I,' and his laugh hit the roof. 'Is it a ghost, Stoney?'

'Nope,' said the boy. 'And nor's that other one, either.'

'Oh,' she breathed. 'Two ghosts?'

Stonewall squirmed, torn between silence, a sense of loss and a desire to do whatever Rick suggested. He could feel an undercurrent here, adding to his normal anxiety and the constant challenge to make Rick believe him and never send him away again.

'What would you like?' she asked. Rick shouted with laughter again.

'Don't ask a lady that, she might tell you.'

'Ice-cream?' Stonewall said mournfully.

'Two,' she said cheerfully.

Rick got up to order, none of this sitting around politely when he knew he could jump the queue as long as he grinned. He swaggered a little.

Stonewall looked at Sarah and Sarah looked at Stonewall. She was all right, he thought desperately, must be all right, Rick likes her and she isn't no woman I ever saw before. She, on the other hand, simply considered him beautiful.

'It's a ghost,' said Stonewall, when his ice-cream arrived in a big glass dish stuck with wafers like a ship in full sail. 'Went into Miss Gloomer's.'

'I'd told you to go home and stay there,' said Rick sternly. The boy ignored the interruption. What else was a window for, but to afford an escape?

'I seen him go in. I seen him last night and I seen him down the beach when I was getting bait. Ed Pardoe knows him, this ghost.'

Rick looked worried.

'Tell me about me,' Sarah teased, not quite lightly. 'Me, before I was the ordinary mortal I am now. Whose ghost was I? What did I do?' Cold ice-cream in too large a mouthful made Stonewall swallow with a gasp. Everyone listening: he could make them wait.

'You used to go in the doctor's a lot. You were married. To that other ghost, I think. The one who sits and talks with Edward Pardoe. You got run over by a bus. You went off walking into the sea, didn't come back. I saw you, but it wasn't you, it was someone else.'

Stonewall could guess what Rick was going to say. He'd say, You shouldn't eat all that ice-cream so fast, makes your brain go soft; but the woman with the hair listened intently, her skin suddenly paler, so that the red hair looked redder than ever. All Rick could do was grumble, even though he was outrageously happy.

'Why didn't you do something when you saw the ghost go in Miss Gloomer's, you twerp?'

Stonewall ducked his head. 'Cos my mum would know I was halfway out the window, wouldn't she? Don't be daft.' He looked hopefully at the empty plate, the last icy morsel trailing down his throat.

Anything else would require a bigger fee from a

stranger. Despair filled his eyes. Everyone was more important than him.

After they had gone, Sarah rubbed her arms beyond the confines of the full, elbow-length sleeves of her shirt, her fingers feeling instinctively for the tiny scars which adorned the fleshy part of her upper arms. They'll grow smaller in time, the surgeon had told her with manic cheerfulness; no-one will notice.

Enough. Saturday afternoon, holiday time: families, ghosts, moral obligations and bleaker memories had no place. She wanted to shrug off the whole human race, their unhappiness, their miseries, above all, their presence, sink them into the sea with her own inadequacies. Wanted, as she walked back to the top of the crowded street, to cleanse herself and all her fears in the vastness of the ocean she had been craving. Once inside her car, the sun beating down on the roof to make the sense of confinement worse, she looked briefly at the Ordnance Survey map, propped it against the wheel, drove back through the town and miles beyond. Such a flat, deserted coast. She wanted what she knew she could find: a place where others did not go. A desert with water, the emptiness she had been searching for to heal her own sickness.

She drove fast, then swung away into narrow lanes where the meadowsweet lurched from the banks and touched the roof. She kept the coastline ahead of her as she bumped down tracks designed for smugglers and bird-watchers, until finally, land ran out. The map had led her to a place where no-one needed coke or ice-cream.

Two more cars were parked on the same spit of terra firma. Four people, muffled despite the heat, sat on shooting sticks, binoculars aimed towards the hinterland, each looking as if breakfast and lunch had passed while they waited so long for the sight of the rare bird which had drawn them, that they seemed to have become permanent features of the landscape themselves. Sarah ignored them as they ignored her, left her car unlocked, handbag and keys under the front seat, jogged towards the sea. A year's rigorous punishment of her own body left it lean, shapely, hard. She stopped a hundred yards from the indifferent spectators, peeled off every stitch of clothing and left it with her shoes balanced on top as a marker, the bright purple of the silk shirt iridescent in the sun to guide her route back, then jogged on towards the flat horizontal of blue. The sand looked as smooth as baize, dipping into valleys which were velvet on the feet. She ran on and on, but the ribbon of waves seemed to recede. Then, when she stumbled into a narrow stretch of shallow water as warm as a bath, she gave up the pursuit. The water was soft as silk and the breeze a silent fan. Lying with her naked limbs tickled by salt felt utterly natural but at the same time blissfully decadent. The sand bank acted as a couch, moulded to the shape her body had designed for itself, while soft water crept up her neck into her hair. Some sybaritic millionaire would pay a fortune for this. As she lazily splashed water on her flat belly and her thighs, she felt again, with a little frisson of disgust, the tiny white scars on her abdomen which mirrored those on her arms and her back and reminded her of maggots. She wanted to scrub at them with sand until they disappeared, but somehow, in the water, they were less offensive and she could no longer imagine them shifting and moving like the vermin on a carcase, eating away at sanity, and the will to live. The sun was hypnotic; she could not be sombre under the merciful glare, sprawled like a cat before the fire, dozing to the sound of soft breeze and silence.

Ten, fifteen minutes; she could not guess how long she had lain in her feline pose. Neither did she know what woke her, whether it was the sound of distant shouting or the sudden sensation of a deep chill curling round her. When she opened her eyes, she saw the greater expanse of water all around her, lapping greedily at her bare breasts, colder water mounting above her knees, pulling slightly as if inviting her to float away. For a moment she was tempted to let go, simply drift like a rogue vessel, but sat up, watched her pool expanding before her eyes, the surface corrugated by breeze as she scrambled to her feet, alarmed, disorientated, still in a muddle of a dream. From the rim of the rise on which she stood, the ribbon of sea seemed ominously closer and clearer, the wind on her face sterner. She looked back to the shore for her clothes and could not see them; two pin figures stood by their toy-like car, waving and shouting as if cheering some invisible team, dancing in a fury of agitation. They seemed a long way off and the rim of the sea even closer.

Sarah began to run. The route back bore no comparison with the careless route out, when she had imagined the golden surface felt beneath her feet. Now the sand dipped and rose before her into gulleys where water collected into swift rivers, pulling at her knees like an hysterical child. The first channel was easy; the second brought the breath to her chest and fire into her veins; the third rose against her like an engine fuelled by hatred. She did not pause to look again for her clothes, pushed through the skin-ripping flood with her hands above her head, bending into it, the tide tearing at her waist until it receded like a tease at the moment when she thought she could no longer fight the relentless, inland pull. The steps became firmer; she splashed through a dying current, shrinking to a gentle tugging at her calves, and walked unsteadily up the incline to her car. The prickling of thistle and sand grass marking the point where the tide did not reach and land began, felt like a blessing. A woman stood with a brace of binoculars round her neck, stout shoes on her feet and tears of consternation on her red face.

'How could you be so stupid?' she yelled. 'He wanted to go for you,' pointing to the man on her left who stood shivering, leaning on a stick. 'Wouldn't let him! We've been shouting for hours, you'll give him a heart attack, you wouldn't listen, I could kill you!' Then her face crumpled into lines of relief. 'Oh, you silly, silly girl. Don't you know about tides? You must have been so frightened.'

Sarah stood before her dripping and shaking, humbled and ashamed.

'I should have thought. I'm sorry I gave you such a scare. Thank you. You woke me. The shouting wasn't wasted. Thank you both.' The shivering grew worse.

'Your clothes,' the woman said, softening more. 'Your pretty coloured shirt.' So much for assuming they would not notice.

'You'll probably get them back,' said the man, helpfully, needing to say something to control his own shock. 'They'll probably wash up in the harbour down the coast. Or somewhere.'

She felt a terrible desire to giggle, put her hand over her mouth.

'I think I'll get in my car where it's warm.'

'Do you want a blanket or something?'

'No, thank you, thank you.'

She had to get inside, start the engine and move because until she did, they would watch, without prurience but with an honest concern which made her feel far more exposed. The heat from the driver's seat spread through her buttocks, she dripped into the fabric, the steering wheel was warm on her white knuckles and through the windscreen she saw the advancing sea, marching inland like an enormous army with white halberds and a silent war cry, unstoppable, irresistible, the oldest enemy. She watched until the chill subsided and she could flex her fingers. From their own vehicle, the couple watched her.

The back wheels of the car spun in the sandy gravel, a satisfying sound. The bumping, jolting progress back to the main road made her want to sing. For the joy of survival and for the revelations it entailed.

First, if Elisabeth Tysall had lain in such a pool, warm, drunk, drugged, to make her own death simultaneous with blissful and uninterrupted sleep, she had chosen a tempting method, full of dignity, and that was an obscure comfort. The nature of Elisabeth's death had always tormented her. Secondly, Sarah could now see how she had never possessed such a well-matured desire for death, even though the number of temptations were beyond counting on the fingers of both hands. She had so often wanted to die. She found a cigarette, lit it awkwardly, and felt a moment of euphoria which was warm and wild.

Late Saturday afternoon, people trailing back from their beaches, passed Sarah's car, not looking, but seeing enough to notice a naked bosom level with the wheel. And that was another thing. Death and risk made clothes seem irrelevant. A man stalled and whistled as their cars paused alongside, each waiting to turn right. His children in the back giggled and squirmed. Sarah waved at them demurely, laughed at the minor traffic jam outside the amusement arcade as holiday-makers looked for places to park, and pulled into the side, still grinning. A small bullet of a head with hair on end appeared at the nearside window. The face of Rick appeared on the right. While the boy averted his eyes, he did not.

'Lost again, are you?' She had time to notice how the bruises round one eye had darkened into purply striations, well on the way to recovery.

'What's this then?' Rick said grinning. 'Legal services?'

'Doubt it. They'll fire me. I just went swimming.'

'You go indoors like that,' Rick said. 'They'll keep you for ever.'

The early evening was warm, but the sky had grown troubled. Edward loved that phrase, a troubled sky. When he owned his birthright, he would paint a troubled sky, with angels interrupting the clouds and coming down to bless him. He shut his eyes and thought of it, until Julian called everyone downstairs into the horrid gloom of their Edwardian dining room, where the chairs cracked shins, and dead flies fell from the plum velvet of the curtains as soon as they were drawn. Edward stayed silent while Julian conducted the meeting like a headmaster in front of the assembly hall, telling them all, Mother included for all that she would either notice or care, how the solicitor sent by Father's executor was not suitable for their purposes, did they agree? Mother laughing herself sick, saying nothing except, No, no, no, you've got it all wrong. Joanna upset, wondering if it was her earlier referrals to their guest as the cow, or the arguments at breakfast yesterday which had made Julian so obdurate. Edward merely nodded his agreement, thought of the easel waiting upstairs and the man waiting on the beach tomorrow. They did not need a disruptive lawyer who made his sister cry as she cried now.

When he watched Joanna weeping, he felt on his own skin a flush of irritation which was the very opposite of desire. If only he could, for a minute, imagine wanting someone else: boy, girl, woman, whatever the body was, as long as it was not the plump, snivelling, beautiful child.

'We're decided then,' Julian said without turning it into a question.

Edward now sat facing the long windows where the paint blistered off the frame and the glass was

cloudy with salt from the shoreline which they
owned, travelling across the drab marshes, which
they owned, to the house, which they owned, while
he owned nothing. Bitterness rose like a painful
cough. It was warm and airless: the windows were
stuck in the dining room. Mother, giggling in her
evening dress, plucking at the hem, finally picking it
up so the fabric hung around her knees while she
chewed at a thread, suddenly springing into life as a
car drew level with the front door and she rushed to
the window. They all followed.

'Oh,' said Mother in tones of wonder. 'Oh my
dears!'

Joanna and Julian moved to the window where
Edward stood, languid but transfixed.

'Whoever it is she needs a drink and so do I,'
Mother said. She stood very still, none of her normal
twitching and constant adjusting, a wistful note in
her voice, a hidden chuckle. You wicked old crone,
Julian thought with more than a hint of fondness.

Sarah Fortune stepped from her car, presenting a
perfect half moon of buttock with a well-defined
swimsuit mark as she reached inside for her handbag,
then stood up with the strap parting her bobbing
bosom as she slung it across herself and stepped
back, naked as the day, to slam the door with a careless foot. Her hair was a frenzied cloud, her shoulders tanned and she was perfectly controlled. Joanna
felt she should not look, stared and held her breath
instead. Sarah walked away across the lawn towards
the cottages, resting one hand on the handbag as if
she were wearing a suit and strolling to a business
appointment, no hurry or anxiety in the stride, careless or oblivious of the scrutiny. Julian bit his lip in
a rare moment of sympathy, Oh Lord, how terrible
for her, not to know they were all there, judging her
finest details with the scrutiny of a jury; she would
be mortified. But then as he watched, Sarah stopped,

looked at the ridiculous appendage of her handbag, flicked it off her shoulder into the long grass
and raised her arms in the air. The grass was warm
and moist; she seemed to enjoy the sensation of it
round her feet. Expensive tan leather bounced on the
lawn: still they watched. The sky was pink in an
early sunset; she seemed to glow as with an unbearably slow and graceful precision the perfect figure
turned a series of perfect cartwheels, hand over
hand, twirling in front of their eyes with only the
damp red hair marking where she was. Then she
picked up her handbag, placed it on her head,
walked towards the cottage where they had put her,
strolling with her arms outstretched to keep her balance, her naked feet swishing through the grass.
Hettie the sheep followed, keeping pace, bahhing
piteously. There was a shred of bright orange nastur-
tium hanging from her jaw as she trotted after. The
sun sank like a big, red stone into water.

They were spellbound, until Edward let forth a
bellow of delighted laughter. Joanna expelled the
breath she had held for a full minute, joined him in
a frothing of mirth which made her eyes water.

'Well,' said Julian, shaking himself. 'Proves my
point. About her not being suitable.' Edward caught
on his brother's face a terrible, naked look of despair.

Mother turned on him, dropping the hem she had
chewed. Her voice was cooing and fluting, talking as
she would talk to a baby.

'Will my little boy sack a lady from her job for
taking her clothes off? Would he? Would he be so
silly? Should know better. No man got sacked for
taking his off, not even a doctor.' Her voice sank by
a whole octave, emerged as a grim rattle, whining
but perfectly articulate.

'If Julian gets rid of this lady, his mummy will
break everything in sight. Is that understood?'

He turned sharply, met for a moment a pair of eyes

hard with purpose, moved towards her. She sprang back and began again her chewing of the hem, saying nothing, looking away. Then he looked towards Edward for moral support, found Edward also looking away, gaze fixed on the footsteps through the long grass of the lawn. Joanna evaded his glance, arms crossed resentfully, her ever-ready tears still in her eyes, but her body obdurate. He felt the meeting had passed without a definitive vote, but if asked, he would not favour the initial resolution. Oddly, he did not mind.

'Look,' said Joanna desperate to break the ice, 'I'd better go and ask if she's all right. I'll take her something to eat. I mean,' she added, flustered, 'she must have had an accident.'

'I doubt it,' said Edward drily.

'Fuck off,' Joanna replied with far more calm than she felt. Edward was always on the outside, never feeling anything, always analysing: he didn't care if a person felt cold, and stared at her in the way she had found disconcerting for as long as she could recall. He moved nonchalantly to put an arm round her shoulder.

'What would you give for a body like that, eh, Jo?'

She turned on him, furious and pink, picking the arm from round her neck and throwing it back as if it were inanimate.

From the kitchen came the sound of breaking glass. The Mouse was making her point.

CHAPTER SEVEN

'Left you, has she?'

'You could say so.'

'Thought she would.' Squinting across the table top towards Malcolm Cook, Detective Sergeant Ryan, his erstwhile colleague in many a case, neither looked nor sounded sympathetic, not through lack of affection for his friend, but simply a well-tried patience with the whole breed of men who called themselves lawyers, a breed deficient in common sense, particularly regarding women. Ryan knew his own record was far from perfect, his attitude to the fair sex ranging from possessive passion, through the straightforward lust which could not remember names, right down to daily fondness and the acceptance that there was nothing you could do to keep them, since life and women were in one great conspiracy. His own contribution to Malcolm Cook's loss was going to be the provision of as much alcohol as he could get the man to take.

'I have to say, Malc, you were more fun before you two got together. Was a time when you were a great big lad, liked a pint and never moved your bum off a chair. Then you took up running, fell in love with a redhead, lost all the fat and got serious. You never sit, you bloody well sprint. She's worn you out, old son.'

'Get me a drink.'

'Surely. Doubles. Few packets of crisps?'

'No.'

Ryan didn't like the way Malcolm stared into the middle distance like that, ordering a refill every five minutes and showing not a sign of Saturday-night fever, not a tremor as he raised his hand. All the makings of an expensive night even in the sort of downmarket pub they both preferred. Malc was a mate, as far as any lawyer could be, but that wasn't the same as wanting him crying on your shoulder. It got your jacket all wet.

The drink went down quickly, not quite as quick as the last. Malcolm smiled. When he did that, he was a different man.

'Look, I'm not here to weep, I'm here to drink, understand? And I want to raise an old, dead subject, OK? Charles Tysall, your friend and mine. My father's been nagging at me again. No, I don't mean directly, just getting under my skin as usual. The man's not well, supposed to keep calm, but as soon as I mention Charles, he has an apoplexy. He's recreating that man as a plaster saint, all because he's dead and was a client. All clients are heroes, the hypocrisy makes me sick. I want to tell him what Charles did to Sarah—I told you we kept all the details from him at the time—and spell out to my honourable old dad what his client did to other redhaired women. I want him to know. People should know the truth, even sick old men.'

'You really aren't happy with him, are you?' asked Ryan, mockingly.

'He sent Sarah away. To Merton, of all places. He . . . precipitated things.'

'Oh, I see. Revenge, is it? One good turn deserves another. You lose the girl and give the poor old git a heart attack. Come off it, Malc, it wouldn't help anything, would it?'

'No.'

'Anyway, what that Charles did to your bird never

came to court, did it? She refused to give evidence of
the attack. With your support. I wanted you shot.'

Malcolm raised a hand in protest, let it drop.

'She had her reasons. I didn't want anyone looking
into her motives, still don't. Besides, Tysall saved
everyone the trouble. When his wife's body was
found, off he goes and follows her into the water.
What I want to know is how did he come to do that?
I never really understood. He never struck me as the
suicidal type. All those times we tried to nail him for
fraud, and you for the women he plundered . . . He
always wanted to live.'

Ryan looked smug.

'Nothing to do with me. I just happened to meet
the sly bastard in a coffee shop. Made the suggestion
he'd like to go and see where his lady wife was
buried. It might not have been the tide covered her
up, see? It could have been, course, probably was,
but I made him think she's been buried. Last rites delivered on her lily-white body by another man's big,
chunky hands. I knew it would drive him mad. He
might have beaten his own wife to a pulp, cut her
face to ribbons, but he couldn't stand the thought of
anyone else touching her. Listen, I couldn't have
prayed he'd walk into the sea like he did: I just
wanted him suffering.'

Ryan took a sip and it was gone. Time to go on to
pints. Whisky was fine in spots; he'd go back to it
later. Something nagged him, something he didn't
like and knew Malcolm wouldn't either.

'So Sarah's gone off to the seaside, has she? Not
her kind of place, I wouldn't have thought. Not very
classy. Fish and chips, big amusement place, caravans down the beach. I can't see your Sarah in a
place full of yobs.'

Malcolm smiled again. Ryan decided the smile
was sadder than the scowl.

'You don't know Sarah. She has . . . simple tastes.'

He seemed to hesitate, draw back from saying more, plunged on. 'What I want to know is anything which may affect and upset her. The sort of things people might still gossip about, take her unawares when she ought to forget. You got to know the local cop in Merton when you were investigating. You know what people said, I never did; lawyers never do. How long did it take them to find Charles Tysall and what did he look like?'

Ryan was wearing that shifty look, the one Malcolm knew all too well as sending shivers of alarm up his spine. The expression worn by a police officer choosing economy with fact, sitting where he was, assessing the odds on the consequences of truth, a hesitation complete in the second it took to weigh up the fact there was nothing to lose.

'They phoned me up when they found a body,' Ryan said carefully. 'I gave them a description, and it tallied. Tysall was seen walking out of town with the tide coming in anyway, so it's pretty clear already. Then this doctor turns up on site, used to know Tysall a bit, and, oh, yes, by the way, according to local rumour, knew the wife quite a lot better.' He let that sink in. Any deceased, in Ryan's eyes, had few virtues and high nuisance value, especially women.

'Anyway, the doc is told in advance the body is probably Tysall, and he agrees, so Tysall it is. Mind,' he added, shifting with ever greater discomfort, 'they also say they get three or four bodies per summer off that coast. Unidentified. Tramp steamers, suicidal fishermen. Christ, I'd hate to live in a place like that. Three pubs, one church, nothing else to do. The wife loved it.'

He knew he should not have spoken. His own reservations about that flimsy identification should have remained exactly what they were, his own. If he talked long enough round the subject, maybe Malc would forget where he was. No chance, Ryan thought, looking at the calm face only slightly flushed with alcohol while his own was glowing; should have known better. Malcolm was staring at him. Once you've let some cat out of a bag, Ryan thought, you can't shove it back in.

'I wouldn't regard identification by a slight acquaintance of a drowned man sufficient beyond reasonable doubt,' said Malcolm, refusing to register anything but polite curiosity. A policeman under attack, even friend, could become as wooden as the table. 'Do you know that close relatives misidentify their dead with monotonous regularity? If you believe a person is dead and you see a dead person, it seems to close the circle. I think we need another drink.' He walked to the bar with the bouncy step of a runner, one hand feeling for his wallet. I should never fool with lawyers, Ryan thought, especially when they can drink. He patted the silky red head of Malcolm's dog which grinned in response. Now there was a good female, constantly obedient, loving, asking no questions, telling no lies.

'Just one thing more,' Malcolm was saying as he sat. 'You gave the locals a description of Charles which tallied with the corpse. What description?'

Ryan wrinkled his face, genuinely struggling for memory. He knew Charles Tysall, oh yes, knew him from the files and the cheats and the women. Knew he was a murderer perforce, a man with a passion to destroy, looking all the time for perfection in ideas and the opposite sex, knocking it into pieces when he did find it, but for all Ryan knew, he'd only been face to face with the bastard twice. The dead wife, whom he'd taken to hospital in his car, he'd seen more than twice, each time less recognizable than the last, sometimes talking, sometimes not. His brow cleared.

'I gave them the description Elisabeth Tysall gave

me. I sat with her, waiting in casualty. She told me
what he was like.'

'How?'

'She said he was hung like a donkey.'

The man in the beach hut made tea. He had a small
gas stove stolen from an empty caravan, water which
he collected from the lake near the small caravan
site, a camping gas cylinder stolen from another
beach hut. These wooden edifices he liked above all;
they reminded him of doll's houses. They stood
along Merton's public beach, stringing away down
the coast with all the grace of wet washing on a line
in a downpour, irregular, highly-coloured, lumpish
and graceless, decorated to individual taste as if they
could ever be permanent. They were a series of garden sheds with stable doors on stilts, hired for the
season, subject to wind and flood, raised far above
the sand to cope with the high tides they were so unlikely to withstand. Some did, more by luck than
judgement, remaining upright with peeling paint and
all their romance gone long after some family moved
on to where the children had alternatives other than
an amusement arcade in the rain, and the parents
were not sick of a caravan, the cold, the moaning and
the spartan splendour of the beach. Merton's claim to
holiday-making fame was for those with old-
fashioned stamina, a taste for chips, sticky sweets,
pints of ale and mugs of tea. The leftovers were
abundant. The man with the white hair was grateful
for that.

My name is Charles and I have no name, he
chanted, rocking back and forth in the small space of
the hut, watching the dawn rise on a Sunday morning. I rose from the sea like Christ from the dead.
Sunday is a day of grace for sinners and I am not one
of those. My name is Charles. There were occasions
when he almost forgot. Just as he forgot what it was

he had been when he had the name, until he remembered again. The beach hut, last of the line, was slightly askew; the stool on which he sat also slightly crooked, so that he leaned constantly to one side. The stick with the carved duck's head assisted him to redress the balance. It was against the local by-laws to stay in a beach hut at night, in case the wind got up and encouraged the endless hunger of the tide. People obeyed the rules. Charles held such people in contempt. Also those who treasured the small possessions he stole, but left them out for him to steal all the same.

People without names cavorted on the beach in front of the hut by day, looking to their own pursuits, their games, their dogs, their delicious children, never to left or right and never towards anyone old. He could walk amongst them as if he were invisible. When there was a crowd, faintly excited, they sounded like the geese which had travelled over his head the autumn before, when he decided his new existence became his so much it was better than the one before. Who needed prestige, when they could reach out and reclaim it whenever they wanted? Who needed a fine apartment when an empty holiday cottage would do? Places like the one where Edward found him. Looking for Elisabeth and who had buried her, giving himself a reason to live. When he had done that, meted out his own version of justice, then he could go home.

It was necessary for a man without a name to have a reason. From his casual and contemptuous observation of humankind, no-one else needed such a thing. They just existed, like lumbering animals.

A child was attempting to clamber up the rickety steps of his beach hut. A plump little thing with a nappy rump and curly hair, grunting with the effort. Charles peered over the top half of the stable door, hissed, bared his teeth, watched as the child met his eyes, waddled away, crying. Good. Oh, it was a clean little thing. He could have cooked it. The thought made him dizzy.

The tide was out again this morning, fickle bitch, leaving a huge expanse of mud and sand for the fools to play on. If only they knew how difficult it was to keep clean. It was the desire for fresh water which drove him the half mile into town, made him careless.

Between the daily business of eating and cleaning, cleaning was the worst. He slithered down the steps of the hut with his stick, dived behind and up the bank into the dunes, to find the place where he met Edward, if the young man deigned to arrive. Sandwiches would be nice: he could live on sandwiches and save himself foraging time. It was only when he was hungry that the urge to destroy became so paramount. A hypoglycaemic rage, he would have said, when he had a name. Which he didn't, now. Nor half the command of words. Snippets of poetry was all. The haunting and cynical voice of Browning, all he remembered from a thousand books.

> 'That moment she was mine, mine, fair,
> Perfectly pure and good: I found
> A thing to do, and all her hair
> In one long yellow string I wound
> Three times her little throat around
> And strangled her . . .'

He sang the words to the tune of a hymn.

From inside the worn pockets of the track suit rescued from behind the church hall, he pulled out the crumpled letters, the medical record card and the envelopes he had taken with such fastidious care from Dr Pardoe's desk in the surgery.

'Darling Julian,' he mimicked, reading in a high and breathy voice. 'How wonderful to know that I shall see you soon . . . Your loving Elisabeth.'

Oh yes, he loved you, darling Elisabeth; the good doctor loved you to death; look at what he did for you, in case you should cause him a scandal. Look at the record of what he did. The last billet-doux, a prescription on the record card for enough diazepam to stun a crowd of women, let alone one.

Charles without a name looked out to the sea. 'Escape me?' he murmured. 'Never.'

Flames danced in front of his eyes, the morning sun blazing over shallow stretches of water left by the tide, moving and dazzling. He could burn down the Pardoe house, that was what he could do, a house he had entered and left a dozen times, all of them so mad or so preoccupied they never noticed. Charles could hear the crackling sound of fire, imagine the sight in the dark, as they rushed out screaming, for him to pick them off with a knife or a stick, one by careless one, until finally, he would stamp on the hands which had touched his wife, buried her without permission.

The images were soothing; Sunday was a day of grace. Charles without a name listened for the church bells, hearing nothing but the wind in the pine trees at his back and the desolate mewing of the gulls on the beach before. One day soon he would go home. He wondered how he would ever get clean enough to go home—and where home was.

Edward despised the mere notion of going to church, quoted religion as the opiate of the masses. Joanna went to accompany her mother, also to put flowers on her father's grave. There had been no ordinary plot for Mr Pardoe, of course: he could not have been buried in the serried ranks of the others who now stretched out into the field behind, not he, but in a plot in the old graveyard, bought from the vicar long before as the price of charity. Joanna thought of it now as she sat in the congregation with her

mother, saw for the first time how people might resent Pa's privileged resting place. She was thinking
too, of how much better her own life would be if the
family did not own so much, how pleasant if she
could ever present herself as an ordinary contender
for friendship instead of a race apart, unable to enter
a shop without putting someone in mind of owing
rent. Perhaps if she had nothing, Rick would love
her, but on this footing, she could never be equal,
never belong, even here with her elders, singing the
same hymn in a great, slow groan of tuneless sound.

Mother sang lustily, Da, da, da da da daah, her
voice loud and cracked, humming without words, the
feathers from her hat curling over her face, another
evening gown of purple trailing round her pink-shod
feet beneath the mackintosh, her face flushed from
yesterday's sun. Nobody minds, Joanna thought defensively, so why should I? Mother was popular, always had been; men flocked to say hallo after
church. Men had always flocked in that direction,
Joanna realized, surprised at her own observation.
Poor little Mouse, to be so pitied.

On the other side of the feathers, Julian gently
took his mother's hymn book and turned it the right
way up so that she could at least pretend she was
reading the words. She ignored the gesture. On the
last hymn of the service, he sensed rather than saw
Sarah Fortune slipping out of the pew behind, late ar-
river, first to go, with her hair concealed under a
straw hat. He shut his eyes for the final blessing, seeing nothing inside his own skull but the vision of her
body in those circus cartwheels, hand over graceful
hand across the lawn.

The sun struck with cruel brilliance as they
emerged blinking from church, the sound of the organ receding behind them, the bells taking over.
Groups formed on the paths between the graves,
women with women, men with men, a division as

old as time. Julian counted a small congregation of
largely advanced years, hinged together by habit and
the continuity of their lives rather than belief or com-
mitment to virtue. That was certainly true of Rick's
dad, from the amusement arcade, sedulous as ever
towards the doctor even though he must have known
the evidence Julian had seen on his own son, signs of
drunken violence which were always explained away
as the boy falling downstairs. Rick's dad, his cousin,
PC Curl the village copper, others who may have
needed God's forgiveness as much as Julian felt he
did himself, but never prayed for it, believing, perhaps, as he did not, that a visit to Church wiped the
whole slate clean. There was a murmur at his elbow.

'Can we have a word, Doc, before you have to
rush away?'

He liked the presumption that he was always busy,
always in demand, disliked the deference. If it had
been towards him for his qualifications and his value,
he would have been pleased, but they bowed to a
Pardoe for the supposition of money and influence.
It was that which put him beyond companionship,
nothing more, not even his own brusqueness, which
they tolerated.

'What do you think, Doc? Time we began to take
this ghost business seriously, don't you think? I
mean, after Miss Gloomer, not fair, is it? Could have
been this white-haired bastard did the fishing shop,
other places too. I mean, he's real all right. He ain't
a ghost at all.'

'He hasn't hurt anyone, has he?' Julian said
sharply. He couldn't make himself care, except about
Miss Gloomer. If there was a poor, summer vagrant
wandering about at night stealing the surplus, it
wouldn't be the first or last to go of his own accord.
The idea of hunting him was vaguely repellent, although not to Rick's dad, nor to PC Curl who always
dramatized problems of law and order.

'My nephew seen him plenty,' Curl murmured. Julian laughed. Stonewall Jones was his favorite child, stubborn, discreet, incredibly brave in the face of a cut arm, chickenpox and anything which had ever ailed him, but not, surely, a reliable source of information.

'S'not funny, Doc. Something's got to be done.'

'Such as?' he suggested lightly, refusing to take the lead. They were silent. No-one else wanted to do anything other than talk.

'Such as locking doors, keeping your eyes open and letting him be?'

They nodded, each following the other. Pass the word, that was it, the full extent of civic duty on another day so warm it should be treasured, Sunday lunch beckoning as a prelude to an afternoon's doze. The heat made them lazy, turned their minds to other things. Rick's dad fingered his tie, tight at the throat, uncomfortable. The mood of vague purpose fragmented into nothing; Joanna called for her brother. The vicar stood next to her, the verger on the other side, planting a kiss on Mother's powdered cheek while she embraced him, the powder falling on to his dark jacket without him seeming to mind.

We could set off through the streets, Julian thought with sudden, savage amusement, in my car, with Mama waving to the locals like the Queen. She's the only one of us they can love, because she requires so little. They passed through the churchyard gate. There was no sign of Sarah Fortune's car with the dented wing.

'Just a minute,' Julian said. He walked back to the gate, sprinted through the old graveyard, into the newer environs of the field where Elisabeth Tysall was buried.

The same temporary headstone, disgracing him; the rest tidy. His old dead roses spirited away and at her feet and her heart, fresh flowers in new vases.

* * *

The chimes of the ice-cream van rang out to the faithful long after the church bells ceased. Down by the beach, they rang to a greater effect and the formation of a sporadic queue by mid-afternoon. They were parked on the edge of the caravan site, by the main track over the dunes on to the beach, ready to catch the comers and goers, who came forward as if the van, next to the refreshment hut, but somehow more enticing, was a mirage in the desert.

'What's the matter with you, Stoney? You suffering heat sickness, or what?' Rick was doling out a double 99 cone with Cadbury's flake on top, watching it melt even as he presented it out of the window to a lad who'd have to be quick to get it all down in time. All down his vest, more likely. Talking over his back to where Stonewall lounged, ready to dive into the freezer for a Mivvi or a raspberry split or those iced lollies built like space ships which were so popular this year, but so phallic in appearance, he and Rick sniggered over every sale especially to girls. Nothing was funny this afternoon.

'Nothing's the matter,' Stonewall said sulkily.

'Whenever you say that, I know you're lying.'

Oh, Rick was on the ball today, jokes to customers, the bruises round his eyes making him look like a pirate, hands over the ices quick and deft, shirt shining clean and his hair falling over his forehead so he could flick it back and wink. There was a pause in the line. Give it half an hour, when they all started trailing home, business would be brisk. Rick checked stocks and whistled.

'Come on, Stoney, talk to me.' There was a shuffling. Stonewall looked out the window.

'Are you going out with that redhead, Rick? Are you?'

So that's what it was, a little *frisson* of jealousy, a little bit of the old insecurity creeping back, as if it

had ever gone since the boy lost his own father and
screamed in his sleep.

'Course not. I like her, that's all. You be nice to
her if you see her, Stonewall. She did me a good turn
on Friday night.' Rick laughed uproariously. He'd
been laughing like a hyena all weekend, imploding
with silent jokes Stonewall didn't understand.

'What about Jo, then?' Rick stopped what he was
doing, and the laughter.

'That's something else,' he said sharply. Stonewall
kicked his frayed training shoe against the door. He
was miserable without knowing why.

'Cheer up. We got things to do after. My dad says
we got to go looking for that ghost. Your white-
haired ghost. Typical, doesn't want to bother himself,
lets us do it.' He whistled again.

'Did you really believe me, then?' Stonewall
asked, his voice quivering. 'No you didn't. You just
pretended you did in the caf, to please her. You never
believed me until other people did. You never believed that ghost got my dog.'

He had carried the stiff, twisted collar in his
pocket for the two days since he had found it. Rick
could see it now, protruding from the side of his
shorts above the thin, pale brown legs with their covering of freckles. Stonewall was such a thin, sandy
boy: even his legs weren't significant.

'And,' he was saying, his voice high with anxiety,
'when you go looking for the ghost, you'll send me
away. When you get a girl, you'll send me away.
That's what you'll do. Everyone does.'

There were tears now, coursing down his slightly
dirty face, leaving rivulets made worse by the smutty
hand which attempted to push them back. The face
of a customer appeared at the window. Rick produced three of the phallic lollies, took the money,
slammed the window shut and sat on the floor
among the refrigeration humm, pulled Stonewall

down beside him. He grabbed a sheet of kitchen towel and applied it roughly to the boy's face, absorbing phlegm and tears, put his arm round the skinny, shaking shoulders.

'Now listen here, you snotty bastard, and listen properly. You're my mate, my very best mate, you hear? And if I can't have you round me all the time, that doesn't make any difference. You're still my best one. I used to go about with Jo Pardoe when I was your age, bit like you and me now, loved her the same way, only it changed, and it all had to wait. My fault, I suppose.'

Stonewall grabbed the kitchen towel, blew his nose, failed to stem the tears.

'You love her more'n you love me,' he whispered. It choked him with shame to mention the word. Saying 'fuck' or 'cunt' was easier.

'Well, well, well,' said Rick, wonderingly, running his spare hand through Stonewall's stick-up hair, a gesture the boy would always pretend to dislike, but loved as much as Sal had loved a stroking. 'That's a damn fine haircut you got there, boy. And as for love, well, I'll love you for ever and nothing in between, you hear? And if I love someone else, they'll have to love you too. Jo would, she does already, even if her brother never pays you for digging up bait, like you did again this morning. He never catches anything, you know, don't do it again, you hear?' He paused. Another face pressed itself against the window of the van. Rick stuck up two fingers. He had to get to the end of what he was saying, since whatever it was, was important.

'There'll be times I'm busy and you're busy, but there you'll be, first and last, bad moods, good moods. Any fucker comes near you, meaning harm, I'll tear his fucking head off. Course I love you, Stoney, better than anyone. It'll always be the same until you tell ME to fuck off. See? I'll love you to death, boy, just you try and stop me.'

There was a knocking at the window. Rick got up, turned on his chimes and began to whistle again. The sky overhead had darkened; for once they came off the beach early. A week of heat, a season of drought; even for business and his dad's pleasure, he could not be sorry about the rain. One day, he and Stonewall might have an empire. Then they would only be nice to people they liked.

'Three Mivvis,' he yelled over his shoulder. 'On the double!'

Stonewall kicked him in the shins to show he was alive, sauntered to the freezer like a millionaire bar lizard in a small, select space, obliged the order with flourish. Four Mivvis, then they ran out, two double Ds, five phallic symbols, four caramel torpedos, nearly as bad in shape, six straight vanilla tubs and a bombe, Stonewall grinning throughout. Felt a hand on his shoulder, Rick's of course, there was no room for anyone else and no need either.

'Stay down there, boy, just sit down. I think I seen your ghost.' Preternaturally tall, striding down under the darkening sky which made his white hair look as if it shone, was the man with no name. Had he shuffled with an armful of family burdens, whinging kids, bags of windshield, Thermos flasks, towels, damp clothes and plastic bottles, he would not have stood out. The others were purposeful. He looked confused.

'Tall,' Rick said tersely to the figure at his feet, clutching his ankles. 'I mean, really tall.' He didn't say handsome instead of long, tall, lean, regular featured, a face and frame tending towards the cadaverous: neither of them reckoned anyone over fifty could ever be called attractive; they just didn't count at that age. 'Big thatch, white hair, can't see his ears, bit of a beard, not much, trousers don't fit. Track-suit bottoms, too short?'

Stonewall nodded in the sheer ecstasy of being believed, not caring. The white-haired man paused in front of the window, sunken cheekbones presenting themselves first, the patrician voice echoing next.

'I'd love what you have for sale,' he intoned, 'but I haven't any change.' Rick leant forward confidentially, so that he was half out of the van and still looking as if he was telling a secret, putting his hand over one side of his mouth as he spoke in a hiss.

'Tell you the truth, mate,' he leered, 'we've had a good day and it's melting. Have one free. On the house. Only don't tell,' he added, tapping the sides of his nose in a cockney parody, unconvincing to his own ears, not to Stonewall, still clutching his ankles in a paroxysm of terrible giggles.

The ice-cream fridge was on the right. Rick dived in, scooped out from on top a double cone, filled both, delivered it. The man did not pause to offer thanks or smile. Rick knew it was a giveaway to stare, so he pretended to prepare for the next on parade, noticing at the same time how the creamy floss had gone down the man's throat like a mouse down a Hoover, all in one, in a great big gulp, terrible, Adam's apple going in then out and a whole cone gone in a swallow. The man could have eaten a dog, the thought made Rick swallow too. Something wrong with his teeth. Another queue had formed behind him, discretion overcame the ghost's obvious desire to ask for more and he left without a wave.

'Think he's hungry,' Rick muttered.

'So he isn't a ghost,' said Stonewall, finally, lazily, leaving hold of the ankles, standing up.

'Four double cornets left,' said Rick. 'He could have ate the lot.'

'Perhaps he ate Sal.'

'Give us the mirror, Stoney. He made my hair stand on end.'

Her hair stood on end like a series of wire fences, and nothing a soul could do. Mrs Pardoe wore it squashed under a hat or turban, depending upon occasion or season. She maintained her feathery boa and frightful hat as she tripped across the grass to the small terrace of three cottages on the right of her overgrown lawn, her feet landing neatly without the high-heeled shoes which might have dug in so far as to root her to the spot.

The roses round the door looked glad of the rain which fell out of the sky in droplets as big as petals, weighing down her hat and waterlogging the feathers. Mrs Jennifer Pardoe knocked on her own property with a terrible urgency. The door was open. In she went, all of a flutter, which stopped like a toy with a run-out battery as soon as the door closed behind her.

Sarah Fortune stood up from behind a pile of papers in the lounge area. She looked tired as if the heat had struck and she was glad of the rain. So was Mrs Mouse Pardoe. She shed her toque and her mac and sat down comfortably.

'Oh, lord, what a relief,' she said. 'Do you think you could make some tea? I can't stand this any longer.'

The movements were deft and forceful. None of the tottering, none of the giggles; a normal old lady of sixty-five years, oddly dressed, nothing more than eccentric. She sat herself comfortably among Sarah's papers, picked them up casually, glanced at a copy of Mr Pardoe's will, put it down with a smile.

'Working, dear? It's so bad for your eyes. Don't you like this simple will? It was all my idea.'

'Shall I draw the curtains?' Sarah said thoughtfully. 'In case we have visitors?'

'They're all out, dear. Don't worry, I have ears longer than stalks, and why do you think I insist on keeping a sheep? I'll know as soon as I hear a car and if anyone comes to this door, Hettie will bleat for me, then I'll just go back to being senile and you humour me, all right?'

'Of course,' Sarah murmured. 'I quite understand.'

Mouse Pardoe beamed. 'I knew you would. Ernest said so.'

CHAPTER EIGHT

'The late Mr Pardoe,' said Jennifer Pardoe, 'was a bit of a bully. Full of charm and also full of shit.' She belched slightly after the use of a rude word whose sound she obviously felt was agreeable. 'He was very lovable and very forceful and I was always known as the Mouse. I loved him greatly, hopelessly, but also realistically. I didn't have much option, even if I thoroughly disapproved and consider them, as I do now, that most property is theft. My opinion was never heard, my wishes never considered, until, when he grew older and beyond temptation, he started to listen and I suppose I got the upper hand. He had a passion for respectability, although he wasn't in the least respectable. It's a shame so many things come too late.' She sipped tea out of a mug with all the grace of a thirsty labourer, looked at Sarah over the rim.

'No,' she said, answering a question which hung in the air. 'I myself am not in the least respectable. Neither are you. I have always regarded the mere notion of respectability as such a waste of time.' Sarah nodded a mild assent.

'Anyway,' Mrs Pardoe continued, 'we made certain confessions to each other, my husband and I, long before he died, which somehow put us on an equal footing. I won't elaborate now. He ceased to care about property and such, and made the will you've read because he trusted me. He trusted Julian too, but Julian was on a bender at the time, not booze, you understand, the other kind of addiction, misguided love. Then my husband died in a typically stupid fashion. People surrounded me, immediately, telling me what I should do. They hemmed me in, and even if I'd finally got my better half into the habit of listening to me, no-one else did. The children, never. I knew they were going to push and pull me in all sorts of directions, and I knew exactly what I wanted to do with all this property we own, so did he really, getting it in the first place was only a sort of game to him. But I wasn't going to be allowed to have my own way.'

'Who,' Sarah asked, 'was going to stop you?'

'I merely made a suggestion about what we should do with all this property and Edward hit me. I ruined Edward as a child, let him get away with everything. He was such a pretty baby,' Jennifer Pardoe said simply, as if that was explanation enough. 'No-one was going to listen, as I said. The tradition of not listening to me was far too well established and I really can't stand confrontation and conflict. So I decided to go mad. Remove myself into the realms of the harmless and also make sure I got attention. You get a lot of attention when you're mad. I've rather enjoyed it, even though it is a bit of a strain, sometimes. When mad, you can be a total exhibitionist, something I was never allowed to be, wear what you like, say what you like, marvellous, you ought to try it.'

'Lying in the cabbage patch?' Sarah asked.

'Yes. Wonderful. But if I did it without being mad, some fool would call an ambulance. I've realized I'm probably quite a bit mad to begin with. It must help, don't you think? I like walking about with the sheep too, and talking to the birds, why not? Only I couldn't if I were supposed to be sane, could I?'

'I don't see why not.'

'My dear,' said Mrs Pardoe, patting her knee, 'I know that you have the uncanny knack of understanding almost everything, but one thing you can't know at your age is how much power you lose in the world when you grow old. You have to create another power base as your own crumbles. Basic politics. Mine, by the way, have always been slightly left of centre. Ernest Matthewson never used to approve.' She peered at a Mickey Mouse watch. 'I'd better go. We'll have to continue this another time. I wonder, will that boy Rick come up with ice-cream and my newspaper today? Probably not, what with the rain and all.'

She gurgled her tea again and proffered the mug. All confessions, Sarah noticed, needed some kind of liquid accompaniment. They could not emerge from a dry mouth.

'That boy Rick is in love with your daughter,' Sarah said. 'The feeling is reciprocated.' Mrs Pardoe nodded.

'Calf-love, I hope.'

'Calf-love can be real.'

'Well, there couldn't be a better candidate. A nice working-class boy, just like Mr Pardoe once was. Given the right chances, he'll go far. I must go.' Sarah wanted to stop her but there was nothing she could do against such steely determination.

'I suppose,' Mouse was saying, 'I should get a stick if I'm going to keep up this doddery charade. By the way, girl, have you any idea what should happen to this estate?'

'Yes. You've just endorsed it. It was you gave the instructions to Ernest, wasn't it? Not Julian?'

'Of course. Only it was supposed to look as if it was Ernest's idea, I mean anybody's but mine. I told him I wanted the children to realize that they had everything they needed already. I wanted them to realize of their own accord, without anyone telling them.

I wanted them to know how you work out your own destiny and money only makes it harder, sets you apart.'

'And why did he suggest me?'

Mrs Pardoe looked away, put on her hat and let the feathers hang down to her chin.

'They're supposed to go at the back, these feathers, more fun this way, aren't they?' Sarah's gaze did not waver; Mouse met it.

'My old friend Ernest never does anything without a dozen motives, you know?'

'I never knew he was quite so clever.'

'He isn't, he's simply cunning. What he really said about you was . . .' she paused, her first hesitation, as if the symptoms of insanity were resumed with the hat.

'Yes?'

'You were a catalyst. Does that mean a very sleek cat? Can a catalyst do something about Hettie the sheep? She's been driving me mad.'

Mrs Pardoe lurched across the wet lawn, singing in the rain.

Catalyst is not what Ernest said, Sarah thought. He would never have used such a word. Nor would he have understood that someone who acts out another role, like Mrs Pardoe's madness, becomes the part they play.

Miss Gloomer was dying. When Julian came back from his ten o'clock call, he drew level with the house he could never quite love as home since his father had died there, although he had loved its classless eccentricity once. He pulled into the drive, sat where he was with his hands on the steering wheel, watching the windows through the rain. Mother woke and slept early; no light shone from Edward's room with its sweeping view of the coast. I should not think of him as a spy as well as a failure, Julian thought. I should not delight that he and Joanna are likely out of the house in separate directions for fear of what they might do to comfort one another on a wet night like this; I have an evil mind.

He watched the lawn, noticed with weary guilt the way it resembled a hay field. The night was cooling fast; drizzle made the grass glisten. Tomorrow, time allowing, he could scythe it, tonight all he could see was the ghostly vision of Sarah Fortune, naked against the green. Then he was out of the car, walking automatically towards the cottages, his feet soft on the surface, hissing in the grass. He could say he thought he had heard an intruder; he could say he had come to enquire after her health after Joanna had told him the story of the rogue tide; he could say there was no time to come sooner, which was a lie. He could mention Elisabeth Tysall's headstone and ask Sarah's opinion, but he was still afraid; it was ridiculous and he turned to go back, saw the lamp outside the cottage they had given her, illuminating the scrubby roses and against the block of light from the open door, her figure, bent double. He heard the pitiful bleating of the sheep, heard Sarah's voice, soothing in return. Julian quickened his step. She did not seem remotely surprised to see him.

'Oh, it's you. Look, we've got to do something about this sheep.'

'Why?' His own voice sounded like a bleat of protest.

'She's been making a noise all evening, that's why, all afternoon too, butting her head against the door. Took me a while to realize it wasn't a simple desire for my company. One of her horns is growing into her eye.'

Julian squatted on his haunches. The sheep flinched; Sarah pressed the fleece against the frame of the door. He noticed that the left horn was partly swathed in a steaming rag, then saw with horror how

the tip had grown at a crooked angle, so that instead
of being level with the forehead, it grazed the ball of
one bloodshot and weeping eye. There was a hideous
sore patch beneath.

'She's in pain. She'll be covered with flies in the
morning,' Sarah was saying, matter of factly. 'I've
tried to yank the horn back, she's been very good,
but the horn's too hard. So I wrapped a hot dishcloth
round it. Thought it might soften it. Is that the right
thing to do? She doesn't like it.'

Julian swore under his breath, trying to remember
any jewels of animal husbandry his father had
learned in that last of his many enthusiasms. What
was it Father had wanted to do at the time, or was it
Mother's idea, collecting rare breeds of sheep? Put
something back into the land, Mother had said.

'I can't see properly,' he muttered, feeling the animal tremble beneath his hand. 'Do you mind if we
take her inside?'

It was bizarre, standing in the cruel light of the
kitchenette where a kettle bubbled on the cooker,
with the sheep trying to back away from where he
held her between braced legs.

'The heat does seem to soften it. Here, hold on to
her muzzle.' Sarah obeyed with both hands. The terror in the wall eyes of the animal seemed to fill the
room. Slowly, with considerable strength, Julian
lifted the horn with a wringing motion of both his
arms, twisting it up and back, well clear of the eye.
Quickly Sarah wiped the moisture which had gathered round the wound below. Hettie bucked and
reared. Enough was enough. They let her bolt for the
door in shambling haste, dishrag unwinding as she
went.

'She looks like a woman coming out of the hairdresser's, half done, I never knew sheep needed similar attention.' She had turned to wash her hands in
the sink, up to the elbow. Julian did the same.

'I wouldn't have seen you in the nurse's role,' he said lightly.

'Oh, I wouldn't know about that,' Sarah said with equal lightness. 'Would you like a drink? Plentiful supplies.'

Any animosity between them was gone. He felt himself shiver, remembering the crumpled horn, boring into an animal's head like the memories penetrating his own skull. The cottage was cool indoors, designed to repel heat in summer, preserve it in winter. Sarah was dressed in a cotton sweater, short sleeved with a deep V, buttercup yellow, her hair springy clean, the smell of soap, shampoo and perfume easily overpowering the farmyard traces of sheep and the lingering medicine smell of Miss Gloomer's bedside. They sat in the small living room. A large shawl of many colours was flung over the sofa; an ugly table lamp had been removed to the floor to diffuse the light, transforming the place so much that even the single bar of the electric fire seemed cheerful. On the first sip, he noticed that her whisky was excellent and she sipped her own with the evident pleasure of a connoisseur.

'Did you detour this way to tell me I was fired?' she asked without rancour, as if the answer did not much matter.

'No. You're retained for having a certain expertise with a sheep. How did you learn that?'

She shrugged. The sweater fell away a little at the neck; he noticed two small, raised scars, as if a mole had recently been removed.

'I really don't know. I don't have any skills, animals are easier than people. Would you like some more?'

The whisky had gone in the twinkling of an eye. He nodded. She rose gracefully, her arm catching the light and he noticed three more of the little scars above one elbow, white against the golden brown of her skin. There was nothing disfiguring in any of the scars, but the sight of them filled him with a peculiar anguish.

'We spoke on Friday,' he said abruptly. 'About the late Elisabeth Tysall. What do you know about her?' Sarah followed the direction of his gaze to the marks on her neck, pulled the neck of the sweater closer to her ears with both hands.

'Nothing while she was alive, but I came to know of her. I know that her husband considered I was her double. I know that he abused her badly and she killed herself off the coast down here. Let herself drown. Yesterday, I almost found out how. Do you know, if it had been warm, like yesterday, if she was drunk enough, drugged enough to lie down and sleep, it would have been a peaceful death, a simple letting go. No pain.'

'Do you think so?'

'Provided she had no terror. Provided she had consumed enough to want to drift away.'

Julian looked at her closely for signs of flippancy. Now he could see they were not the same, Elisabeth Tysall and this woman at his feet. They had little resemblance apart from the hair and the membership of the same league of female beauty.

'I should like to know about Elisabeth Tysall,' said Sarah wistfully, 'because no-one ever asked.'

Julian took a large swallow of the whisky and put it down. The prospect of shifting the burden of guilt by speaking of it made him react like the sheep at the end of the unexplained pain, silly and slightly skittish.

'The Tysalls had a cottage here,' he began. 'At least, she made it very much theirs with improvements, but it was rented from us. They appeared to be enormously rich. I suspect the kind of rich who actually owned very little. Not our kind of rich. This isn't a glamourous place, but Elisabeth Tysall liked it. Charles, her husband, let her come here alone, although he was extremely possessive. I supposed he reckoned there was no temptation in a little seaside town. We aren't exactly endowed with adult attractions. No casinos, no places to be seen. You don't get in the country calendar if you sit in the amusement arcade.' He looked at her meaningfully, met an innocent stare.

'She used to walk a lot. So did I, in those days when this landscape held magic for me.'

He remembered to sip slowly, feeling slightly intoxicated already, speaking faster.

'So I walked with her. I'd met Charles twice, when Father had had them up to the house for a drink. Charles saw me as a boring country bumpkin, the plain man I am. I met Elisabeth for longer in the surgery when she came in for a prescription. I don't know how it happened. I couldn't keep my eyes away. Life became a vacuum between meetings. A week when I didn't see her, and there were plenty of those, was a week in hell. She wrote letters in between, teased me, made me stand back. She was a wise flirt, warned me about Charles's savage jealousy. I told her, leave him: I'll take on the whole world for you; but she said no, you don't know me and no-one ever wins with Charles. Then all of a sudden one weekend, she succumbed. I can't describe it,' he said simply. 'I'd sound like a boy if I tried to describe it.' Julian sat back, exhausted by the memory.

'I remember telling her, you are so beautiful, you'll immobilize me completely with any other woman. What am I to do if you don't stay with me for ever? Leave him, marry me. I shall never react like this to any other woman, you're so perfect. Don't say that, she kept saying. Please don't say that.' He began to tremble, reached for his glass, let the good whisky slop on the floor.

'A fortnight later, she came back. You know how it is when you miss someone so much it hurts. I'd got myself into a pitch of anger because she hadn't been in touch in any way, no letter, phone call, nothing, and of course I couldn't get in touch with her because of Charles, but I was still mad to see her. My perfect Elisabeth, the fulfillment of all dreams. She wasn't perfect, though, not even remotely beautiful any more. In fact, when she barged into my surgery, she was hardly recognizable apart from the hair. Her face had been cut to ribbons. It might have been glassed: it was difficult to tell with all the stitches and the swelling. I couldn't look at her.'

Julian put his head in his hands, briefly, toyed with his glass, his palms sticky with sweat.

'I asked her how and why, of course. I think part of my reaction of revulsion, no more or less, was guilt, in case our affair had triggered what had been done to her. It was difficult for her to speak clearly; her mouth had been slit in one corner. She said it was nothing to do with me, Charles had done it on a whim. I didn't believe her. I was stunned and revolted and frightened, so I behaved like an impatient irresponsible doctor. I prescribed for her massive doses of tranquillizers, sleeping aids, told her she'd do best by the healing process if she slept for twenty-four hours. I rang the pharmacy, didn't even volunteer to stay with her. Instead, I went out and got drunk. Paralytic.'

He emptied the tumbler.

'May I have some more of this please, with the reassurance that I'm not going to repeat the exercise now? I've never been drunk since, though God knows I've tried.'

He closed his eyes and listened to the sound of the liquid gurgling into his glass. A generous measure, enough to make him shrug to attention. The hand touching his as he took the glass was warm, encouraging.

'I suppose it was the next day she disappeared, when I couldn't raise my head off the pillow, cancelled Saturday surgery, where I gathered later, she called to see me. She might not have received a friendly reception, despite her state. They thought she was bad for me and they'd never exactly liked her manner, which was imperious, to say the least. I suppose a woman as beautiful has the right to be rude and defensive, so many people must want to touch.'

He was nursing the whisky rather than drinking it. Sarah sensed a man of iron self-control, who drank not for pleasure, only for oblivion.

'I assumed she had gone back to her husband. I got a letter from him, some time later, terminating the tenancy on the cottage. I felt, as I should have done, extremely guilty, also relieved. The guilt then was nothing to the guilt a year later, when she was found in the sand banks, half a mile from the quay. The buried body, come back into the land of the living.'

'How did she come to be buried?'

'No-one knows, or if they do, they won't be telling now, but the creeks change shape all the time. A section of bank could have fallen on her, buried her, then split apart again after months. There was a storm tide the day before she was found. It was the growth of hair, mainly, which indicated how long she'd been there. Then the police investigation, her husband saying she'd never gone back to London at all, he thought she'd gone home to America, which is where she came from originally. Elisabeth was under the sand from almost the day I spoke to her last. I wish there was some doubt: there isn't. I shall always know it was I who put her there. She came to me for help. The one who was her lover gave her the means for suicide. The last straw. I may as well have ordered her to go and die.'

The whisky was untouched and the room was silent. Julian coughed, painfully.

'Charles came to look at the body of course. He phoned me and I told him he could stay in his old cottage if he wanted, but all he kept asking was how his wife came to be buried in the sand, as if I should know. I was angry with him, short, said I didn't want to know, shouted at him, he should have loved her. It was the same week Father died, my behaviour before that might explain why he didn't trust me. Charles simply wouldn't accept any of the explanations of how Elisabeth had been interred there so long, he wanted me to take him to see the place. I couldn't, wouldn't. Then I was called to remove his body from where it was washed up. I knew it must be him. Do you know what I did? I kicked that sodden bundle in the ribs, put the last nail in the coffin of my self-esteem. Then I came home to bury my father. I knew then what I've known ever since.' He began to count on his fingers. 'Namely, I'm not fit to be a human being among all these decent people here, let alone a doctor. I killed her, you see. I may as well have killed myself.'

Sarah got up and moved into the kitchen area where he could see her putting the kettle on the stove, lighting the gas. A moth came in through the window, fluttered in front of the mirror Joanna had used to dress, reflecting the light from the floor. Julian wanted to stop the sound of the flapping wings round the light.

'Coffee?' Sarah was asking.

'Yes.' He waited, leaned forward and caught the moth in both hands, got up and released it through the open window. Sarah came back, put the coffee on the floor beside the lamp, sat where she had been at his feet. There was nothing submissive in the pose, only a command for attention.

'Now you listen,' she said. 'There's something you should know. Don't ask for the sources of information, just believe, Elisabeth Tysall did not kill herself on your account. She planned it before she came here that last time and nothing was going to stop her. She had written a letter to Ernest Matthewson, deposited with her bank, to be forwarded to him only in the event of her death being confirmed. The bank followed her instructions to the letter. Ernest was ill, his wife intercepted the letter and finally, gave it to me. I showed it to a friend—no-one else. Elisabeth stated on page one exactly what she was going to do, how and where. She said she'd had several affairs in the past, all as revenge against Charles for not loving her any more, but the suicide was pure revenge for her disfigurement. She couldn't tell tales about him while she was alive, but she planned for her body to be found, her injuries examined and him exposed. She didn't know much about the workings of the law, it wouldn't have stood up in court. Also, she didn't have the remotest will to live, something she had lost a long time before. She didn't need your tranquillizers either since she already had an arsenal of pills. There was supposed to be another sealed letter on her when she was found, but that was lost.'

Sarah twisted to sit on the other hip, gracefully. Julian could feel a wild heat course through his veins. Anger, relief, remembered, unexercised desire, until now, dormant along with the dead. Fury, guilt.

'That doesn't mean,' Sarah went on softly, 'that your reaction to her face was not horribly cruel, something to be ashamed of. But it does mean that it didn't influence events. You didn't kill her. Charles killed her. As for kicking his corpse, a corpse has no feelings, leaves those with the living. Your father had just died. Grief makes us all knock on the doors of insanity. When my husband died, I wanted to kill, maim, torture. You hardly did that.'

Julian was leaning forward, hungry for hope, staring into her flecked eyes, finding them fathomless, generous, lonely without sadness. He did not move when she took his face between her hands and kissed him. The kiss went on: he recoiled slightly, then responded with a groan, drawn into the embrace with a long, shuddering sigh.

'Sarah, Sarah . . .'

'Don't think,' she murmured. 'Just don't think. Except of killing demons.'

He thought he also heard her say that Charles Tysall could not be allowed to claim so many lives, but he was not sure of anything she said. He heard only the rustle of clothing, himself climbing the stairs in her wake, entering the dark bedroom where the moonlight shone, pulling his shirt over his head, falling with her into a warm tangle of silky limbs, joined again by the kiss which seemed never to have stopped. Remembering her slenderness, feeling her strength, trying not to claw or to grasp. Shivering until she calmed him, guided him into one cataclysmic moment when he knew he shouted. When he swam back into the planet, he wanted to cry. Instead, he slept like a child.

The wheels of Edward's car spun on the gravel; not the swishing sound of a well-raked, richly coated drive, only the spinning of worn rubber on worn pebbles sunk into mud after warm rain. Fishing: why ever would a man want to fish? Especially the way he fished, a sort of clandestine activity, often at night, for the romance of moonlight on the waves, but mostly for shame, because fishing was something he did to acquire a skill other men might envy, because a man of his vision should have been able to pull fish out of the sea as easily as far lesser men and he had to make his attempts at night because so far, they were conspicuous failures. The fish would not bite, even after the hours he had spent over two years, they stayed beneath the water and laughed at him. The rods were state of the art, the bait was right according to the books, and that boy Stonewall swore it was, managing just a touch of scorn in his silent servility. Edward admitted he needed a teacher, if he were humble enough to learn. He could cast, but he could not catch. It was like everything else—his failure was in proportion to the effort. If only Dad had taught him.

The house felt empty. 'Joanna!' he shouted up the stairs, careless of whom he might wake; how dare they sleep when he needed company and food in that order? Silence. Her car was gone, out with one of her bitchy friends, as long as that was all. He slammed down his fishing tackle on the kitchen table, emptied his jacket pockets of boxes of hooks, floats, casting weights, the detritus of failure, along with sandwiches in grease-proof paper, silly cow. The light-weight plastic of the box of hooks cracked, spilling them on the table, small things these ones, no bigger than a thumbnail. Edward scooped some of them into the kitchen drawer. There were signs of his impatience, signs of his desire, all over the house. New rods, new reels, hooks in every drawer. Mother, Julian, even Father before had let him spread this litter. They all thought fishing might make a man of him. If he had heard that once, he had heard it ten dozen times.

'Joanna!'

Nothing. Edward went up to his room, hungry and bored, and looked out of the window. The rain had eased to a soft drizzle; the sky was clear for another day's fresher heat tomorrow. He was suddenly forlorn, still angry. The doll's house stood covered. He brought his fist down into the plywood roof, heard it crack and crumble, the contents inside skitter as the edifice tottered, groaned and stood still. Unable to bear examination of the carnage, he turned to the window; unable to look towards the sea, he looked towards the cottages.

A light in a window over there. Hettie the sheep grazing in front of the one door out of the three which had roses. An upstairs light and a downstairs light. Julian's car parked by the front door of their house, as usual. Edward suddenly knew where he was. The knowledge made him feel sick.

He clattered downstairs in case he was wrong, passed via a wide detour to the back of the house where Julian's room stood next to Jo's, both doors ajar, both rooms empty. Back to his own room, looking out again. The light above the front door shone out to welcome everyone home, illuminating the grass. He could see Sarah Fortune in the nude, walking away from him like a contemptuous ghost, a model for a painting with her handbag balanced on her head and her arms outstretched for balance in perfect poise. Save me from desire, he told himself with all the fervour of the prayer he despised. Save me.

Back down in the kitchen, he tripped over his rod, swore, tripped over the newspaper on the pantry floor, swore again. He seized a fistful of bread, felt a tickle on the back of his neck, turned. Mother was behind him, still in the feather hat she had worn that morning, a tweedy coat over the same dress. She was clearly startled. More satisfyingly, she was also frightened. Retreating before him like a slave, back into the kitchen, putting her hand on the hooks on the table, screaming short little shrieks like a parrot, raising her palms as if about to pray, before he hit her. A punch was all, to the side of that ridiculous hat, but hard, making her fold, clutch the back of a chair with a hook or two still in her palm. She gasped but would not fall, straightened up, clasped the table for support with the other hand and stood straight, swaying slightly. The hat was knocked even further sideways, the feathers curling and brushing the left ear lobe, from which a drop of blood began to form and slowly fall. She opened the palm in which two fish hooks were embedded and sighed theatrically.

'What did I do, Ed dear? What did I do?'

There was a draught of cold air from the back door. Joanna stood, hair damp, frizzed by rain, looking at the tableau of mother and son. Mother sat with great precision and began to tease the two hooks out of her palm, wincing only slightly, tut-tutting under her breath. It was the barbs, pointing backwards, that got under the skin and went into the bone of a fish without causing pain; Joanna had listened to a thousand expositions and explanations from Edward. The hooks did not look painless inside a hand.

'There!' Mother said, triumphantly, easing out the first, holding it to the light and going to work on the second. 'You just have to do this and then you go this way, see? Easy peasy.' Joanna was comforted. Accidents will happen, fishing was silly sport. Then the drop of blood oozing from behind Mother's hat, a single drop, plopping on the table before Mother caught it in her injured palm, sucked greedily. All gone, that bright red speck, all gone. Then she saw Joanna for the first time. Her voice became defensive. She looked at Edward, fearfully.

'All gone!' she said, gaily, retrieving the second hook. 'Time for bed! Time for bed long ago! Should not have got up!'

Edward was filling the kettle at the sink. Joanna looked long and hard at the hunch of his back as she guided her mother out of the room.

'Want a sandwich, Ma?' she asked as they went slowly upstairs. 'Are you hungry?'

'No, thank you, thank you no.' Then as an afterthought. 'Mustn't wear ear-rings, darling, they hurt if you fall over.'

Joanna was glad Mother wanted nothing like a sandwich. She did not want to go back to the kitchen, with all its lingering body heat, the claustrophobic warmth, the accusations, the denting of faith in the brother she had trusted. Not yet.

The tide receded. Hooked against a rope in the quay, looking jaunty in the moonlight, hung a purple shirt like a church gown left out to dry at the end of the Sabbath. A pair of sandals danced and sank, moving on elsewhere with the fish.

Julian Pardoe stirred in Sarah's arms, bereft of guilt or pain.

'Sarah?'

'Yes?' Moving closer.

'When grief makes you insane, what do you do? What did you do the first time?'

'This,' she murmured sleepily. 'Only this.' Then later, another murmur. 'I never was much good at the law, you see, never much good at anything, but I am good at this. The law is so slow. It's no fun at all. It should be more than arithmetic . . . There are so many better ways to cure an ill.' He did not understand: it did not matter, he pulled her closer, back into the kiss, felt those strange scars on her arms, too late for questions, let himself drown in the oldest medicine of all.

CHAPTER NINE

They could go fishing for the ghost and earn themselves glory. Stonewall and Rick were down in the boat, a battered old rower with a put-put engine, half a horsepower, Rick said, but good enough for the creeks and if you let it go with the tide, it could win the Olympics. They were waiting for the water in the kind of milky sweet dawn which made Stonewall shiver. The boat lay snug against the harbour wall. He leant over the side with his line, looking for the crabs he could sell for bait or more likely throw back if he caught them, found instead a purple shirt drying on the mooring rope, wrapped it round his skinny middle and felt absurdly happy with his prize. Rick lay supine and looked at the sky.

He stood to stretch his legs and yawn, his head below the level of the quayside wall when he heard Edward Pardoe pass in his unseasonally heavy shoes. Rick balanced himself on the central bench of the boat, clutched the wall and sprang over. Intent on his own progress, looking briefly at the swans which dithered with the tide, Edward noticed nothing else. Rick put a finger over his mouth as Stonewall sprang to attention beside him. Both silent by common consent, they leaned with their elbows propped on the bonnet of a car, looking through the windscreen and out the back to watch Edward walk towards the road which led out to the beach, the caravan park and the woods.

Rick snapped his fingers and jerked his head in Edward's direction in a parody of military command, instantly appreciated. Stonewall made a mocking salute, trotted away in his filthy training shoes after the disappearing figure. Rick shaded his eyes with his hand, still acting the role. The sun was brighter by the minute; Stonewall's mum would blame him if the lad was not home by breakfast, time enough for that. Now what was that bastard Edward doing? He wouldn't rise early in the morning for nothing, wouldn't rise at all if he could help it. Rick turned and spat on the ground, always did him good to spit, even if it was a habit recently learned and one which shamed him.

He'd acquired it first a few weeks since, when Edward came down the arcade and warned him off Joanna. What's it to you who she goes out with? Rick had said. I'm not going to do her any harm. Just lay off, that's all, she doesn't even like you, just pretends, laughs at you behind your back, Edward had drawled, so leave her alone, or we'll see about your amusement arcade, your job and your dad's living, plus all those other souls who work in there from time to time. That's when Rick spat, more in response to the first half of the message than the second, powerless, the way he often felt, story of his life.

Pardoes and fathers have the last word. Not any more. He looked across the road at the kingdom of his arcade. Even with a dad like his, he was good enough for anyone. He'd been thinking about it all. Today was the day to find Jo.

Rick folded back the doors to the arcade, went inside, moving from switch to switch. The place was suddenly full of flashing light and wonderful, raucous sound which gave him strength.

* * *

Stonewall thought he had got the drift of Edward's purposeful direction, since on this road there was very little choice. Maybe the lazy sod was going to dig up his own bait for a change, but he carried nothing. The road could only lead to caravan site, beach or woods; Stonewall couldn't see a Pardoe having much to do with caravans. Edward walked on the bank parallel with the silent road, with Stonewall shadowing, shielded from view even with the piece of purple flotsam round his waist, as he trailed behind, slightly excited, more irritated than thrilled, for once, slightly insulted by being so inconspicuous. He was hungry, he was following Ed who owed him money, committed to the pursuit, even if he was cross enough to risk a short cut. Stonewall launched across the caravan park, flitted like a shadow between the sleepy, slug-like vehicles where morning life was just beginning, into the woods where the wind moaned softly. Ed must have gone to the beach; he would head him off. He followed a series of tracks which led through the scented pine woods, dipping through sandy valleys, up and down to the final ridge of trees on the edge of the sand. There was a path across the ridge, again dipping into gaps where entries and exits had been forged or grown. Stonewall scanned the beach, moved slowly left. He had first seen the ghost talking to Edward, right out there. They had met in the middle of the wilderness, like two people about to fight a duel.

That was weeks ago. This time he heard the voices first and almost stumbled across them, sitting halfway up part of the steep slope which led from woods to beach, out of the breeze. Two of them, Edward and the white-haired man sitting in his old clothes with the palms of both hands on the pummel of a stick which Stonewall also recognized. Miss Gloomer's stick. Stonewall fell flat to earth as if he had been shot, lay with his hands propping up his head. He could scarcely hear them, what with the wind in the trees behind him and the mewing of the gulls on the beach below, struggled to listen for the sake of having something to report. His stomach grumbled, he farted and almost apologized aloud. People did not do that on videos and the prospect of doing it again stopped him crawling closer.

Rick loves me: he said so.

The sun was beginning to filter through the branches above him and warm the back of his head, not the sand beneath. The light was intermittent, like being in the disco above the Ark Royal with strobe lighting. Stonewall shivered with an uncomfortable sensation of fear, watched the sand flies leaping in front of his nose. What did you do with my Sal, you, you with the white hair like the headmaster? Sal's collar still dug into his groin; fear was displaced by anger, then by his own importance in seeing the ghost in which others now believed. They'd catch him all in good time, Rick and he.

Rick loves me. We can do anything.

A spider was creeping along a dew defined tight-rope of web, suspended in front of Stonewall's freckled nose. Edward and the old man beneath were certainly not talking with the ease of old pals. The conversation was clipped, infrequent, with much staring out to sea and long pauses, not men at ease, not like him and Rick.

'That's a new stick you have,' Edward was saying. 'Where did you get it? I thought you hadn't any money.'

'Oh, I stopped by to visit some old dear, for tea and chat, of course. Somehow acquired the stick on the way out.' Edward made a tut-tutting sound of warning, played with a blade of grass.

'You shouldn't do things like that,' he said petulantly.

'A man must eat. I shouldn't break into your

brother's surgery either, but you didn't have qualms
about that.'

Silence, the wind moaning, blurring sound.

'. . . did you find?'

'The medical records of one Elisabeth Tysall. Details of a complicated prescription for soporific poi-
sons. Particulars of an adulterous murder, to my
mind.'

'Oh no, not quite that,' Edward protested. 'Not as
such.'

'Yes, as such. Letters from her which he received.
Bitter letters to her he never sent. Why did he keep
them out of his own house?'

'Because my mother is so inquisitive, I suppose.'

'I could kill him,' said the man calmly. 'That's the
idea, is it not?'

'You mean Charles Tysall could kill him?'

'With his bare hands,' said the man laconically.
'Although I daresay, he'd endeavour for a little more
subtlety.' Edward wriggled uncomfortably. The man
shifted in sympathy and moved further away. His
piercing blue eyes abandoned their constant survey
of the shore and bored into Edward's own. They
seemed slightly out of focus, the man himself more
of a vagrant than he had ever been before. Only his
speech was perfectly controlled.

'Which would suit your purposes, I presume, as
we discussed, however obliquely. It would suit you
even better if your mother perished in the same accident. You and your beloved sister, lord and lady of
all you survey, now that would be a lovely landscape
to play with.'

'I suppose so,' Edward muttered, still uncomfortable, but his body tingling with excitement. He would
still have preferred his ambitions to be guessed, remain beyond definition, carried out without his
knowledge. In the light of morning, his dreams became violent and vulgar; he wanted first to cherish

and then, postpone them. Plans were so much more pleasant before they became real.

'We've still got this woman staying,' he said hurriedly. 'Makes it a bit awkward.'

'The one your sister called the cow.'

'She doesn't do that any more. Look, we ought to think about this.'

'Of course. I think all the time.'

'I mean, lay low, for a while—'

'Are you changing your mind?'

'No, no.'

'You would prefer, perhaps, not to know?'

'Can we just arrange another meeting, say two days' time? I've brought you a key to a caravan, all mod cons, fourth row down on the left, on the end ... What's the matter?'

The long, thin man was heaving with mirthless laughter, an unpleasant wheezing sound which shook his whole frame and made the stick vibrate.

'Nothing. It's too late to change your mind. Do you really think I'll stay in a place of your choosing, where you can find me.'

'I can turn you over to the police,' Edward blustered.

'For what? And have me repeat our conversations? Really!'

Again, there was that revelation of the balance of power between them, which Edward tried to pretend did not exist, but had been there all the time, since the very first, denying his control of the man, giving the lie to the little illusion that he was a grand benefactor and this was the grateful servant.

'Just don't do anything until I tell you.'

The man raised his eyebrows, spread his hands. 'Would I? Did your sweet sister make you sandwiches today?'

'Yes, sorry I forgot them.'

Edward left without a backward glance, breaking

into a jog along the beach, running awkwardly, disturbed, anxious to be away. The man rose too, moved to the left, out of sight.

Stonewall had missed most of the talk, apart from the odd bit about caravans. Something froze him, belly down, the inertia of hunger which stopped him getting up and following the ghost, the sun on his head, his long squinting at the spider, the light falling in lumps through the trees. Thinking of his mother's wrath, wondering if it was better to wait here longer until her anger would be tempered by anxiety, thought after ten minutes' indecision how that might well make things worse. Thought, too, of which lies to tell to explain sneaking out of doors so early on a Monday morning, drawn by the allure of Rick's boat, not able to mention where he had been in case that meant a total ban, and somehow, in between all these anxious machinations, something more than the memory of Sal nagging at him, like being halfway to school on games days and realizing he had forgotten his shoes. Stonewall hated Monday mornings like that: they were the days for guilt.

Rick loves me.

Reluctantly, he scrambled to his feet and turned to run downhill back into the woods. Stopped, took a step back, heart in mouth, tripped, fell heavily on his bottom, winded. The white-haired man was standing there, towering above him from nowhere, looking at him, leaning on his stick like a man who had no need to lean.

'I know you,' said the man. 'Don't I? And you know me.'

Stonewall shook his head in frantic denial, tried to scramble up, but the sand slipped from beneath his feet. Oh yes, he knew the man now. Almost a year to the day, that man striding out over the channels, Stonewall trying to stop him and tell him about the tide coming in faster than anyone could run, getting pushed over for his pains. A man who seemed to have grown taller and thinner and acquired this halo of bright white hair. He must have lived like an animal to change from that to this. His arms were like sticks, he was dirty.

'You're a spy for the good doctor,' said the man softly. 'You're just a spy. You even look like the doctor. Did you help to bury her? Did you put your grubby little fingers all over her, you and the doctor? Is that her shirt I see on you? Did you touch her tits? Did you?'

The boy was opening his mouth to protest, I never did nothing. I don't know what you're talking about, lay off, leave me alone, what did you do with my dog? There were no words, only a single sharp scream.

Stonewall's hands had flown to his head: the pummel from Miss Gloomer's stick broke three of his fingers. The second blow thudded into his skull; he could feel the crunching without pain, like a tooth coming out at the dentist, hardly felt the third blow at all. His body, halfway upright, curled into itself, fell forward, rolled down the slope through the pine needles and spiky grass, the thistle and the brambles tugging at his shorts, nothing hurting or feeling, his eyes awake to the light sparking through the pines, the moaning of the wind turning into a roar and then into a great big silence. He ceased to notice the sun, felt a mild surprise as his body jerked again and then lay still, foetally curled with his hands to his head the way Rick had taught him to land if he fell. The final sensation was of resting against a brown tree trunk where the bark scraped his cheek and at last, that graze caused pain, humiliation, a vague sense that he was in the wrong place at the wrong time, foolish, just a baby who wanted to cry and not be teased like this. He could not close his eyes but there was nothing he could see.

Rick loves me.

The man looked down dispassionately. If he followed to finish what he had started, he would probably tear his clothes and he did not have clothes to spare. Nor enough clothes to go home. Wherever that was.

It was a mild breakfast, big brother in mild humour, Joanna noticed. Mother took hers out into the sun; there was no sign of Edward and no ill will from anyone. Mother had dressed in Monday best, wore a turban with a brooch. With a reluctant sense of fairness, which had always distorted itself to champion the younger of her brothers, Joanna was admitting to herself how it was that Julian was best with Mother, adapted to her childish level, played her games except sometimes when she went near the stove. There was a bruise she had noticed to the side of Mother's cheek, the imprint of yesterday's ear-ring neatly reproduced, a lower level of attention-seeking in her lunacy today, uncharacteristic, a deviation from the way she never failed to hide her battiness, always thrust it under their noses. The dress beneath the turban was turquoise and shimmery with leg-of-mutton sleeves, the pink plimsolls the same as yesterday. Joanna could see her now, beyond the kitchen door, feeding the birds by scattering crumbs in large, unnecessary flings. Joanna sensed her restlessness. She was restless herself, wanted to tell Julian about the scene she thought she had seen last night, Edward and Mouse, something terrible. Loyalty forbade revelation, even to herself. Edward would never do such a thing; her imagination was playing tricks. It was all part of some spirit of energy which seemed to have afflicted them all since Sarah Fortune had arrived, a long few days before.

'Jo, don't bother cooking today,' Julian was suggesting pleasantly. 'Mother doesn't much care, seems a waste of the heat. Look, I meant to ask you ages ago, what happened to that boy you were seeing? Rick, from the arcade? Nice lad. I stitched his knee last year, he was extremely brave, I know we don't talk about these things, but I mean, I never even told you I liked him—'

'First I heard!' Surprise and the restless energy made her hiss.

'What on earth do you mean?'

Mother came back indoors. The full turquoise skirt was tucked into her knickers on one side. She did a waltzing turn, then beckoned to Hettie the sheep to follow from the doorway.

'Can Hettie come in?' she enquired with smooth politeness. The sheep seemed to snigger; they were only as silly as one another. 'Only she's so much better today, I've asked her for coffee.'

'Not on weekdays, Mother, you know that,' Julian admonished calmly. 'Joanna, what do you mean? What happened to Rick? You two fall out or something? I hoped, well—'

Joanna exploded in fury. How could he be so calm and concerned when all he wanted to do was put Mother in a home where they would never let her wear her own clothes? When it was he who wrecked her chances with Rick in the first place, drove him away with threats?

'I mean,' she hissed, 'that no, we didn't fall out. But it's a bit difficult for a man to go on taking a girl out when her big brother tells him not to bother because if he doesn't, he might lose his living. See what I mean? And don't lie about it. Rick was shy enough already. You just made it worse.'

She was shoving breakfast dishes into soapsuds with shaking hands. Julian's calm only fuelled her fury.

'Jo,' he began.

'Don't call me Jo!' she screamed. Mother erupted into laughter and then went back outside, humming in some strange sort of satisfaction. Julian let it all ride for a full minute until Joanna's frenetic movements became slower, then joined her at the sink, drying as she washed, sorry all of a sudden for not doing more often as he did now. Unbidden, Sarah Fortune came to mind. Life is too short to bake cakes, she'd said, sometime early this morning; made him laugh, made him smile now. I love my sister, he thought, only I never say so. I love this place, if not this house, I'm not the worst doctor they ever had. I can live if I let myself live.

'There's the door,' he said. 'Go down to the quay, I should, and ask your Rick which brother it was gave him a warning. All I can say is it wasn't this one. Oh, and do bear in mind the fact it could be simple nervousness makes a man give up on a gorgeous girl like you. You beautiful women never seem to know how terrifying you are. You scare us to death.'

She was still defiant, horribly doubtful. So much easier to blame rather than act, so much simpler to wallow.

'Gorgeous!' she spat.

'Oh, ever so, ever so gorgeous,' said Mother, nodding like the sheep in the doorway.

'Extremely good-looking, if you want to be pedantic,' said Julian gravely. 'If only you saw yourself as other people do.'

'Such as?' she flung back, still defiant, tossing her hair out of her eyes. He pretended to consider, think of an opinion she might value. Not the vicar, the genteel verger who kissed Mother after church, not any male in their small circle he could quote.

'Sarah Fortune says so. She told me, I didn't ask. Takes one good-looking woman to know another.'

The front door slammed. Edward's distinctive cough echoed in the distance. Joanna couldn't face Edward. She stuck two fingers in the air, roughly towards Hettie, aimed towards all present, speechless, mollified, flattered, unable to say anything with grace, still trying to suppress all those warning chords in her head which had been humming with the strength of the church organ, about anything Edward had ever said.

'Come in and have some more coffee, Mother,' Julian was saying. He was trying to distract her from her obvious efforts to introduce Hettie into the kitchen, as if she needed a watchdog, but also to turn attention away from Jo's dilemma since the girl could never make a decision with the spotlight on her. Look at them both, Jo thought with fleeting concern, would he ever put Ma in a home, like Edward said? In the end, she didn't want to think about either of them at all, she simply wanted to run.

The dramatic stripes of her light cotton skirt flowed round as she walked briskly down the road, the effect of it reassuring. Sarah Fortune's influence had made her root through her wardrobe and the local shops for things which actually pleased her. If she were Sarah, how would she tackle Rick? Calmly, directly, without going pink or beating about the bush, saying, Can I talk to you, please? That's what Sarah had said when they talked about it. She said, Find out the truth and then, if you have to, find someone else. A long talk it had been, with the clothes.

The amusement arcade was an empty hall of sound, not yet fit for the crowd who would filter through later, clog the quayside with cars and sit like dummies munching chips. Joanna did not smooth her skirt or preen her hair, but went into the relative darkness, temporarily blinded. Rick was polishing. Thunderbirds V, she read; Street Fighters, Space

Wars X, Kung Fu, a veritable graveyard of fun. He stopped and looked at her.

His face broke into a slow smile. From the darkness behind, his father's large, florid countenance appeared. A gnarled hand laid a warning grasp on his son's arm, while the opposite hand tipped his cap to Joanna. Hypocrite, she thought, bully and hypocrite. Rick's bruises were still faintly shocking. She looked from him to the old man and back again, challenging. He seemed to shrink in front of her eyes.

'We'll take the van,' Rick said.

Driving out to the woods by the beach, Rick rang the chimes, ignoring the early posses of children who waved. Joanna sat upright. Beyond the caravan site, where a pitted road marked 'unsuitable for vehicles' led into the woods, Rick turned left, stopped after two hundred yards. The human compulsion to congregate had always amazed him in its sheer perversity. Once off the beaten track, even so short a distance from two thousand other souls, there was rarely anyone at all. You'd think, he'd told Stonewall, that human beings really loved one another the way they went on.

'I've been wanting to talk to you,' said Rick to Joanna, resting over the wheel of the van. 'But you called me out, so you go first.' Her hands were in her lap; he could see she had been biting her nails and now she was taking an extra deep breath.

'Rick, do you like me, even a little bit? Oh, that's a silly question, you can't really say no, can you?'

'Yes I could, but it wouldn't be true. Course I like you.' He was furious about the tremor in his voice. 'You and Stonewall, you're all there is for me.' Then he copied her deep breath, entirely without affectation. 'Only your brother Edward said you were only playing games with me and I couldn't take that, could I?'

'Edward?' she said slowly, in tones of despair.

'Who else? He also said he could take away the arcade. I shouldn't have listened Jo, should I? I shouldn't, should I?'

She had begun to cry, whether from a sense of relief or one of betrayal, she did not quite know.

'No, you shouldn't. We wouldn't do any such thing. Dad wouldn't, Julian wouldn't, Edward . . . You know what we should do with all this stuff we own? We should just give it all back, all that stuff we have, get rid of it, let other people have it.' The tears embarrassed her.

Out in the woods, it was cool. They walked for a while in silence, moving by instinct towards the sea. You could live here ever so long and never fail to be drawn to the sea: all steps led in that direction, winter or summer. Rick wanted to make love to her there and then, on the pine needles, the way he had wanted to for months, too nervous to try because it mattered too much and he was so terrified it wouldn't work, slid his arm round her waist instead. The crying ceased, slowly.

'I've been so miserable, Rick,' she said with a great tremulous sigh. 'I've tried to stop being miserable, but I can't.'

'You and me both.' He tightened his hold. 'You're fading away. Don't you go getting any thinner.'

She wanted to laugh, still wanted to cry, turning to him as he turned to her, burying herself in his chest, her hair floating over his face, him stroking it into smoothness, looking down at the top of her head in wonder. Then moving on, arm in arm, looking for an even quieter place to sit down, somewhere where the sun would reach them but not intrude.

'I could kill your brother Edward,' Rick murmured. 'He was out and about early today, though. I got Stonewall to follow him, for a game.' Joanna did not like mention of Edward. She wanted to believe that the conjunction of Edward and mean little lies was a kind of mistake, all to be made clear, some other time.

'Stonewall didn't do so well then. Edward came home as I left.'

Rick stopped, faintly perturbed, not enough to distract him from the beating of his own heart. Much further and he would die; as long as he could sit with her, hold on to her, the rest could wait.

His feet felt the smoothness of sand in a couch-shaped hollow to the left of the track, shielded by a crooked tree halfway up the last slope before the top ridge and the alien openness of the beach where two seekers of kinder light knew they did not want to go. They sat together, peaceful but awkward, he suddenly with all the patience in the world, wanting to do everything right with time as his ally.

'You do want me, Jo? Are you sure?'

From out of his mouth, the shortened name was fine, she loved it, gazed at him, and then, the expression on her face changed slowly. From one of dazed and mesmerized beauty, her huge pupils narrowed, defied the love in her eyes, became a mask of puzzlement, almost pain.

'There's a person, watching us,' she murmured. 'Over there.'

Rick twisted away from her, shouted loudly, 'Who's that?' focusing in the alternate light and dark made by the waving branches, listened, heard nothing but the sighing of the wind. Looked round in deep suspicion, fists clenched, ready to fight, saw a flash of purple.

A sleeve and a hand extended from the other side of a tree, a thin stream of blood forming into a bright red drop at the end of the fingers, suddenly caught, looking as if it would never fall. Rick would not have recognized a mere hand, but he knew the colour of that piece of silken flotsam. Stonewall, the stupid spy, always playing games, the silly little runt.

'Come out, you daft bugger!' Rick bellowed.

Slowly the hand slipped. Both watched, hypnotized, ready to be amused. Stonewall's face, contused, streaked with dirty red, his eyes staring wide, emerged first. The hand moved in the semblance of a royal wave, making a big, slow, theatrical gesture until gently, violently, a slight trace of foam around his mouth, Stonewall slumped towards them.

Shortly after Julian had left, before eight o'clock, she supposed, without checking her watch, Sarah felt that great stab of pain which made her sit on the side of the ancient bath, holding her head in her hands. The clanking of the plumbing which produced steamy hot water by chance rather than science, pipes reverberating inside walls like the tuning of an organ, stunned recollection, forbade thinking, encouraged screaming. The same with the pain itself, intense, dying slowly, inducing panic because she knew it was not hers and there was nothing she could do, could not divine the source or the cure, only feel and pray it would go.

It was the same old affliction, an excess of vicarious knowledge. She was always able to sense loneliness across a road or a room, similar to an Exocet missile finding heat, but now all pain, physical and mental, seemed to find her, echoed from another body into her own and settled in her limbs, to be treated only by her own equivalent of prayer to no known god, the prayer as often a curse for the empathy she had somehow acquired.

A sort to telepathy, Malcolm said dismissively. Grist to her mill, in the days before Charles Tysall and Malcolm when she had augmented her income by discriminate prostitution, less concerned about profit than fun and freedom, merely a woman in pursuit of a talent. She had never considered herself a therapist, simply a person without conventional morals of the kind which seemed both irrelevant and obstructive. Besides, she loved sleeping with men provided she liked them. Affection or respect was the key; either would do. Some of them preferred to chat: not many. Being a tart with a heart meant listening first or after, it did not matter what they wanted, provided she gave value and as often as not, received her own reward.

Sarah washed with thoroughness, killing the smell of sexual contact with some regret. Losing the habits of genteel promiscuity because of being with Malcolm, did not mean losing either the empathy or the instincts. Malcolm's kind lived by one set of rules, she lived by another, was all; she could not even see anything odd about hers, could not even see it as a strange way of going on.

Or even a strange way of being, until she looked in the glass, as she did now, with the steam melting on the bathroom mirror and all the smell of sex gone, the pain receding into a dull ache, somewhere around the head, the ribs, the hand. She wanted not to stare at herself and could not close her eyes, they seemed to be stuck, staring wide. She turned on the basin tap to make more steam, scratching at those little grubs on the back of her arms where Charles Tysall had been, knowing he was alive, leaving his scars on her skin, like Elisabeth, now on someone else. The pain increased. She stared into the steam. There was a brief wish that someone, anyone, would stare back, that a hand could appear over her naked shoulder and brush away the worms, as no-one had ever done, not Malcolm with his best efforts, no-one, since no-one ever did.

Sarah did nothing, stared towards the blurred reflection of her face, concentrated to keep her eyes open, in case other, more innocent eyes, should close.

CHAPTER TEN

'All gone! Everybody gone!'

Left to her own devices, Mrs Jennifer Pardoe tended to potter and talk to herself, a mild eccentricity, she thought, a measure to preserve sanity in the face of the constant charade. The trouble was, it was becoming difficult to tell which persona was which. She kept finding herself acting oddly, even in privacy. Daily domestic help was long since vetoed: acting mad in front of the family was exhausting enough, though less of a strain recently. Mouse Pardoe was more than happy to justify her own existence in the meantime. By a gentle, none too efficient polishing of the furniture, a little playful baking, the occasional stroll with the vacuum cleaner, since it was not as though she had ever intended Joanna to be a slave, although it had often crossed her fertile mind that excessive domestic burdens could provoke the child to rebel enough to get the men to do it. This ploy had not worked: Joanna as housekeeper had a dedication well beyond her years.

Mouse sighed. A pretty girl of eighteen should find better things to do than think about the kitchen, or allow her brother to impose his presence everywhere by the clumsy means of all his fishing mess. Look at it, always taking up one end of the long table, reels, weights, ugly things, all there to exert male power. Mr Pardoe had done the same. In Mrs

184

Pardoe's languid tidying of the kitchen and pantry, there were vague, but varied purposes. It allowed her to hide the tracks of predatory forays into the larder in the early hours of the morning; made it easier to blame her own, quixotic, greedy tastes on the men of the house. She could succumb to the desire to make another truly ugly cake which no-one could eat and that gave her magnificent licence to irritate. No-one had eaten the one she made to greet Sarah Fortune.

'They're all in their own worlds, dear,' she said to Hettie who stood sentry at the back door, a cunning watchdog who would warn if anyone approached by the simple means of a subdued bleating, which reminded Mrs Pardoe of someone coughing in church, a polite little rattle behind a handkerchief. Thinking of which, the verger who had greeted her so affectionately on Sunday was coming for tea this afternoon, which would be very nice indeed, the way it had been for years of Mondays. Mrs Pardoe laughed, a snuffling, giggling, finally trumpet-like sound which she smothered with a tea towel, her chin resting on the table. I'll be coming for tea, oh yes. There were certain phrases did this to her, such as the vicar saying, I'll give you a tinkle, meaning he would phone; Joanna asking, Where is the crevice tool for the Hoover? Such rude descriptions, shouted aloud with such innocence. Mouse sat at the end of the table with her head on her knuckles and chuckled until the onset of the sobriety which usually followed private laughter except on special occasions demanding silence, when the giggles would go on and on until she wanted to be sick in a sort of secret drunkenness. Share this with another and they became a friend, a bit like a joke with sex, and that, she told herself firmly, was enough of that.

There was something she had meant to tell Sarah Fortune. Something important. Oh dear, oh dear, oh dear. Memory gone. Perhaps she was really going round the twist after all.

Her tidying at table level had disturbed a collection of hooks in packets. Similar, but larger than the feathery, coarse fishing kind she had collected in her palm the night before. She looked at them with caution and dull hatred. Edward's little toys; Edward, fishing to compete with his father, using fishing as an alibi, like his father. Then the same suppressed levity came welling up within her again, a desire to play with things. A mischievous impulse. She would hide all the reels, throw away the weights, tie knots in the lines, sweep up the hooks. Then say, I was playing, dear. I was only playing; like you were when you hit me.

There was a dish of soft butter on the table, along with the milk, a bowl of soft liver pâté in the larder, cheese, soft sliced bread in the bread bin. She would make the men a sandwich. Then she would make, not a cake, but scones to greet them home. They would never eat them, and the waste of what they would not eat would really rile them.

Julian thought he would be haunted for ever by the sound of the ice-cream bells. They met him on the road on the way back from the graveyard where he had gone to make his peace with Elisabeth Tysall, measure with his eye the small length and breadth of her grave, pray mutual forgiveness, consider the headstone. The Big Ben chimes, distorted by speed, met him as he strolled back to the surgery. When he clambered inside, shocked by the sheer amount of blood on his sister's clothes, impressed by her quiet lack of hysteria and the way they had arranged the boy and kept him warm, it seemed best to continue as they were. The country ambulance could take some time to arrive; the hospital was several miles distant, the van a stable machine and he himself a pragmatist.

A doctor was always presumed to know what to do and he did not; everything was obscured by blood and anxiety, while for the sake of everyone else it was imperative to pretend. The lanes through which they rode were full of meadowsweet; the vehicle proceeded like a hearse. Joanna drove with cautious competence. Rick kept a loose hold of Stonewall's hand while the doc kept a dressing pressed to his head and a commentary of competent clichés between the boy's ramblings, disjointed words, slurred through a thick tongue.

'Talk to him,' Julian said to Rick. 'Tell him things. Make him blink.'

The eyes of the child were wide and rolling. Rick told him things.

'What do you think, eh, Stoney? I reckon that Omen III game is a load of shit. I thought we'd get that one with tigers in. Street Fighters VIII? Bit easy, you reckon? Such a smart arse, you are, just 'cos you can do 'em all. Tell you what, you can order one all of your own. I'll get you a special cushion for the seat. Like the Queen. No? I'll get you a pin-up then, Madonna. Who done it, Stoney?'

'Ghost,' the boy said loud and clear. 'That one. Drowning.'

'You were right about Omen, I'm telling you,' Rick was saying in a conversational murmur. 'Crappy game, that was. Could do with a game about drowning. Ghost, you said? Didn't know about that one.'

'Ghost,' the boy said. He raised a hand in protest and closed his eyes. Rick turned his head away, fierce with fury.

'Is this any good?' he muttered. 'That bastard. Is anything any good?'

'Perfect,' said Julian. 'Perfect. Keep talking. Everything's fine. Keep talking. Ask him things.'

'About ghosts?'

'Anything to make him blink.'

The day had been long. The people were fractious, holiday-makers fussy, demanding the spice of the Mediterranean to go with the weather, rebelling against chips. There was a near riot down by the caravan site when the shop ran out of ice-cream and the van did not appear. Inside the hairdresser's, the heat was stifling, the gossip stifling too, old repetitions of everlasting tales without topical edge, no-one wanting, yet everyone needing a storm, not a mild belt of rain like the day before, but a storm with noise.

When the news filtered through, about Stonewall Jones somehow running into a tree, going off to hospital in Rick's ice-cream van because Dr. Pardoe reckoned it was quicker than waiting for an ambulance, it was no more serious than the accident that morning on the Norwich road, or someone failing to return a rent-a-bike from Mr Walsingham, getting drunk and throwing it into the quay. Someone went to see Stonewall's mother, but she was out, gone to pick up the pieces, the way a woman did. Inside the hairdresser's, where sweat trickled out behind cotton wool under the three dryers (40 per cent discount for senior citizens), they could have done with Mrs Pardoe, simply for the colour and the smell, turquoise or gold or silver, and the wafting scent of Yardley's lavender.

They waited for her at noon, again at one; then they looked at the sky and waited for rain.

Charles, coming off the beach, noticed before the others the signs of preternatural darkness, waited for his turn for obscurity. He watched the other fools from the stable door of his beach hut, all of them,

English holiday-makers who should have known that
rain and cold were never more than a breath away on
a coast which did not have a climate, only weather;
watched them balancing the act until beyond the last
minute, gazing, commenting on the lowering sky as
it sank so low it merged with the land, continued
watching, saying, Will it rain? Scrambling for cover
only when the big spitting fell and it was far too late
to avoid a soaking. Like other Anglo-Saxons further
afield in fêtes and garden parties, the result the same
as with these bewildered troops trailing away from
the beach, along with Charles, wondering if he could
beg another ice-cream on the way as long as his
white hair was plastered to his head, his shirt sleeves
rolled, trousers turned, his jacket over his arm, his
eyes pink and full of sand.

No van, no food, simply the burning which spread
from gut to brain and back again, an infection which
began to consume, while he began to march, like a
prisoner, along with the others who shuffled away
into caravans, the bedraggled few who could still
laugh, aiming for the town down the causeway.

He was beyond food; the paper in his back pocket,
dry as his bones, crackled when he touched; hatred
replacing hunger. Other visions, fables of revenge
and failure. Lying, rolling, groaning in the dark while
a man went on kicking. Sticking glass in the neck of
a red-haired bitch. The dog on the beach, his hands
round a neck, what was her name? Sarah. What had
he done to Sarah? There were benches along the
causeway. Towards the end Charles sat. The sky was
black, each feature of every building clearly defined.
The short and vigorous shower stopped, temporarily
out of mischief, leaving the light of thunder, the fan-
tastic, promising light before a storm.

Sarah, that was her name. One of the other red-
heads, the whore. She who had so captured his fancy
when he had seen her flying through the foyer of Er-

nest Matthewson's office, the soul of innocent perfection, grinning like a little girl who found life nothing more than a glorious joke. Wearing a red coat
which clashed with her hair in a deliberate anarchy
amounting to a kind of brilliance when combined
with that untouched sophistication which seemed to
be her hallmark. So Ernest had said, through several
layers of suspicion, when asked. Ernest always answered questions from valuable clients like Charles
Tysall, not always truthfully. Our dear Sarah, he had
said; such a celibate young woman, devoted to her
career. Charles had pursued. Asked her out to dinner
and made her wait; discovered in her an unnerving
indifference, followed her, had her followed. Felt
himself hounded by her, the facsimile of the old
wife, the ideal model for the new, touched, as yet, by
nothing but loyalty. Perfectly pure and good, fine,
fair . . . Other women jumped through hoops like circus dogs, responding to the click of his fingers. Not
this one. Not this whore who slept with old men and
young, judges, silks and boys, sullied herself with
life's lonelier inadequates, ignored his superior gifts
for a careless, dirty life like that, and so disgraced
him. Imperfectly pure, imperfectly good.

The thought gnawed at him, like a rat on leather.
Nothing could meet his hunger then, or the different
kinds of hunger now. Charles examined his hands,
noticed the veins, the knuckles made more prominent
by receding flesh, then saw with a shock that his in-
tertwined fingers were resting on the pummel of
Miss Gloomer's distinctively stolen stick, clutching it
like an old man. Foolish, stupid, beyond bravado, sitting on the edge of town nursing a prop dishonestly
obtained by local standards, if certainly not by his
own. He had taken it because he wanted it, therefore,
logically, it became his. Like a wife, or a lover, or
money. Until one of them refused and made a man
descend into this darkness. A man had beaten him.

He had lost all his power until he had floated out of the sea.

Scornfully, Charles donned his damp jacket, buttoned it over his thin chest with the stick concealed, the pummel forming a lump inside the shoulder and the end of the stick protruding like a shortened third leg. He began to walk, across the quay, by now deserted save for those sitting inside cars in a state of martyred enjoyment, obscured from view by the rain outside and the condensation within. The amusement arcade heaved with people, music, electronic sound, the smell of candyfloss and onions making Charles faint. He swallowed, turned up the collar of his coat, went on walking down east quay and beyond, as innocent as anyone hurrying home. His home was the beach hut, the barn, the church porch. He knew no other.

Remembering his purpose, to make the hunger work, he turned towards East Wind House.

'More tea, sweetheart? I'll go.'

Mouse Pardoe lay on her bed alongside the verger, each with a cup of tea in one hand and a cigarette in the other, the coverlet over their knees. Everyone applauded the verger's good works in visiting the sick and the elderly (of which breed he was one of the more able-bodied), while only himself and his friend Mouse knew that these weekday visits were not exactly philanthropic. They simply knew one another, in the biblical sense. They had known one another for a very long time, a knowledge of herself which Mrs Pardoe had shared with several men of the village who had the right qualifications. Namely, that they must treat her with an entirely non-possessive affection during Mr Pardoe's long business trips, and that their discretion should be bigger than their body weight. She liked them small and neat, in direct contrast to the bulky physique of Mr P. Such teeny-weeny infidelities of hers began as a game of tit for tat, then they became quite a delightful habit. One had to get on with life.

These days, she and the verger were usually content with a cuddle and the delicious comfort of secret trust. In both their eyes, a proper christian attitude only meant refraining from judgement, hurting no-one, and taking God's gifts wherever they could grab them.

The verger was about to agree to a little more tea and perhaps a soupçon of alcohol to go with the splutter of the rain on the windows, when Mouse, as much by instinct as by fine tuning, heard the watchdog bleating of the sheep at the front of the house below her window. She did not spoil Hettie for nothing. She put a finger to her lips; the verger replaced cup in saucer with elaborate care, grinned without alarm since this was not the first time they had been interrupted. All he had to do was to move to the chair by the bed, adopt the less comfortable position of a Church of England comforter while Mouse adjusted her dress and put her hat back on straight. Then she would start talking loudly and that was all there was to it. This time she shook her head.

'Wait,' she said. 'No car. I'll go and see.'

The pain in Sarah's head somehow lifted when the heavens opened to release the rain and the sky began to rumble like a giant's indigestion. She had spent the morning working on the estate, tabulating lists of properties, how long the lease, how easy to sell, value per area, inspired guesswork dogged by the stabbing behind the eyes. Frequent trips to the kitchen window showed the absence of cars outside the big house, all except her own. Another was parked well short of the grounds, probably a walker. Perhaps Mrs Pardoe, all alone, did not like the rumblings of thunder; Sarah did not fool herself that she

crossed the wet lawn for charity but as much for
company, the continuance of yesterday's conversation, which had begged more questions than those it
had answered, left her curious for more. There was
something about Mouse which made her feel kin-
dred: something she liked and a degree of unscrupu-
lousness she could only admire.

The sheep cantered towards her and then wandered
away, appreciating friend rather than stranger. Sarah
went through the open back door into the kitchen,
where all was quiet with mid-afternoon languor. A
pile of crazy-looking sandwiches lay on the pine table, bread cut to the size of slabs, the fillings of yellow cheese and pâté uninvitingly solid and nasty
against the white dough, the whole edifice like some
comic, plastic joke, a sandwich made by a child in its
first stumbling lesson in home economics. Next to it,
a row of sunken, sultana scones which made those in
the tea shop a study in refinement.

There was another motive in her visiting, apart
from the desire, part personal, part professional, to
intrude upon Mrs Pardoe while she was alone. Sarah
needed milk. It seemed impolite to call through the
house as though summoning a dog, so she crept instead out into the hall which led to the front door,
into the dining room and living rooms, sensing the
warmth of recent presence, the smell of erratic polishing, noticing the dead flowers left on a table from
last Thursday's dinner, the half-drawn curtains and
on the first rung of the stairs leading up, a feather
from a hat. Knowing she was an intruder, Sarah went
on upstairs, stood on the landing at the top. From one
of the front bedrooms, she heard the murmur of
voices, backed away, then paused. Another door was
ajar. Sarah went towards it, peered inside.

Edward's room, she could tell at a guess. There
was an easel by the window which commanded the
best view in the house. It was the view which drew

her first, then the easel, depicting its strange, over-precise, hate-inspired version of the view. She turned away from it, disturbed. Then she looked inside a doll's house, the roof of which had collapsed, the rooms inside intact. Little figures, grotesque, clutching one another. Books on the floor, the room of a dreamer. Embarrassment flooded over her: her behaviour was that of a spy. She could not call out for Mouse now, not when she was already upstairs. Quietly, she crept out, back down to the kitchen.

She could just collect the milk then, for the fourteenth coffee of the day. A large and venerable refrigerator rumbled in the corner of the kitchen, *circa* 1955 with a rounded shape and a crusted handle. Inside, a medley of food and leftovers, but no milk, and she could not somehow take the milk from the table. Then Sarah remembered Joanna getting pints from the larder and went in that direction.

She stood inside the door, amazed. The place was armed for a siege with durable products, jam jars by the dozen, full and empty, honey and lemon curd, sugar bags in rows, enough tea for a year, six pints of milk, two open and rancid, as well as four half-eaten pies, some weary lettuce, two cabbages from the garden with a faint smell of age, four loaves of bread, a side of ham, a dish of pâté, a half-eaten trifle, a dozen tins each of peaches, pineapple, tuna, sardines, sweetcorn and beans. It looked like the style of provisioning suitable for a bunker. The crooked chocolate cake she had seen before, untouched and not improved by the keeping, although the air in here was as moist as a cellar. On the flagstone floor was newspaper, damp and messy, incongruous among the food.

The door swung to behind her, the pantry suddenly dark with some light from the storm-laden sky penetrating from a single, small window, covered in wire mesh to deter the flies which had penetrated in small

numbers and circled round the light bulb lazily, ignoring all else, especially the cake. Sarah felt the per-
verse desire to lift that paper on the floor, a test of
strength and curiosity, a way of manufacturing bravery, since she knew what dwelt in a state of inertia
beneath. Their brothers had been on her kitchen
floor.

'Oh, bugger . . .' someone swore beyond the door.
The someone was in the kitchen. A hacking cough.
Sarah froze, suddenly conscious of her squatting, in-
terfering pose, doubled up further at the prospect of
embarrassment. She was a licensed visitor, sir, so the
law would say, allowed across these portals by common consent, but not to grub around on the flagged
tiles in a pantry while no-one else was looking.
There was something else, an ear for sound, which
told her the cough, the shuffling out there, was neither Edward, Julian, Joanna nor the Mouse. Each
voice had a pitch, an intonation as unique as a
favourite singing star who could not be copied, and
this, while still a faintly familiar, patrician voice, was
not one recently heard. Outside the wired pantry window, Hettie the sheep was bleating with a pathetic
aggression, the sound first in the distance, hidden by
rain, moving closer as if she had turned a corner and
yelled in surprise.

'Oh Lord.' It was not the tone of prayer, only a
curse, but mixed with wonder as whoever it was
bumped against the kitchen table. There was a scrab-
bling sound: paper, a chair scraped back, a sudden silence, a gulping noise, a burp of satisfaction, all
seconds apart. Sarah knelt and moved towards the
pantry door. It was not a door which could ever quite
shut, warped by decades and no-one ever noticing it
should be able to shut, a door which banged but
never quite closed. Through the aperture, at the
wrong angle to see more than half, she tried to look,
in desperation moved the door a fraction to see the

man at the table. A long tall hobo. Whitish hair scraped back into a small rat's tail, not the friendly rat of a cartoon character, seizing the last of the monumental sandwiches, gulping at the open pint of milk, eyeing the scones, not for taste or shape, merely for size . . .

Mouse Pardoe clattered downstairs, cramming her hat to her head. She seemed to have lost a feather, picked it up on the bottom step, stuck it into her bosom, made her walk the one of dignified senility and entered the kitchen. There was a man sitting at the kitchen table with his finger making imprints on a single scone, digging at it once and then putting his fist in his mouth. He was wearing a jacket, something she had seen before; something which may have been collected out of a wardrobe upstairs where all things worn by the late Mr Pardoe still remained, unlooked at and forgotten, she recalled, later. For the moment, she remembered only her lines. Adjusted her hat to a daft angle, twirled the feather picked up on the stairs between her fingers, flipped the skirt of her evening dress over her knee and stepped lightly into the room.

'Hallo . . . oo,' she cooed. 'Hallo, haloo . . . ooo!' It was a salutation fit for a pigeon, soft and dulcet, but commanding.

'Are you making tea?' she demanded, moving in the direction of the sink. 'Oh, do be a darling. I want some too, but I don't know how. Nothing like a man to help.'

Dumbly he rose, lifted the kettle from the edge of the Rayburn, shook it. She took it from him with a manic beam, and banged it down again, her ample hips swinging to some unheard beat, humming throughout, the humming emerging into operatic singing, accompanied by operatic gestures.

'Say, gentle ladies,' she trilled, 'eef love you know . . .

Is love this fever, troubling me so . . .

Ees love this fe . . . ever, troubling meahh, so?'

Then she beamed at him again, leant forward as the kettle, still warm, began to simmer, pulled the lobe of his left ear playfully and whispered into the right.

'Got a friend upstairs, if you see what I mean,' she said with a lascivious wink. The act was going well. Sarah could see from her vantage point, good to the point of ludicrous. Mouse Pardoe deserved an Oscar, but the man did not like a flirt.

'Do you come here often?' she trilled. 'Oh yes, of course you do. I've seen you before. You're a friend of my son Edward and I think you're wearing my husband's coat. Oh dear, oh dear, you've eaten those sandwiches. Silly boy!'

She was on the other side of the table from him now, leaning across, scooping the scones towards her with frantic movements, her back to Rayburn.

That was too much for the intruder. He had winced when she pinched his ear; the touch was overdone, broke the trance in which her performance had held him, as if Mrs Pardoe had suddenly stepped out of the spotlight, become human, threatening. Her scooping up available food before his hunger was sated confirmed his irritation. He moved swiftly and clumsily, the stick beneath the coat knocking against the chairs as he lurched round the table towards her. He picked her up roughly by the straps of her dress, hoisted her upright so that she stood with her body pressed close against his. Then he whisked her round and in one swift movement, grabbed hold of both her hands, clamped the palms firmly to the sides of the kettle and held them there. There was a delayed reaction, both of them breathing deeply.

From her viewpoint, Sarah did not immediately

comprehend. Actions of sheer malice were difficult
to fathom, created paralysis rather than instant response. A high-pitched shriek of fear and pain burst
forth from Mouse Pardoe's lips; she began to strug-
gle, but Charles braced her sagging frame upright,
his knees pressed into the back of her thighs, held
her hands in the vice of his own, pressed them firmly
as the kettle began to boil, and then Sarah understood.

There was no thought in her reaction. As the
shriek descended to a whimper, she crashed through
the pantry door holding the newspaper, flung the
contents at the same moment as the scream descended into a pleading moan. Something brown,
damp and inert suddenly moved on the neck of the
white head; squirming animal life landed on the
Rayburn with a hiss. Lugworms met the heat of
the kettle and the stove, more landed on the man's
arms and round his feet. He sprang back, slipped on
the flesh, steadied himself, staring at the floor, seeing
a serpent.

He raised his eyes slowly until he met those of
Sarah, standing three feet away with the newspaper
still in her hand. Their gaze locked in confused recognition. She should have known, she thought later,
should have known from the first glimpse who he
was, the style of his embrace, the clutching to himself of the thing he was about to torture. She should
have known, from what she remembered.

Mouse Pardoe's whimpering rose again to a cre-
scendo, descending into a sobbing. Then there was
the sound of heavy footsteps overhead. The man
backed away from the two women and the worms
writhing on the stove and floor, without taking his
eyes away from Sarah's face, his hands reaching for
the scones and the milk on the table, grasping them
blindly but accurately, as if he had rehearsed and
memorized their position, shoving them in his pock-

ets. The stick, banging again on the legs of a chair, made a loud sound. Against her own judgement, Sarah found herself advancing towards him, possessed by an anger which knew no fear, acknowledged no risk, desired nothing but violent retribution, a growl in her throat. Her hands had formed into claws; her voice emerged like a spitting cat.

'Charles . . . you shit.'

The door from the hall crashed inwards, the verger cannoning through and into Sarah with her hands poised to strike and her face white with fury. He grabbed her, holding her wrists shouting, 'Here! what's this?', blustering with breathless energy while she twisted. Charles melted away through the door, into the rain. Sarah felt the rotund, miniature shape holding her own, shrieked in turn, 'Let go, you stupid shit, fucking let go!'

'No,' Mouse Pardoe shouted, shaking but suddenly firm. 'No, don't, not yet. That's the last thing you should do.'

Sarah came back to earth and knew the Mouse was right. No-one should pursue a ghost.

The thunder rolled away, but the rain persisted, tumbling out of the sky in sheer impatience. Miss Gloomer liked it. After a particularly satisfactory tea, she had risen from the chair to look for her stick, an automatic reaction for which she chided herself, reaching instead for the substitute, a lesser favourite, then decided not to move at all and drew a rug round her knees instead. The nice doctor, who did not know he was a good man, would call at six. There was no need for him to do that and he might not stay long because he never intruded, he was brisk and respected her privacy. The burglary had shaken her, left her weaker, but not so weak she could not think. What one needs in life, she was telling an imaginary audience, as she would tell the doctor when he

called, is an infinite capacity for forgiveness. People
are only little, busy things, babies and animals, you
see, they do what they can; they are thoughtless and
selfish, they love nothing better than their own flesh
and blood and that is the way they are. If you want
to be on the inside track, Doctor, get yourself a family.

On that thought, of what she would say when he
came in for a small glass of sherry, Miss Gloomer's
small and obdurate frame gave up the task of living.
She died in her upright chair, wearing her winter and
summer shoes, thinking of children and how little in
life she really regretted including her inability to
make a cake, why bother when you could buy better
from the baker? This was one of life's greater mysteries. Julian found her. He sat and held her cooling
hand, called for the ambulance, which would take
some time. Composed her eyes and her mouth,
watched the instant, facelifting effect of death.

Rick took Joanna home, with the kind of absent kiss
she understood without trying, then took the van
back and parked it outside the arcade. Course he'd
live, daft little sod, he had to live, made of metal, the
doctor said, hit that head one more time and a stick
would bounce. A weary sickness made him slow getting out, drawn to the row and the smell and the
noise and the temporary end of thinking. He did not
walk straight inside; he saw sense and went further
down the quay where he bought fish and chips and
ate them without tasting anything, standing in the
wet without noticing that either. Getting food down
and keeping it there was vital. He belched but did not
spit and went in to work.

'You're late, boy, we've been taking serious
money here, where the fuck you been?' his father
said. Rick seized him by the lapels of his jacket,
shook him until he rattled and then sat him on the

floor. There were no words with this brief exchange of views, only the breathy sounds of a precedent being established. It was enough.

'Listen, Dad,' said Rick, picking him up with absent-minded strength, 'you got to do something useful tomorrow.'

'Oh yes, what's that, son?' his father asked, almost respectfully.

Rick paused. 'We've got to have this place for our own so we don't owe anyone. But first we got to get our act together and find this ghost. He might have done for Stonewall. We got to find him.'

Malcolm Cook looked round Sarah Fortune's London flat, standing disconsolately and a little defiantly, facing the elegant mirror which dominated the narrow hall, giving a view of anyone who entered and also the rooms either side. He never expected it to be quite the same as the last time he had seen it, since Sarah, who loved and acquired beautiful things, also gave them away with the same ease and moved them round restlessly. Malcolm was the opposite, preferred the spartan and the durable objects he would preserve for ever.

Next to his flank and keeping close, the red-haired dog, ever immune to the reverberations of the place, could not resist the introspective mood.

Start again. Open this door and think about it. Look at it from her point of view. Would the new paint on the walls have changed anything in her mind? Would she miss the place at all in view of its history? If he was ever going to understand her, he would have to make himself go over every step of her ordeal. At first, he could only see himself in here, using his enormous energy to clean up all the stains, so much blood he could only marvel, forced himself not to remember, but to feel, shivered.

So this was what he had done for her first, swept

through the flat while she recovered, covering all traces with gloss and emulsion, three coats each. Maybe that had been wrong, just as encouraging her to forget the finer points, put the whole episode to one side like a useless gift, had also been mistaken. Perhaps she should have been forced to relive it again and again, exorcise the helpless pain of it, come to terms. Instead of which he had been saying, Look at me. Look at me, please, take me instead of looking back; I'm here for you, all yours.

The apartment had the stuffy heat of a place enclosed in summer. He wanted to fling open the windows but desisted, imagining instead the place in darkness. Forced himself to think. What would have been the worst thing about that one night last July, the importance of which, as far as he was concerned, was to thrust Sarah, bloody and bowed and needing, into his arms?

He walked back to the front door, turned, as if coming inside for the first time, as she had done in the near dark, careless, lovely, amoral Sarah. Entering her own domain with a slight feeling of trepidation. Seeing through the mirror in the hall, Charles Tysall lurking in the room to the right, waiting. Turning to flee, too late. Charles behind her then, embracing her, making her watch herself in a mirror like this mirror, making her strip in front of her own reflection, teasing, taunting, announcing his litany of hate and disappointment, calling her filth. Then flinging down the mirror which had rolled and broken into a thousand shapes, large shards, sharp-edged pieces and smaller slivers, twinkling. Charles, pressing Sarah's naked body into that bed of bloody pain, holding her there, while she writhed against the glass and he waited to end it, to cut her face, her throat, whatever he could reach as she twisted away and he slashed, not caring if he cut his own long fingers.

Malcolm shuddered again, his mouth hanging

open, his eyes seeing again what he had discovered then. Led by the dog and her merciful passion for open doors, strange places, raw meat smells, they had come upstairs. Charles had penetrated the dog's russet-coated neck with the biggest piece of glass, almost killed her. Canine blood, mixed with the human; the same smell.

So much blood, so much glass, he had not known how to move her. There was all the gore of an abattoir, none of the convenience. He had wrapped her in the white towels she had soaked, all contact with her skin giving rise to small, breathless screams, which she bit back so hard her mouth bled too. She could not stand, sit, faint, or recline, a creature flayed by the glass, the place reverberating with her whimpering.

What would Sarah remember most, when she touched those little scars which marked where the myriad shards of glass had pierced so deep, leaving her arms, part of her abdomen, her back, her shoulders, littered with souvenirs? She touched them often: they itched, she said, excusing herself as someone would with the hiccoughs. He tried to analyse the pain, in a way he had never quite tried before, because he had been busy offering (instead of imagination) comfort, warmth, forgetfulness and the panacea of love.

Humiliation, that was what Sarah would remember. She would be most crippled by the inability to fight back, by her cowardice, by loss of control, by the obscene pleas she would have spoken to make the taunting stop. There would be the shame at crying in his presence, begging for life and a scintilla of dignity. It would be the poison of the shame, for doing nothing to prevent him, for letting it happen without seeing it was coming, for never fighting back until too late, misjudging, becoming helpless. That would kill the soul and leave the vacuum full of hatred.

Facing the mirror, he could feel it with her. Malcolm had been ashamed of his own furious ineptitude, but it was nothing like her shame. He should have made her talk. No-one earns a future by repressing the past, and pain like that, he saw clearly now, never goes away. He had merely done the equivalent, he supposed, of treating a wound with a bandage when only surgery would do.

The dullness of logic prevailed. Tomorrow was a full day's work. Also the day after. He could rearrange his life to go and find her, a quest fit for a man who professed to love, rather than merely possess.

When he was calmer. When he could think of her not as what he wished she would be, but as what she actually was. Imperfectly pure: good by her own standards only, indelibly scarred.

CHAPTER ELEVEN

Edward came home shivering. The almost tropical dampness made him long for foreign territory and a bath, but he could not bring himself to go indoors. All morning he had sat in the estate agent's office where he worked, unable to get the white-haired man out of his head. If he looked out into the street, all he could see was white-haired men. Even his white-haired boss seemed threatening instead of contemptuous.

Edward hated working in the estate agent's, hated working full stop. This latest of jobs, a sinecure, was one he liked least, reminding him all the time of what his family owned in property and making him incubate the worst of his dreams. The Pardoes did not own a single beautiful building, he explained; nor was there one he could see in the village. Otherwise he might have cared about his work. The place needed pulling down, how could a man of taste love it?

Today, both his aggression and his defensiveness seemed to have disappeared. He felt naked, vulnerable and mean. It made no difference, working in an office which the Pardoes virtually owned. Conscience could always undermine money.

Edward knew he should have been able to identify the white-haired ghost by at least a name, but it had never been important when all they were doing was playing games. He should have been in control of the

205

trespasser he had found, but he was not. With his estate agency knowledge, Edward had housed, sometimes fed, the malevolent spirit for three months. All in the interests of fun and the somewhat malicious, somewhat romantic dreaming which fed his own daily existence and made it worthwhile. It had made him walk taller but now made him want to hide. He had meant mischief, but the reality, the look of hatred on the man's face, somehow extended it further than his own cowardice allowed. Edward might have hit his own silly mother from time to time, he might have detested his brother, but wanting them to disappear was not quite the same any longer as wanting them dead.

The discomfort, which had begun when he heard about Miss Gloomer's burglary, increased somehow because of the mere presence of Sarah Fortune and solidified into an indigestible lump after this morning's conversation, like much of Jo's cooking and all of Mother's playful cakes. Increased threefold when his two colleagues came back from a makeshift lunch at the pub which the Pardoes also owned, talking about the ghost. Above the cheese-and-onion which Edward could smell as they spoke, the pungency overcoming the waft of a pint of lager between them, he learned all about how Stonewall Jones had met the ghost in the dunes and had his head caved in with a stick. The lady behind the bar worked in the surgery up until noon, then moved sideways into a less sterile atmosphere. Best gossip around, she was, with her dual sources.

Edward's blood ran hot, the slow digestion of the news creating a sweat under his cotton shirt, once perfectly ironed by Joanna and now a mass of wrinkles. The news made him itch all over, as if bitten by insects and carrying poison. Edward had never been anywhere where he might catch malaria: he had never dared, no money, no courage and no stamina, preferring the sneering discontent of home. Sitting outside his own house, he longed to go as far away as any aeroplane would take him. To any other kind of jungle where no-one knew him.

There were cars lined up outside the front door as usual, Jo's, Julian's, the visitor's, plus another, the house apparently the scene of a conference. The rain was easing. Edward felt allergic to them all, especially Joanna. On the wet grass of the lawn, another ghost, that of naked Sarah Fortune, still travelled, pale and tantalizing, in smooth circles across the green, the only thing of objective beauty he had seen in weeks. Oh, come on, he told himself, as the rain drizzled mildly against the windscreen of his car, come on. Be manly or something. A man should be able to fish, like his father, a man was not ashamed to be whatever he was, even if that made him idle, artistic, self-seeking, incestuous. A man should be large, not small, indecisive and afraid. Edward looked at his own neat hands in a hot flush of realizations he wanted to avoid. The hands shook, more than they had shaken when he lost his temper and hit his mother last evening. A man should achieve control of his actions. He should also have someone to tell.

Wavering lights, out there, as he sat looking over the marshes towards the sea which he wished would come closer, even though its proximity made him afraid, as well as the house itself, lit like some ugly Christmas tree. One thing he knew now, above all others: he had loathed this place for as long as he remembered. Squinting through the glass, he could see two things. First, the strange car belonged to PC Curl, their only full-time member of Constabulary; second, from the near distance, the light outside Sarah's cottage beckoned like a flickering star.

Nine-thirty, he read on his watch; the mere beginning of a summer night. Closer, the light shone more like a keep-out sign than a welcome, a warning, a weapon against this early dark created by the long, mocking storm. It was ironic, he thought, beneath the lingering anxiety, that he should follow his brother's footsteps so meekly, treading the same route with similar humility. He knocked loudly on the door, making a tune out of it, rat-a-tat, rat-a-tat, instead of just banging once, something to prove he was a nonchalant son of a bitch who would go away whistling if there was no response, waiting all the same.

She answered after a long delay, less winsome than before, still beautiful. A woman with a fierce look on her face as she looked out of the window first, then said, 'Come in,' with a purely neutral friendliness.

'To what do I owe the pleasure?' Sarah said coldly. 'I've been visited here by all members of your family. You give me the impression you're more comfortable out of your own home than in it. Sit down.' The charm and the warmth was back, the teasing note uppermost, some of the edginess gone.

'Have you been home yet?' she asked in that steady, reassuring, conversational way. Edward, in common with his colleagues after lunch, smelled slightly of the pub where he had gone and sat for an hour or more after an abortive and hesitant search of the caravan site and the dunes had revealed nothing of the white-haired man. Emptiness and sunset had ended the search: Edward was secretly afraid of the dark. He shook his head.

'I went to look for someone,' he muttered. 'Why?'

'Ah, you might not know then. The village ghost took human form this afternoon. He came up here and attacked your mother. She's all right,' she added, watching him closely, standing away from him, arms crossed. Edward sat heavily, rubbed his eyes with a pathetic gesture which made him look like an over-grown baby.

'Not the first time he's been here, though, is it?'

Edward did not answer, his silence an affirmation.

'I was present, you see,' she went on, 'when this non-ghost arrived. Your mother said to him and I quote, "You're a friend of my son Edward, I've seen you before." She sees a lot, your mother. I suppose I imagined from that that it was you who acts as his liaison officer. Difficult to see how any man, even one as resourceful as Charles Tysall, could stay alive in secret when he's supposed to be dead. Not without assistance. Not much, perhaps: he likes to move alone.'

'What do you mean?' Edward was suddenly angry. 'Charles Tysall? He was drowned, last year. My . . . acquaintance said he was sent by the family, the wife's family, that is. Maybe the wife's brother. He was having a long holiday, he said, experimenting with living rough. He said he wanted to know—'

'Who had buried Elisabeth Tysall in the sand,' Sarah finished for him.

'Yes,' Edward said, dumbfounded. 'How did you know?'

'Edward,' Sarah said, 'I'm beginning to think you're an idiot. Not the genuine article maybe, but a very good pretence.' She unfolded her arms. He looked up at her like an animal waiting to be whipped. She smiled slightly. It scarcely lessened her intimidation.

'I offered your brother a drink, so I suppose I'd better do the same for you.' It was grudging. Watching her move about, Edward was paralysed with the sense of his own weakness and an awful physical desire which he knew, even then, was going to loosen his thick tongue.

'I knew Charles Tysall,' she was saying. 'I also know he was obsessed with the fate of his wife.

There's no doubt about identity, so where do you come in?'

'He hit Stonewall Jones this morning,' Edward burst out, ignoring the question. 'I can't believe he did that. I can't think why. He's not a ghost, he's a monster. The boy's badly injured. Oh God, I never meant this. Honestly, I never meant this.'

Sarah's hand flew to her head with a brief cry. She felt along the side of her face where the pain had been, tears welling in her eyes.

'Oh, poor boy, poor child. Oh, I wish I knew how to pray.'

Edward sipped his drink, wondering if he should respond to that since he felt nothing for Stonewall Jones, could only see in his mind's eye the relative sizes of tall man against small, helpless boy. Julian would have liked sitting here, sipping excellent Glenfiddich, he thought by way of distraction. The thought came upon him without a trace of bitterness. Jealousy merely lingered.

'I shouldn't play games, should I?' Edward asked. 'I found him squatting in the cottage next door to this.' He jerked his head to the right, winced. 'It seemed amusing not to report him. I didn't want tenants in the place this summer, hate them, kids, buckets and spades, cars, spoiling the view. So Charles, if we must call him that, started a small fire for me. Nothing too drastic. Nothing which would spread.'

She inclined her head, as if understanding completely.

'There were also a few of my paintings in there. Joanna in the nude. Didn't want her to see them if she spring-cleaned, didn't know how else to get rid. They were a bit . . . suggestive. Watercolours, easy to burn. Painted from imagination, of course. Wishful thinking.'

'Are you in love with her?' A gentle question,

without criticism or condemnation. He was grateful for that.

'Am I? I don't know any more.'

'Jealous of other men, though?'

'Yes.'

'Jealous of Julian?'

'Yes! Yes! Yes!' he shouted. 'He's so dependable, so bloody adult, so sodding disciplined and my father loved him. He doesn't even need to learn to fish!'

He subsided as suddenly as his voice had risen, flung himself back against the plaid-covered sofa, petulantly. His own native defences of self-justification surfaced. He looked at her unforgiving eyes, looked away.

'Anyway,' he mumbled, 'owning a ghost was good sport for a while. I'm so bored, most of the time. Then he began to ask about Julian, how well he'd known Elisabeth Tysall. Well, I knew all about that. Julian just about lost his mind over that bitch, I watched him. The ghost wanted proof that Julian had something to do with her death. I pretended it existed but I knew it didn't. Julian's too soft to hurt anyone.'

'Elisabeth Tysall was a victim,' Sarah said sharply. 'Don't dare call her a bitch. You don't know what she was.'

'No,' Edward conceded. Guilt was corrosive, it caught in the throat like a fishbone.

'So,' Sarah said, 'you played make-believe with Charles as your creature. Thought you had the upper hand. Where is he, Ed?'

'I don't know,' Edward whispered. 'I just don't know. I gave him the key to an empty caravan. He isn't there. Maybe a beach hut, somewhere on the beach, he likes the beach.'

She was so powerful, she seemed to draw the words from him, like a fish on the line with no power to escape. Still standing in front of him, Sarah pulled her shirt over her head. A pretty colour, russet silk,

Edward noticed, thinking at the same time, Christ, she's mad; she's going to strangle me with it. She pulled the shirt as far as her shoulders, left it bunched round her neck and turned her back on him. The gesture was shocking and bizarre; made him recoil with a small, half scream.

'Please look at my back,' she commanded. 'Go on, look. With your artistic eye. Look closely, report what you see.'

He wanted to avert his eyes, escape from this threatening action, but he stood awkwardly and looked. A graceful spine, curving into a tiny waist, the silky flesh criss-crossed with scars, three or four larger gashes, the majority small pit marks, white against the brown of her skin, ugly. She pulled the shirt back over her naked torso abruptly, leaving him relieved, shivery, revolted but aroused.

'I just wanted to make a point,' she said wryly. 'Cuts like that are what you get for playing games with Charles Tysall. He makes you roll in broken glass. He holds you down among the fragments of a broken mirror. And when you've finished bleeding, although you never really do, he'll leave you thinking it was all your own fault.'

Edward had stared. With his eye for colour, he could imagine the vibrant blood welling from those wounds, flesh and skin mashed in ritualistic flogging. He could see the cool smile of the man this morning, the precision of his movements, the air of efficiency.

'He did that?'

'Oh yes. Slowly.'

Edward stumbled into the kitchen and retched into the sink. Bile was all he could produce, the residue of a day without food, no sisterly sandwiches to fill the gap, nothing but two pints, three sips of whisky and a diet of anxiety. He drank some water, looked out into the dark, recovered himself, came back with a mumbled apology.

'That's all right,' said Sarah, equably, but dry. 'I confess I don't usually receive quite such a flattering reaction when I take off my clothes.'

Edward blushed, relaxed more than slightly. Even like this, so serious and frightening, she was able to make a man think there was nothing incurable about his own condition.

'What shall I do, Sarah? What on earth shall I do?' he asked humbly.

She noted that he asked nothing about her own history, nothing about the scars, nothing which expressed concern about anyone other than himself. Men *in extremis* were always thus; she was used to it in the adult version, and this was a mere, play-acting boy. She sized him up, considered her own code for dealing with misery by the simple if tempo rary means of bodily comfort. The men in question needed to command affection and respect, this one commanded neither. All he deserved was a chance of redemption.

'I don't know. Stop dreaming of wealth and changing the landscape into something you might like. You hate this place, leave it. You're the younger son, the underachiever, your sister says. You'll always be powerless here. Make a break for somewhere else, before your last friend rumbles you.'

'Leave? With nothing?' he asked incredulously, glancing at the table, full of papers, brief notes in neat handwriting, valuations, lists.

'Yes. Enough to sustain you for a while, perhaps. There won't be much of an inheritance anyway. Not after your mother's finished with it.'

He looked at her, the pink spots on his cheeks an alien version of his sister's. Sarah spoke patiently.

'She wants to give it back, Edward dear. She wants to give back all this property to the local people who need it. That's what she wants.'

He started to laugh. A whinnying chuckle which went on and on until his eyes streamed.

'You need food and an injection of sense, Edward Pardoe. You never felt this way before working up at the estate agent's and discovering how much you might have, did you? You can get away with dreaming and painting and doll's houses, Ed; you might even make a living at it, but you can't get away with murder.'

Food. The thought was no longer beguiling. Charles lurched in the narrow alleyway which skirted the back of Miss Gloomer's cottage, leading by a route as twisted as her frame into the high street. The village was criss-crossed with similar environs, ancient rights of way, coal-and-fish-delivery routes before the days when anyone would even dream of pulling a horse and cart in front of their own small doors, when families lay cheek by jowl in houses Rick found adequate for one.

Food was not the problem for Charles: enough for the day was all he could contemplate after the sandwiches which had scarcely touched his rotting teeth. Something in the solidity of the scones, like hairs tickling his throat, made him cough, stand where he was and gag, left him thirsty even after the milk which had washed them down.

There were fresh-water taps on the caravan site, easily found by dark when no-one looked. Too soon to go back to the beach, too far to go without water.

'Give me water,' he whispered, 'and there is nowhere I cannot go, nothing I cannot do, even if I am beaten by women; rendered impotent by the weaker sex, when I could have snapped their necks like killing chickens, just like that.'

He had no plans, there was no point in planning, but a dim feeling that he was running out of time for revenge. The image of Sarah Fortune, snarling at him, superimposed itself on the image of his Elisabeth's face, but then these two images had always been blurred. Red hair, red bitches; a feeling of weakness. Was I always like this? Was I never strong? Who loved me?

There was a tap in the graveyard. Perhaps if he went to the second grave of his wife, where he had left the thistles, she might let him in to sleep. Come back to him, chastened, beautiful, the way she was before. Porphyria. Perfectly pure and good. He would tell her he forgave her, raise her from the dead, the way he had raised himself from the sea.

His footsteps were quiet in the dark; an old man padding through a village, unable to force himself to the brisk military walk, tardy, irritated by his own lack of strength, spitting on the ground in contempt of his own sloth, failing to see the blood in the phlegm on the road by the wicket-gate. By the side of her grave, he could almost believe she would rise and greet him; knelt, suddenly humble, felt for her shape in the dark.

His hands felt the petals. Someone had prepared her. The ground was covered with fresh flowers, damp from the rain, smelling of heaven. Gifts for a lovely lady.

Someone. Some man, some thief in the night had borne these tributes. Charles scattered the flowers in a fury of moving hands and kicking feet, ignoring the onset of pain as he bent and tore at roses and daisies, breaking the stems, flinging them as far as he could, kicking the containers, not caring about the sound, stamping on petals as if putting out a fire in a ritual dance of fury, finally lying down on the naked earth which covered her. An innocent piece of earth. Even beyond death, even now, just as he forgave her, someone else had laid their claims first, just as they had before. It had all been for nothing.

* * *

No-one has claim to my image, Mouse Pardoe thought, not liking the indecision, not one little bit. She was being allowed only one ally at a time, most of them leaving her for diplomatic reasons, the verger first, Sarah later. They had talked a little about the ghost and who he was, and all this time, Mouse kept her hands in icy water. The verger, fisherman born, had dealt with the worms; there was now a ghastly smell of roasted flesh about the place, centred round the Rayburn, drifting through windows but determined to linger.

The sky remained the colour of gun metal. Mouse thought she would always remember the colours of the room; the verger's black against the pinkness of his skin, Sarah's pallor, her freckles, the hair, the russet colour of her shirt, then the colours of the best Pardoe hat with old feathers on the table, the surface of which seemed to glow a dirty yellow. She only noticed then the total absence of the yellower scones with their little bullets of burnt sultanas. She must have been mad. How could she? She talked to Sarah, a little irrationally and over-expansively, about her life, burbling, she said in apology, and all the time she looked at the space where her baking had been. There had been no-one looking when she had made those scones and still she had made them.

Mouse was chill beneath her evening frock and woolly dressing-gown, a combination of garments she would otherwise enjoy. A little lonely, too, but not enough to shout down the earlier suggestions of getting a doctor. 'I've got one of those,' she said to Sarah, 'and a daughter, although I hate the thought of relying on either.' Mouse noticed, quietly, that dear Miss Fortune had been uneasy as well as practical about calling the police. They met each other's eyes over the dialling in a mutual suspicion of authority. The police might question, Mouse thought, the quality of her baking. And the motives, which she could not now remember.

Then Joanna came home. After thirty minutes of PC Curl's questioning, a process as slow as Sarah's delivery was quick, she took the Biro from his hand and wrote it all down for him. Then Sarah left too, just before Julian arrived and there they all were, the whole business protracted by news which put it in perspective. *En famille*, with all the complications of being so. Oh dear.

The trouble was, Mouse Pardoe did not know whether she should go on being sweetly mad or loudly sane. It had been so pleasant, even with blistering hands, to talk to the only two people in the world who knew she could think. She missed it sorely, could not decide whether to keep up her act with her daughter and son, could not even quite remember when it had started or why, could not imagine above all, how she would explain herself for all these months of calculated pretence. Julian was looking at her closely. The stuff he had put on her throbbing hands had been applied, she noticed, with peculiar gentleness. No. Good Lord, no; she could not keep up her twittering birdsong, not after hearing what the same ghost had done to Stonewall Jones, the boy who had waved and danced for her in the garden whenever he brought up bait for Edward. Her own hands, her own fortune, were not important enough by comparison, and besides, her children were listening to her, really listening, not even pretending.

'I think the shock seems to have cleared your mind a bit, Mother,' Julian was saying, without talking as if she was deaf all the time. She glanced at him slyly. He did not seem to be playing games; like Joanna, he was honestly and simply concerned, listening with both ears. Jo flitted round the kitchen, bringing back bits and pieces of bland food, the panacea for all ills; Julian offered the wine. Each time Jo passed, she hugged her mother. Mouse had missed the hugging which was something a mad woman denied herself, if not with the verger, certainly with her children.

'Yes, dear,' she said demurely to Julian. 'I do believe my mind is feeling better. Now, what is PC Curl going to do?'

'Send out a patrol car regularly overnight to us, then organize a search party in the morning. That policeman can't do anything too quickly. He isn't the type.'

His father was not slow, Mouse thought, with a secret, reminiscent smile. Now there had been a neat and nimble figure of a man with a twinkle in the eye to match, oh yes. Tuesday afternoons, for a long time, he was.

'A ghost hunt,' she murmured, forgetting to add a manic giggle. Should she say who she knew the ghost was, or say she had seen him with Edward? She could keep her powder dry until she found out what other people knew. Her conscience was variable in its hints, but he was always on it, whatever he did.

'I don't think the search party should include Rick,' Jo said. 'There's no telling what he would do. Julian, what's the hope for Stonewall? Rick loves him.'

They sat at table, comfortably elbow to elbow.

'Well, I can only say that will help.'

She rested her head against his shoulder, briefly, the first time they had touched in as long as she could remember. He ruffled her blond hair fondly; she did not resist.

Mouse looked at them. Children, love one another; and where is my little changeling, Edward. Love me, love one another, but listen to me sometimes. That was all I wanted. I think. She chuckled.

'When that Stonewall comes home in the ice-cream van, I shall dance like Tallulah Bankhead.'

The kitchen shuddered with giggles and delicious, hysterical comfort. Julian poured more wine. They did not think of Sarah Fortune, united in the forgetfulness of all outsiders, although each of them, with separable and secretive degrees of worry, thought about Edward.

'I expect he's gone fishing,' said Joanna, apropos of nothing, in a gap between laughter.

Mouse looked at the space on the table where the scones had been, and knew how easily laughter sat with grief, how the madness was not always feigned.

The silence had grown longer. Sarah remembered the smell of worms.

'Will they know?' Edward was asking. 'I mean Jo, Julian, anyone else for that matter, about me knowing this man Charles? The ghost?'

'Yes, if your mother tells them so. She could tell them you've let Charles into the house before, and into the cottage next door. If the boy Stonewall recovers and remembers, he'll say if he saw you elsewhere.'

'Christ.'

'Not that they'll know what you discussed,' she said distantly. 'You could have been sorry for him. You could have been passing the time of day with a fascinating stranger.' She spoke with a touch of bitterness.

'And what will you tell them?'

'Nothing to contradict what you say yourself. I'm a lawyer: we only repeat what we should. I'm well-schooled in that.' Ernest Matthewson came to mind, like a malevolent spectre.

'There's a price. Help find Charles. Help save your family, and yourself.'

'Is that all?'

'Enough, not even much. You encouraged Charles. You conspired to rid the world of your mother and brother, even if it was a malicious day-dream. Didn't you?'

'Yes.' The voice was dry.

'Well,' she said with a finality not quite approaching either threat or promise, 'I think it would be best all round if no-one ever knew about that.'

'I think I'd like to go away,' said Edward shrewdly. 'Try living somewhere else.'

'What a good idea,' she said with a quiet approval of such intensity he could almost believe he had thought up the idea himself. 'And I suppose for now, you'd better go home.'

'Do you want to come over with me? I mean, should you stay here by yourself? For your own safety?' The onset of genuine concern upset him with a sensation as pleasant as a warm swallow of tea. She seemed to consider for a moment.

'No. Thank you. Taking refuge isn't the best way to deal with fear. In case it becomes a habit.'

'Perhaps I should stay with you, then? For the same reason?'

She seemed to consider it, shook her head.

'No.'

'As a guarantee of good behaviour in the future?'

'To stiffen the sinews?' she suggested ironically.

'Something like that.'

The wind had risen with the tide, pushing the water, encouraging the movement. Not the howling gales of winter whipping the waves on the open sea, a nudging wind, swollen with rain, eclipsing the shore line as the sea rode gently forward, filling the quay, lapping over the edge, covering the car-park, wavering at the edge of the road, creeping towards the front doors of the amusement arcade and the gift shops, shifting the litter of the evening and finally dragging it back, prudence dictating a pragmatic retreat on the eve of destruction. Stuck behind the hull of a forgotten boat, the bloated corpse of a dead animal was dislodged and floated away to another part of the coast. Two Dutch boys from a tramp vessel borrowed the dinghy and rowed for shore in search of bright lights.

On the beach, the sea nibbled at land, obeying the wind without enthusiasm. Those in the adjacent caravans stirred in the night, the ground beneath them somehow softer, the weight of their shelters settling more solidly after the rain. The sea crept right to the edge of the dunes, way beyond the high-tide level of the afternoon outlined by the sluggish boundary of variegated weed which led the unwary to presume it could invade no further. As the faintest of punishments for man's arrogance, the creeping water brushed the legs of the two furthest beach huts, eroded by similar attacks. The one requisitioned by the ghost collapsed to one side with a sighing groan, settled to sleep like a drunk on crutches as the retreating water sucked from the upended floor Charles Tysall's stolen blanket and other souvenirs.

A yacht suffered for the pride of its owners who ignored guidance and sailed into a sandback where they stuck and keeled sideways. In the early hours of the morning, the lifeboat siren made its own unearthly call, wailing and weeping in anger for the nuisance.

Julian heard it from the depths of a sleep in which he dreamed of murder most foul, his family, the inadequacies of medicine in the area and the body of Sarah Fortune. Heard it like a requiem for the dead, put his hands over his ears, shutting out any message which did not sing of hope.

CHAPTER TWELVE

Rick was running. Running with clumsy grace towards the lifeboat station, the village glistening behind him. The inlet was half full, the banks of the sea defences exposed in muddy splendour. Waddling, wheeling birds he had never bothered to identify, caught his vacant eye, birds which sprang, trotted, screeched in some kind of defiance, part of his landscape and he never even noticed them. Stonewall got down on his knees to talk to birds in the days when he was learning to love the creeks and Rick had laughed at him then; a boy, talking to birds, there's practice for you. How long did it really take to get to know someone?

He ran, one step after another, beginning to pant, wanting the excuse to stop, kept running.

One mile to the lifeboat station, where the inlet met the broader beach, so much further on foot than by transport. Stoney knew all that at half Rick's size, knew all about the birds if not the bees. Rick ran, seeing it all anew, the curlews, the footprints in the mud of the banks, the things which Stonewall saw.

He ran for oblivion, so that the screaming of muscle accustomed to different use would clear his mind from recent conversations of ghosts and retribution, talks with his uncle police officer, the lack of good news, and the tearful insistence of Jo, Don't go with them, Rick, please. If love was a question of conflicting demands, he could only obey the strongest which was not yet hers. So he ran the full mile to the beach, avoiding the woods, passing the lifeboat station, leaping straight down the bank onto the sand. There he jogged slower, the sand soft, his feet wet from patches of shallow mud, the breeze noisy in his ears, a brisk day with a fitful sun, the promise of wind and only the few real diehards out to play. A good day for hunting.

He jogged past the beach huts on his left, saw how two had collapsed but did not know if it was recent, noted it in his mind as just another fact, broke into a proper run on a smooth patch of sand and then began to tire. Perspiration trickled into his eyes; he rubbed them absently and uselessly with the back of his hand, blinked, stumbled, blinked again.

There was a dog running towards him, for a moment he thought it was Stonewall's Sal, the sight so shocking and the expectation of seeing Stoney himself so acute, it made him stop, stagger and choke.

The dog skidded to a halt and then ran round him, barking, ready for a game. Despite his pounding heart and the hairball in his throat, Rick felt the slow beginnings of a smile. Of course this was not Stoney's russet-coloured mutt, but a floppy red spaniel, with nothing in common but the kind of silly, fussy, excitable temperament Stoney would like. It gave Rick an idea, the first positive thought in all the confusing negatives. Buy the boy a new dog: that would make him better.

A man was following the dog, running in the same direction with the sun behind him, moving with the experienced grace which Rick had never mastered, admired for being so different from his own awkward arms and legs swinging everywhere, wasting energy and breath. The man's style of movement was an economical, effortless sprinting, so that when he shimmied to a halt, it was almost a relief to see that he shone with sweat.

'Morning.' A pleasant voice. 'Don't let her bother you. She just likes everyone.'

The hairball in Rick's throat would not go away. He had never quite understood the boy's passion for his dog; now he did as he stroked this one's soft ears and felt against his bare, damp legs those delighted vibrations of infinite trust.

'So did Stonewall's dog,' he blurted. 'Like people. Too much.'

The dog leant against his trembling knees. Having started, Rick had to go on, otherwise this odd piece of information, delivered so randomly to a stranger, would seem even odder. He made his voice harsh, as if his first words had some retrospective purpose instead of weakness.

'You want to be more careful of your dog,' he admonished. 'There's a maniac on the loose round here. Eats dogs for breakfast and tries to kill boys.'

'You're joking.' The man called his dog, which trotted to heel. Rick was stung.

'No, I'm not. The police are organizing a search party along this stretch. We called him the ghost, but he isn't a ghost. So you just watch yourself, running along here alone. Even running as fast as you do.'

He was envious and gabbling. He needed to gabble, talking to a stranger was easier than trying to make sense to himself. The man suddenly struck out a hand. Rick looked at it as if it was a turd.

'Malcolm,' the man said, with a smile which brooked no refusal.

It was such an incongruously formal thing to do, shake hands and announce names in the middle of a beach, that Rick did it, although it made him want to laugh, relaxed him more than a little. Maybe it was the running did that. They fell into step, walking back the way Rick had come. To where the search party formed on the spit by the lifeboat, a motley, serious crew, anxious to do duty.

'Perhaps I can help,' Malcolm said.

'Reckon you can. Just look at 'em. What a geriatric crew. Anyone's welcome. Even with a daft dog like yours.'

There was no-one young in the group. Rick looked at them sourly. This bloke Malcolm was the youngest apart from himself, better take him on. The rest looked like a congregation from church.

They were old enough, though, to work without complaint, with the thoroughness otherwise devoted to their gardens; perhaps Uncle Curl knew what he did when he chose, but even with effort, they did not find the white-haired man by the end of a long day. Not Rick, the London stranger who proved such an asset, three dozen others walking through the woods. In and out of the caravans, taking apart the beach huts, one by empty one, wading across the flats, looking inside boats. Moving into the village, ignoring the populous quay where no-one could possibly hide, sweeping forward from the coast to look inside empty holiday homes, further inland through the council estate, the church, into the barns of the hinterland. The two of them who walked through the graveyard tut-tutted at a mess of scattered flowers until they saw the stonemason erecting a headstone of fine white marble, stopped briefly to admire. Looking for a man with a stick and white hair, a form without needs or substance, otherwise held few rewards and less glory. They began to consider he was indeed a ghost, who had fled or gone back from where he came, into the embrace of the sea.

Rick and his ally Malcolm sat in the bar of the Crown on the Green, Merton's only hotel and a place where Rick had set foot twice, ever. It was Malcolm's invitation, said he was staying there. Posh. Let Dad cope with the arcade.

* * *

Stonewall Jones dreamt of the sea, the amusement arcade, his dog, and remembered someone loved him, best.

Night fell over land, without a whimper. Sarah Fortune was packing her bags, sensing her own impending redundancy without bitterness, preoccupied. She knew, from walking the town, sitting again in front of that unedifying display of cakes, what went on around her and did not want to know more. They would find him, she supposed; that desperation of his would make him careless. But she did not want him found. Except perhaps by herself, as the fulfilment of a whole year's dreaming nightmares, in which she discovered him bound and helpless and made him feel what he had done to her, what it was like to be so diminished. Finding him thus would pacify that burning which ate her from within, that yearning to watch him crawl, to scratch his face with long, polished nails and watch him beg. Naked, as she had been, screaming and whimpering as she had been in an empty house, suffering as she wanted him to suffer, with the knowledge of that helpless loss of pride.

There was a pain in her stomach; she diagnosed it as the result of all her self-restraint, the application of charm and manners to her daily life instead of howling for the carefree person she had been. A pain which came with the incipient grief for Elisabeth Tysall and for herself which would not go away. An ache which was the effort of her own agnostic prayer and the residue of all her violent and foul thoughts towards him. If home was where the heart resided, there was no such thing as home. She packed listlessly, half of her waiting, all of her ignored.

Mouse Pardoe crept away from the bosom of her family, ostensibly upstairs to bed and then out of the front door, bandaged hands lighting her way in the darkness. The deference of the children over a day, their affection, their overwhelming concern brought forth an unnatural sensation of guilt, a kind of emotional indigestion which alarmed her. Guilt of any kind was not second nature to Mouse: it made her tiptoe across the lawn, already resentful of the necessity of Sarah Fortune, who knew too much about them all and was now, for the lack of anyone else to tell, about to know more. Hettie the sheep followed after, but Mouse was not afraid and it was only the reasons why she was not afraid, not of the ghost at least, which made her faintly ashamed.

'What are you doing?' she cried, facing the cottage living room as the door opened without hesitation. 'I came to see if you were all right,' she added with less conviction. Both of them knew it was not the truth. Sarah had fulfilled her purpose. Mouse had plenty of reason to be grateful to Sarah, and that was enough to stop anyone caring. The shawl which had covered the ugly sofa was gone, the table lamp back in place, the room bereft of the flowers which had made it homely, the whole thing back to the anonymity of just another place to rent.

'Packing up my travelling bordello,' said Sarah with a smile. She made it so easy, Mouse thought bitterly, to like her. This was no woman who would kiss and tell, she was as tight as a drum, but somehow, horribly relaxing, all sorts of ideas in her eyes and her mind, but none of them including the slightest critical judgement.

'Packing? Whatever for? We need you, dear.'

'No you don't. I've finished.' She waved a hand towards a neat pile of papers on the floor. 'Valuations. Edward helped last night, that's why I kept him here so long.' Their glances met and slid away in recognition of a lie mutually accepted. Mouse seized a bottle by the kitchen sink, two glasses from the draining board, poured without invitation. She assumed the claret was for her: she was slightly drunk already, aimed to get worse. Such was conscience. Why should she care? If a trespasser ate the food and burned her hands he deserved to deal with his own digestion.

'You Pardoes,' said Sarah without any hint of complaint as they sat, 'tend to be heavy on the rations. Anyway, if you can read the hand-written notes ... I have very clear handwriting, nothing ambiguous about it, what I've done is suggest the properties you can get rid of soonest. Selling them, at absolutely knock-down prices on ludicrously easy terms, to the people who currently own them. Those are the businesses, beginning with the pub and the amusement arcade, then the shops. Give back the lifeblood of the town. Right?'

Mouse nodded, gargling the wine, lovely stuff.

'You don't want to be destitute,' Sarah continued. 'The business end of all this, as well as further education for Edward and Jo, a modest nest egg for all three and fine wines and parties for yourself, will be financed out of the holiday cottages you have. Selling them at very low prices, to be bought by local people to raise families, still leaves plenty, properly invested, for your own old age. Whenever that occurs.'

Mouse liked that touch. She proffered her glass for refilling.

'We won't need Ernest Matthewson to sort it all?'

'You don't need him, no. He won't like it, but you don't. A local accountant, an honest estate agent ... yours isn't, by the way.'

'Awful in bed, Ernest,' said Mouse reflectively. 'Such a hurry.'

Sarah sipped without comment. Mouse sighed with satisfaction.

'Such a relief,' she said brightly. 'I mean really. We've all talked about it today, and they all want the same thing. They live here, they want to belong. Such well-brought-up children. All the right attitudes. They all agree that none of them wants more than strictly enough. Enough is always enough, don't you think?'

'Absolutely,' said Sarah with the right amount of fervour to make Mouse continue. The pain in her own abdomen was becoming intense, beyond the reach of wine, a hunting pain, which sought other places to attack.

'After all,' Mouse went on, accepting more alcohol as if she were a favoured guest, 'wouldn't it be awful if I'd had to tell them in order to get them to agree? Frightful!'

She was back in her hotel receptionist mould which Sarah realized had not been entirely mad.

'Awful,' she agreed warmly.

'I mean, if they hadn't listened? I didn't think they'd ever listen when I got Mr Pardoe to make that will. When he had those little heart flutters, you know? We were getting on so well, I knew he didn't notice how the thing was phrased. All my children . . .'

Oh, yes he did, Sarah thought. He might have seen Stonewall Jones in the drive, delivering bait and known. That boy was going to grow big and tall, like his real dad, with eyes like Julian Pardoe, all his colours and all his stockiness to become in the future the mirror image of his much older brother. When you lay with a man, you knew the colour of his eyes, knew when you had seen them before in another face, along with particular gestures and a way of eating and drinking. You knew.

'I would have told them,' said Mouse. 'I would certainly have done, if they hadn't agreed we should give it all back, all this property stuff, as soon as we could.' She sighed. 'I mean I played the scene a thousand times in my head before I decided to act mad. There we would be, none of them listening, sitting round a table with Ernest Matthewson sitting at the top. Reading out that bit from the will. How does it go? I should know, I constructed it. "To my wife, and then to all MY children . . ." Meaning, his children. Not his and mine, HIS. Those wearing his jeans, sorry genes.' She spelt it out as if Sarah could not see the pun, hiccoughed, recovered her poise, continued.

'HIS children? Well, I suppose Julian is his child. I've every reason to think so. The others? Joanna, probably. Edward, no. It seemed obvious to me. Perhaps that's why he and Mr Pardoe never got on. It's so difficult to tell. Now I don't have to tell.'

'Don't you?' Sarah's question was sad.

'No,' said Mouse. 'Not any more than you have to tell the person before who you slept with last. It's all right for you young things taking the pill. Nature helped me: I could have had lots more babies, but I didn't. Which is just as well, I'd never have known whose they were.'

'I've drafted a separate bequest for your new will,' Sarah murmured. 'Half the residue of your estate, to include a decent house and a piece of his own coast, to go to Stonewall Jones, after your death.'

Mouse nodded, did not even question.

'I entirely agree,' she said. 'I'd already thought of that. I may be selfish, but I'm not dishonest.'

'Well, all's well that ends well,' said Sarah, pouring the dregs into Mouse Pardoe's glass.

'Not entirely,' said Mouse. 'I didn't mean to bang on about my family, now we're all sorted, after a fashion. They aren't really on my conscience, nothing lingers there long. Except these.'

She fumbled in the pocket of the dressing-gown, worn over a frilly nightie up to the chin, and ear-rings which dangled about the pie-crust collar. Produced a small packet, split at the top. *Size 2/0*, Sarah read.

Super-sharp fine wire: designed and perfected for shore fishing. She turned the packet over, read more. . . . *Top-quality hooks made from high-carbon steel.* She shook one of them into her palm. The point was needle sharp, with a neat, inverted barb. The hook was black; she felt it against her own skin, harmless until the barb took hold. The black hooks, each with a small eye at the top of the stem, curled sweetly in their innocent, polythene envelope.

'Only one thing bothers me,' Mouse Pardoe was saying, carelessly, 'I put lots of these in the sandwiches. And the scones.'

She tipped the glass over her nose.

'I only did it as a joke. Edward, leaving them all over the place, drove me mad. Hettie could have eaten one. No-one ever eats anything I make: I only do it to annoy. All those years I *had* to cook; now I can do it for play, like making sandwiches. I would have told them about the hooks before they went near. To make the point to Ed, because then he would never have left anything in the kitchen again, like his father did before. Or hit me. What exactly did you DO to Edward, dear? He's being so nice.'

Sarah saw Charles Tysall, backing out of the kitchen, stuffing yellow scones in his pocket.

'Only that man, that Charles,' Mouse was saying airily, 'he ate all the sandwiches. I don't know how he did it, but he did,' she added with a trace of self-satisfaction. 'Ate the lot.'

Sarah looked at the hook curled in her palm, remembered the sound of the gulping of food and milk. The hook was such a fine wire, one inch long, small enough, only just, for a starving, hungry man to swallow. She pressed the small, inverted barb, between thumb and forefinger, felt it pierce her skin.

'Sharp, aren't they, dear?' Mouse remarked.

The pain in Sarah's abdomen became intense.

'Sleep on it, I would,' said Mouse, abdicating every decision with a smile. 'He deserved what he got.'

Rick never could take drink: a little went a long way, so he had been careful, was not drunk now, merely loquacious. How awful, in the village where he lived, to need the company of a stranger on a night like this. No news of Stonewall: he had checked with Jo and the doctor. He may as well stay where he was with this easy man, both of them dirty, other customers in the smart bar giving them space. Two pints simply brought emotion nearer the surface. Rick wanted Jo to hug, but he stayed, giving Malcolm all the information distilled from Uncle Curl and everyone else. Malcolm's gentler cross-examination techniques worked as well in a bar as they did in a courtroom, especially when the victim was emotional, malleable and confused. Malcolm knew the name, the identity, the local history and the persona of the man they hunted. Like Sarah Fortune, he was all too real.

'Your Cousin Stonewall thought that this Sarah Fortune woman was Mrs Tysall, did he?' Malcolm was asking.

'Only at first. My second cousin in the hairdresser's did too. What do you think the ghost wanted up at the Pardoes'? Apart from it being a lonely place where he might get food? A place with nothing to guard it but a sheep?' Rick's eyes widened, alcohol in flight in the face of realization. The mention of Sarah Fortune made him blush; he thought of her with guilty fondness and a slight tightening of the groin, felt himself pulling his flat stomach flatter.

'You think he might have gone up there for Sarah? Aw, come on, it doesn't make sense. He wouldn't even have known she was there.'

'Listen,' said Malcolm. 'In his other life, Charles Tysall had an obsession with Sarah Fortune.'

'Did he now?' Rick mumbled, foggy again, but leering. 'I can see his point.'

They drank reflectively. Not this lad, Malcolm thought. Surely not, not even Sarah.

'So maybe he'll go back there, then. S'all right. They got someone watching the place, Jo said when I phoned. And there's two men up there anyway, well one and a half, if you count Edward. I reckon he's long gone. He managed months without people, why should he need anyone now?'

Rick drank the last of his pint, did not want to say anything more. Malcolm spoke slowly.

'Oh, I don't think it's a question of Charles going back to find Sarah. Not a question of Charles leading the way to where Sarah is. More the other way round.'

'What do you mean?'

'I mean Sarah leading us to Charles. Sarah will find him.'

Rick did not understand.

'Tell you what,' he said. 'Meet you outside the arcade. Seven o'clock if it's sunny. Eight if it rains. Right?'

Malcolm was silent, the taste of his good whisky, sour.

The room in which he sat had become terrifying. He repeated like a mantra phrase, 'My name is Charles and I have no name.' When at last he moved, towards the cracked, disused mirror against the wall in the opposite room, level with the high stone sink, all he could see was his face glowing yellow, his brown teeth, eyes which were pink and dry. So long without a mirror, the sight unhinged him. If he had even used a mirror in the last year, he would have seen the damage of the changes; seen how impossible it was to go home. He was beginning to smell. Blood and dirt and cold, hot sweat and putrefaction.

Something inside him mortally wounded. Step to one
side and watch me, darling. Dying. He had opened
his mouth and raised his hand many times, let the
hand fall back to wipe the froth which congealed
round his perfect mouth, the lips stretched with pain,
the forehead puckered with the knowledge of helplessness, his long thin body bent. There were portraits on the wall where he grew up. Red-haired
women with the threatening white complexions of
his forebears, himself the saturnine changeling.

Finally, he had bellowed with rage and frustration,
shrieked like a child in the grip of hysteria and heard
his shrieks descend into weeping. Shuffled closer to
the opening when he knew the time was well beyond
daylight. The lights fell across his face and his dirty
white hair; he was ten feet from help, but no-one
saw, no-one heard, the place was full of sound.

The rat-a-tat of machine-gun fire, eerie music,
echoing gongs, popular songs at colossal volume, the
sound of a fairground, the clack of coins and children
screaming from afar, sounding triumphant. In the in-
terludes, a droning voice, 'On the line, fifty-nine,
legs eleven, number eleven, sink and dive, fifty-
five . . .' The sounds bleep, bleep, bleep, wailing
songs, heavy beat, and the mystical calling of the
machines selling their wares to the possessed.

The effort of screaming drove him into a paroxysm of silent laughter, something to excuse the tears.
The irony of a cultured man, enduring this orchestra
of vulgar, electronic sound, with the purple lights
playing upon the yellow skin he felt he could pull
away, while his long hands clutched at his abdomen.

Someone on a misguided expedition to find a lavatory which did not exist, kicked the legs sticking beyond the entrance of the ante-room, swore, went
back. Later, another, ignoring him even while his
mouth opened to scream again, left him for drunk instead of dying. The thought of a drink made his

throat contract; he was thirsty, had only come in here
for water which he could not reach, never left in
twenty hours.

Charles dozed; when he opened his eyes all sound
had ceased and he gazed into the peace of total darkness, the opportunity for rescue ending while he
slept. Panic now, blood in the pee which soaked the
track-suit trousers, the smell of himself disgusted
him. He crawled.

Away from the dead machines, which stood like
coffins in the back room, across the eerie moonlit
floor, illuminated from the windows of the fold-back
doors leading on to the road and the pay-and-display
sign for the quayside car-park. Clutching at the inside handle, feeling it rattle and the whole edifice of
the door shake as he raised himself to his knees and
looked out into the night in an attitude of supplica-
tion, looking for the moon and redemption.

Saw a figure turn, stamp feet, turn back, light a
cigarette to illuminate its uniform, stub out the cigarette as someone passed by and said, Good-evening,
officer. A woman, treating a police officer with polite
deference as her dog bit his heels. Better die like a
dog than live like one.

He began to crawl back, slowly, leaning against
Omen III and Street Fighters IV. Thirsty, thirsty,
thirsty.

'Room after room,' he whispered.

'I hunt the house through . . .

Next time herself! Not the trouble behind her.'

Browning in the mouth. The stanzas a litany for a
shuffling old man who could remember nothing else
but obscenities. Not a self-created vagrant, a real
one. Once back in the room of the dead machines, he
shat himself. The shame was so insupportable, the
act of it so painful, he wept. .

* * *

Stonewall Jones woke, with an urgent desire for the lavatory and a sense of shame in that. He was confused, but very clear about his needs. Coke, not milk; the embrace of his mother, not the nurse.

Sarah had never managed the art of travelling light, nor of counting back into her baggage what she had put in. In the dim light of dawn, she still noticed that there was less, one purple shirt, with the trousers and shoes donated to the greedy sea, one black shirt, with leggings, which she hoped Joanna would enjoy. The child had not been near, which she did not find strange in one normally so considerate; Sarah knew she bore her own kind of contagion, a kind of hidden, moral embarrassment which afflicted those of normal tendencies with a kind of unease.

She bent into the pain. Charles had occupied her dreams, the sense of his presence overpowering. The knowledge of the poisonous hooks in his body consumed her. She woke to the sound of gossiping birds, shrill and cheerful. Perhaps it was the signal they had found him.

The sea mist had descended, the air soft, damp, light struggling through.

Was it cowardly to leave after this fashion, skulking away at dawn in this chilling mist, to a home which was not a home, never had been since Charles had invaded the casual, clandestine, delightfully promiscuous progress of her life and called her a whore? Cowardly to leave, before anyone should find him first and ask her to identify their prize? To go with the same fear, the same lack of a conclusion, the same shame, back to the same hopelessly damaged life?

She closed the door of the car with the crumpled wing, leaving her things inside it. Hettie the sheep bleated with satisfaction. There was no hurry after all.

She walked to the village-cum-town, listening to the gurgling of hidden water. Walked beyond the quay and out on to the causeway. The red roof of the lifeboat station was scarcely visible, the siren, having issued its warning against the fog, remained silent. Sarah paused, turned, scanned the quayside. It was small and manageable, harmless. She could see the folding doors to the arcade slightly open and a man cleaning the windows without enthusiasm before he walked away from the task. Then a shaft of struggling sunlight pierced through the thin mist, illuminated the glass of the windows, disappeared as suddenly as it had struck, like a signal. Sarah knew with a complete and illogical certainty where Charles Tysall was. She began to walk back, watching her feet, feeling the quickening pain in her guts and listening to the vengeful messages of her own heart.

CHAPTER THIRTEEN

She was screened for a minute by the cars which seemed permanent fixtures of the car-park, the shell-fish van and a slow rumbling lorry full of animal feed, the sound of the growling engine ominous in the silence. When Malcolm reached the quay, to meet his appointment with Rick in the expectation that Rick might be late, Sarah had gone. There was an oldish man, with a figure stiff with resentment, coming round the corner, chewing on something, cap over one eye.

'Excuse me, have you seen a chap called Rick? Works here?'

It sounded like an accusation: Rick's father blenched.

'Nope.'

'Only I was supposed to meet him here,' Malcolm said, feeling useless.

The older man laughed, nervously. 'He don't like the early morning, our Rick. Told me I'd have to clean the windows, not him. Thought he'd got some woman in to clean 'em. Saw her. A looker.'

'Where did she go?'

'After Rick, I expect. They usually do.' Rick's dad laughed, taking pride in his announcement. Maybe he'd get some fun out of Rick's conquests.

'Where did she go?' Malcolm repeated patiently.

Rick's dad was thinking of nothing much; comprehension dawned slowly, remnants of another conversation coming back to cloud his early-morning brain, reminding him of the current primary purpose, which was to find a male ghost, not a woman. He supposed the question was related, didn't think why, but guessed wildly in order to please and get this bloke off him.

'Think I just saw someone going up the high street.'

They both turned, uncertainly, uphill.

Sarah could smell him first, an animal in a lair, surrounded by the stench of faeces and fear. He was lying with his back propped against one of the dead machines, levered against it for support. The pathetic outline of him emerged first from the half light in there, then the details. The track-suit bottoms had slid down from scraping along the ground, his thin hands were clasped over his stomach above his genitals which flopped in pathetic splendour. Hung like a donkey. His face wore the rictus of a smile, a dirty face, furrowed with tears.

She tried to make her voice harsh, summon up the hatred.

'Something you ate?' she said, standing over him, willing him to look at her with the unblinking eyes which looked towards the light instead. 'Shame on you, Charles Tysall, you made me offer to rut like a pig, and now, you look like a pig.'

How pathetic an insult, and then, suddenly she was weeping. He had been a handsome man once, lithe as a tiger, long limbed, broad shouldered, a prowler with infinite grace, a predator, but such a beautiful man, proud in his body and his obsessions, fastidious, wicked and still beautiful. Never a man to crawl: it became him as ill as a wounded tiger, a rogue elephant with no notion of human distress. She thought of the hooks which might not have damaged a younger, stronger man, but tore at the weaker fabric of this gaunt and starving fugitive with the terrible glitter still in his piercing blue eyes. The rictus turned into a recognizable smile; he held out his hand, the long, elegant fingers flexing, then trembling, trying to summon into a small gesture some remnants of the old arrogance.

'Imperfectly pure and good,' he whispered. 'Look at me, Elisabeth. Are you satisfied?'

She remembered the hands, slender, manicured soft, caressing her body, spanning her neck, the buckle of his belt biting into her spine, the softness of his balls a cushion against her buttocks before the glass splintered and with it, all limitations on his calculating savagery. Felt the last, great spate of anger against him, remembering that torture, and then even with her own screams in her own ears, the anger died. She tried to retrieve it, hold the need for revenge, felt it slip away as she watched, disgust mixed with compassion, with the treacherous, wasteful pity for him winning in the end. The body was merely a man, a thing, twisting and grimacing, trying now to pull up its trousers in some pathetic attempt at half-remembered modesty. She stooped, indifferent to the smells of sweet, sour and rancid, helped him. He was warm and clammy, screamed when she touched him and there was no satisfaction, even in that.

Water for the saliva crusted round the mouth: she did not want him to be seen this way, sharing for a brief moment the pride which made him want to cover himself, but when she rose from her haunches to find the sink, he uttered a groan of despair. The tap in the other room yielded water onto a rag; when she knelt again and applied it to his face, he moaned again with pleasure, sucked at the cloth with the greediness of a baby on a nipple.

They stayed thus, wordless, she holding him round the shoulders, feeling the bones, keeping the cloth to his face, murmuring nothings, wondering what next to do, with the tears still coursing down her face, dropping onto his skin.

'Do you forgive me, Porphyria?' the voice rattled, bubbling from the chest.

She could not say so, could not utter a clear word. She did not forgive him, either in her own right or on behalf of her friend Elisabeth, but she could not bear to see him suffering either.

The door to the back yard opened with a scraping sound; there were soft footsteps, a pair of training shoes, an increase in the light and then a tall shadow towering above them. Charles had hold of her hand, her arm wrapped across his chest; she tightened her hold, felt the papery skin of his palm, while she listened to a gasp of anger, felt the alien tension of bone and muscle, the intake of breath before effort, the scent of violent rage which would never emanate from Charles now. She held him closer, looked up like a fierce little animal. Malcolm stood above her, fists clenched, legs braced, a fighter ready to pounce. He spoke through gritted teeth.

'Sarah? Is that Charles? What's the matter with him? Christ, he's aged ten years. Is he hurt? The bastard. What are you doing? Let go, for God's sake.'

She looked at him absently, his appearance a secondary consideration, spoke quietly.

'If you hit him, I'll kill you.'

Her own voice came from a great distance, followed by the cough which was Malcolm's effort to control his voice before it became a murmur, strangled by his own, bitter emotion. He had slept with this woman. She had touched him. Now look at what she held, with the same intimacy.

'So, Sarah my sweet. How could you? Is there anything you can't touch? Anyone you don't despise? How could you?'

She could not summon scorn. Could not say,

Look, this is no more than a hunted man who is dying in pain and that is all I can acknowledge. Could not in her contempt of Malcolm's futile clenched fists, even attempt to phrase a denial.

The pain drifted away and she still held him, protectively, knowing only that it was once handsome and proud Charles Tysall who held her hand as a talisman. Knowing too that there was nothing else she could do but hold on and lend warmth. No-one should die alone.

After the room became safely crowded and the rattle in his throat had ceased, she relinquished him calmly, watching the face turn from flushed to waxy pale, the lines of age and pain easing away in the immediacy of death. She walked out of the arcade past a silent phalanx of the men of the town and the hunting party, each staring more accusingly than the last. She walked the gauntlet with her head high, the mist teasing curls into her wild hair, blood on her hands and dirt on her clean clothes. Walked beyond the murmuring crowd, past the rising tide in the channels and the graceful swimming swans, until beyond their sight, she broke into a run. The mist was wet on her face, the sea birds were silent, the earth was still, her stride punctuated only by the fierceness of her sobbing.

Hettie the sheep was still at the door, sporting her unequal horns and endless good nature. Oh to be sheeplike, docile and untroubled, satisfied, until the pointed horn of your life grew into your eye. Sarah picked the roses round the door, they owed her that, and put them in the back of her car. She rummaged in her case on the back seat for clean clothes, stripping and changing where she stood, obscured by the mist, wiping her hands on the garments she dropped, buttoning a clean blouse with shaking but efficient hands. She kicked what she had worn to one side, ever careless with her apparel, whatever it had cost. Clothes did not matter, they never had and they never would. Hettie began to eat her second outfit that week.

Late breakfast in the Pardoe household in a kitchen free of fishing utensils. Edward was giving up fishing, he was going away. Somewhere, he said. Joanna had long since told herself that in doing whatever he had done, he thought he was doing the best, although his notion of the best was no longer hers. It was more difficult to relinquish adoration than it was to relinquish love, everything would be all right in the end.

Julian and Edward were arguing, nothing altered except the tone, the tenor, the result. Edward still with that endless, hard-done-by element in his voice which he would have for ever, and if he ever found out why, he would only be worse.

I shall have to say goodbye, Sarah told herself at the door, look Edward in the eye to make my promise of blackmail stick. Julian was arguing in measured tones. Joanna cooked at the Rayburn, flushed and serene, with that hint of high anxiety which would always be hers. Mouse sat at one end of the mess-free table, eating nuts for breakfast, wearing a swimming-costume under her dressing-gown. She had things to do later; she would never make concessions to clothes, or ever buy new ones. She might, reluctantly abandon the hats.

The appearance of Sarah, fresh and pale, sunny and clean, rivetted attention and brought to the surface of every face a slight blush of shame. Joanna blushed least, for being nothing but inattentive to the guest in the face of greater dramas, but then it took little to activate her guilt towards what was only the hired help and ever so briefly, confidential friend and exemplar. All the same, her skin grew the colour of ripe strawberry.

Julian's blush was more moderate, reaching up towards his sandy hair with the same sting of hospitable conscience as Jo, but also for his confessions and his cure, for what he had said and done so joyfully in the middle of the night. The mild coloration of Edward's sallow skin was merely the result of a temporary worry about whether the guest had come to tell on him, a momentary sense of panic soon dismissed. Sarah's smile, the conscious cheerfulness reminiscent of the ideal girl next door rather than the airs and graces of a high-powered lawyer paid by the day, made all of them feel better. She sat as if she could never take offence in a million years, looking like someone on the way out to play netball with the team. Joanna pushed a mug of coffee towards her which she took with exaggerated thanks. They all began to relax. Except Mother, who kept her nose buried in a newspaper.

'All's well with the world,' Sarah said lightly, looking towards no-one in particular, ignoring the little lump in her throat. 'They've found the ghost. Poor man, dead at the back of the amusement arcade. Something he ate.'

From all sides of the table came a palpable sigh of relief. Julian caught her eye and smiled with full magnetic glare. Sarah wished she could afford dislike for mere weakness, but that, along with hatred and judgement, was a luxury.

And I'm going home now, she was going to say, before the Big Ben chimes of the ice-cream van impinged, first distant then strident, dah da, dah da! Louder and louder, scorching not to the front door of the ugly old pile, but the back, by the cabbage patch, the van itself assuming a new intimacy with this terrain. They would not be the landowning Pardoes for long. Everyone would be welcome.

'Ernest will send in the bill,' Sarah yelled at Julian above the din of scraped-back chairs and the headlong rush to the door, led by Mother, all of them wanting a distraction.

'Of course. Thank you for everything,' was all he said.

When the red car with the dented wing drove slowly past the front of the house, the ice-cream chimes still rang, like church bells at a wedding, the harbinger of good news, so demanding no-one noticed the sound of an engine going away. Rick's news would be repeated a thousand times, like the tune of the chimes. Stonewall, back on the road of living and loving, demanding a video, and could he borrow the sheep for a visit and what kind of dog should they get? And Rick knowing exactly the right kind. And that other fucker, that ghost, well he's really dead. This time.

In a half-hour wake of the van, another car, small, blue, undented, well looked after, pulled hesitantly to the front of the house. Malcolm Cook decanted his long limbs, walked in the direction of celebratory sound. No-one had turned off the ice-cream bell; it grated in his ears. Rick was high on coffee and wine, slow on the introductions. For the moment, the tall, dark man who could hunt so assiduously and run like a dream, was just another stranger.

'Come to collect Miss Fortune,' he said with the half-apologetic, half-aggressive tones of a taxi driver.

'She's gone,' someone said, he was not sure who. 'You're too late.' Rick looked at him sideways, wondering, for the first time, exactly who he was.

'Too late,' he chanted, sounding just like Stonewall.

Well beyond the town, out on the coast road, travelling fast, until she found the turning and bumped down the track she had found before. She moved the car to the very edge where shingle met sand on this flat coast. The mist was peculiarly local: ten miles away from Merton's quay it did not exist. She looked at the retreating sea, the stretch of warm sand, stayed inside the confines of her car, with the bordello in the back, the shawl to decorate a room, the virtue to decorate a life, the odd crate of booze, the remnants of fear packed along with the clothes, and felt no longer drawn to the water. Thought of Elisabeth Tysall's headstone with remote satisfaction. Who loves you, beautiful? I do.

Thought of pleading with Charles Tysall a year ago, standing in front of the mirror in her flat while he accused her. You have no virtue to protect, do you? he had said, despising the offer she had made of her body in return for her life. You are nothing: a woman is nothing without virtue. Looking at the sea, Sarah remembered what she had replied, and what she would say now. She had said then, Of course I have virtue. I do not torment or abuse. I leave when I am not welcome. I do not trespass or take anything from anyone, except my own payment which need not be money. I keep every secret which is entrusted in me. I do not really know the meaning of malice. I like to live without rules, that is all, and that is a kind of virtue no-one values.

Virtue all the same. She left the bleakness of the warm sand with all its temptations, turned away from the coast. Found a deserted lane, full of meadowsweet so prolific, so untouched by human hand, it hid the car from sight. She took a bottle of warm champagne from the supplies in the back and a beaker from the glove compartment in the front. After she had disposed her legs comfortably through the window, she lit a cigarette and wondered, Now where shall I go next? What shall I be next, now I am free.

There did not seem anything wrong with going on exactly as before.

Available now in bookstores everywhere!

A CLEAR CONSCIENCE

A Helen West Novel

by Frances Fytield

Published in hardcover by Pantheon.

Read on for a sneak preview from this
absorbing mystery . . .

PROLOGUE

Life was dull, monochrome. Live dangerously. It was her own perception of herself which made her take the risks. Such as not looking left or right when she crossed the road, staring straight ahead and moving slowly. She did not walk deliberately into the path of the bus, simply did not seem to notice the squeal of horn and fart of brakes. The same sloppy attitude, fed by exhaustion, made her take short cuts, although all she really wanted on the way home was to postpone getting there. It was hot inside her second-hand coat. The pub which she would have passed on the main road would have crowds against the windows, a few pretty girls drooping like half-dead flowers around the pool tables, waiting on busy youths with pectorals like carvings and small muscular bums; the girls so bored, they were looking for something to scorn. Someone ugly. One of them would notice her, point, sneer, and although she seemed to have mislaid the habit of thinking, she knew she did not want to be the subject of comment. In any event, concentration was limited to ten seconds a time.

So she went through the back of the leisure centre instead, into the park. There was a running track round the edge: she liked the feeling of the cinders beneath her feet, the shoddy barrenness of it all, and the sense of importance she got unlatching the gate at the opposite end and walking through as if she was the only person who knew it was there. The park avoided the street. Once, she would have chosen the route rationally. That point in time was a long while ago.

The leisure centre was run like a gospel church and looked like a warehouse from the outside. Local children, disbarred from the place for less than total devotion to either the architecture or the mystical purposes of the building, seemed to haunt it, inspired by a kind of envy for the mysteries within. The leisure centre was not really for the untouchables. She knew the reputation of this particular part of the neighbourhood—she lived here, could read the local paper as well as anyone else—it simply did not make any difference because it did not apply to her and she did not care. This was the way she was going to go.

Muggers on a warm, spring night were unlikely to be fussy animals, she had to concede that. They cared as little as dogs round dustbins. They would knock her down for the contents of her small and bulging shopping bag, but if all they wanted was two bottles of bleach, assorted cheap groceries, a packet of washing powder and her front-door key, good luck to them. And if the motive was rape, they would obviously turn back as soon as they saw her, look around for a better target. They would have to be blind to persist; youth could be wicked, but, surely, never so desperate. Not even a male in heat would do more than sniff at this small woman, twenty-five going on sixty, plodding down the alley which cut alongside Smith Street, led her round the edge of the kiddies' playground, wired in like a prison compound, whether to keep them in or keep them out she did not know, flanked by the tennis courts, also wired in, and skirted by the path which led to the gate, and then up a terraced road to her door.

She could have looked at the tower blocks looming to the left and felt gratitude for not having to live there, never again having to trudge all the way to the top of such spartan splendour. They were like the stars in the darkness—oddly glamorous unless you knew better, which, after a fashion, she did. Bevan was the most ominous, sticking up into the sky; but she was not in the mood for counting large mercies, let alone the small. The hurt, with grief and bruises, was all she knew as she trudged, feeling the slack skin of her arms rub against the worn cotton of her blouse. Her skirt rode up between her legs, bunching in the front under the coat, emphasizing the slight prominence of her stomach, however slowly she walked in her training shoes. She had the beginning of a double chin, pasty cheeks, hair pulled into an elastic band and eyes already laced with fine lines. She walked with a slight stoop. Rape? Don't make me laugh, she told herself, to hide the first *frisson* of fear. They'd pay me to go away. You want good looks, find someone like my brother. He got them all. The niggle of fear persisted, despite her coughing to clear it. It grew like a bubble of air in her chest, felt like indigestion, at first merely uncomfortable, then becoming sharp, sticking in the throat like heartburn.

It was the sudden sound of the wind in the trees which began the alien sensation. Whispering branches, full of budding leaves set too high for vandals, added sibilant volume to the sound of bare limbs. Maybe there was nothing new in the sound, simply a novel ability in herself to notice the symptoms of the seasons. She registered summer because it was hot, winter because it was cold, that was all, but now the sound of the trees made a noise like a whispered command. Don't, don't. The fear grew larger, enraged her.

'Don't do what?' she shouted back, stopping to draw breath. The trees seems to obey, falling silent for a minute, then began again, moaning. Trees were alien here, belonged in another place. They shed dirty leaves in autumn: they made a mess. She had never rejoiced in their triumph of survival. Now she did not look up or down, only straight ahead and did not allow herself any distraction: she would be fine if she kept going at the same pace with her eyes ahead and, all the same, she found herself walking faster.

There was always a point where she had to decide which way to take round the perimeter fence, left or right, to complete the circle, reach the other end and emerge through the gate. One way was longer than the other and she had chosen it by mistake, flustered by the trees. Walking faster with her ungainly stride, she tripped over the lace on her shoe, an accident, because of trying to hurry and the laces being too long, that brought her heart into her mouth, the shock of nearly falling, lurching instead like her brother did when he was drunk, bouncing off the wire fence, the almost falling always worse than the fall itself. She steadied herself, adjusted the bag which bit into a calloused palm suddenly slippery with sweat. Her skin, as dry as the washing she ironed most mornings, felt the texture of rough parchment. She could imagine a knife going through her plump, papery cheek: it would not bleed, not now. What was the matter with her? Come on, come on! No-one could possibly want her for anything, no-one knew her enough to think she deserved malice; there was nothing to fear, but the fear still grew from somewhere. The short route ahead seemed endless, lengthening in proportion to her silly attempts at speed, with the bag heavier all the time and the bathroom bleach slurping about in its bottle. And then when she reached the gate out of the park, it was shut. Not simply shut, six feet high and locked. Keep them out, keep them in.

Turning round with a deliberate, deep breath, she saw him then, slinking away behind a tree. Just someone, some youth who would climb the fence with ease. Probably a black boy: they could climb like monkeys, robbed anything which moved, so she'd been told and so she believed, although she would not know. She only knew that without making any conscious decision, she was beginning to run in the other direction, round the link fence back towards the trees. As soon as she started she knew this was a mistake: there were no lights this side, and it had been the lights which had drawn her to the longer route in the first place. Here there were only dusty bushes by the side of the track, the cinder laid thickly, which made her slip. He was after her now; she did not have to turn to know he was there, jogging along behind her, his feet crunching, his wide, white eyes watching her graceless progress, waiting in the knowledge that she would never manage a real turn of speed. The shoelace snapped; she tripped again, righted herself and stumbled on. The sound of the trees grew louder as she reached them. Only the alley to go, leading out by the off-licence, round the corner from the very pub she had come this way to avoid. Don't, said the trees, don't.

Before the dark alley entrance, she turned, teetered in a staggering circle, letting the PVC bag carry her so she became a whirling cudgel, with her eyes shut against whatever she might see or hit. Nothing. The bag stuck to her hand, making her overbalance, carrying her into the mouth of the alley, before it hit the wall with a crunch and the air was full of the caustic smell of bleach. A large hand, smelling of booze, grabbed at her hair, took a hold, hauled her back.

She came to a trembling halt, dizzy, her arms by her side, the right still holding the dripping bag she could not detach, her mind wondering irrelevantly what had happened to the safety cap, her head yanked backwards, exposing her throat. The skirt was fully bunched round her waist by now, the coat heavy, the sweat pouring from her armpits, she would smell; and he was not even breathing faster, perfectly calm. She could feel the light of a lamp, made skittish by the moving branches of the trees, flickering across her face. Do it now. I shall not scream and I do not bleed: my cunt is so dry, you'll have to push. Put the bleach down my throat, only do not use a knife: please do no use a knife, and make it quick.

The hand released the hold on her hair. The elbow round her neck drew her closer. She could feel a rough jaw graze painfully against her own soft skin.

'I want,' a whisper in a honeyed voice, 'I want ...'

Slowly, she twisted towards him. 'Oh,' she said. 'It's you. Is it really you?'

'Me? Oh yes, it's me.'

The sound of his laughter rose into a shriek of hilarity. She knew that sound: he must have laughed in that same, uninhibited way since childhood. It went on and on and on, cutting across the sound of the trees and a distant yell of celebration from the pub. The diesel engine of a bus grunted in the near distance, and still the laughter went on.

The bleach from the bag dripped onto her shoes. She considered the waste of them and then, slowly, with all the repetitious obedience of passion and terror, she raised her mouth for the kiss.

CHAPTER ONE

If it ain't broke, don't fix it. Don't mess with the system. Leave well alone. Etcetera.

When I am old, Helen told herself, I shall cease even

trying to be good. I shall have no conscience, wear lavender, lace and false bosoms, and, in the meantime, I shall
never learn to wield an electric drill.

She continued muttering and shaking her head as a substitute for obscenities while she stood in her kitchen and
watched the dust settle. An old friend was dead on the
floor after all these years, lying among a shower of mor-
dant flies and the remnants of breakfast. Deceased, still
twitching in the extremities, filthy in parts with her own
sweaty fingerprints. Murderess.

She watched the butter dish teeter on the edge of the table before a delayed landing, greasy side up on the floor
among the other detritus. Someone from a laboratory could
examine the life cycle of the dead flies to give an estimate
of how many summers it had been since the roller blind
had refused to roll further than half mast and only then after gentle treatment. Helen had simply forgotten the habit
of teasing rather than pulling. Carelessness so often led to
death, but, with the fickleness which so horrified her, the
wavering thoughts moved on to rejection. Why had the
blind been there? Why mourn it? Because it hid three
panes of glass, one cracked, two dirty, in a window where
the sash-cord was uncertain; a state of affairs reminiscent
of everything else in the place: the chest of drawers which
demanded pushing and pulling, the toilet roll on one fragile nail, the wonky chairs on uneven floors, the windows
which did not shut. Everything in her domain required
concentrated co-ordination of hand and eye to make it
work, but there was nothing so broke it needed fixing; the
whole place was merely a kind of assault course requiring
extensive training. Strangers would need to know how to
pull the lavatory chain only with a certain force, kick the
hall cupboard before trying to open it, ease the living-room
door over the rug and not touch the kitchen blind without
further instruction. If it ain't broke, don't.

Helen West, hot and sticky after a long day's work, sat and
waited for the resentment to die. The only debate remaining
was between the merits of gin against white wine, but even
such decisions were academic in this house. There was no
ice for gin; the fridge, panting like a dog in a desert, was capable of cooling, but not of making ice after all these years,

so she held the wine while wandering from room to room, only four in all, excluding bathroom, suffering as she went the kind of discontent which felt like the rising damp she could detect in the bedroom. There were also a few summer beetles escaping garden predators in favour of a hostess who hoovered her basement floors as rarely as Miss West did. Helen thought, If I took down the wall between the dark hall and the living room, the place would be lighter, especially without a blind at the kitchen window. The legal mind which was her curse and her profession turned on complications such as planning permission, building regulations and other bureaucratic interference, before moving on to simpler ideas, such as new colour schemes, which required less fuss. Major alteration would only spawn a thousand minor problems; the hell with it.

The second glass of wine began to wane, and the mess from the kitchen floor was inside the rubbish bin when Bailey arrived. Her turn to cook. After three years of evasion she was finally learning how to overcome reluctance by buying only the best and simplest ingredients she could prepare inside ten minutes, but despite that, he usually came prepared for the eventuality of hunger, armed with a polythene bag, this time containing cheese, bread and a punnet of leaking strawberries. Usually she was grateful; sometimes irritated; today, simply neutral. The hug was perfunctory.

'What happened to that blind, then? Finally gave up?'

He was careful not to jeer. Most things in his place worked. He had one efficient floor on top of a warehouse, acquired before fashion knocked the prices out of sight and then knocked them down again. A distinguished flat, clean, clear and easy to keep. She liked it, never envied.

'Drink in the garden?'

'Fine.'

She hated him for knowing when to hold his tongue. Also for dusting an iron chair before sitting down, so that he would rise with the trousers of his dark grey summer suit clean enough for a man who did not like anyone to detect where he had been, while her cotton skirt would be striped with the dusty pattern of the seat. The garden always soothed her spirits, resembling, as it did, a warm, wet jungle in need of the kind of ferocious attention she could not apply indoors, but even while she was admiring the fresh sprung weeds, the controlled shambles of the kitchen remained disturbing.

'I was thinking of knocking down the living-room wall,' she volunteered. 'Or painting everything yellow. New curtains, new everything.'

He nodded wisely, sipped his lager. Two of these and he would feel the difference, but Bailey's diplomacy survived any amount of alcohol, while Helen simply became more talkative, more expansive with the wide-armed gestures which knocked things over.

'Expensive plans,' he murmured. 'You been taking bribes again?' She laughed, the bad mood lifting like a driven cloud.

'Oh yes, of course. Chance would be a fine thing, wouldn't it? Imagine anyone paying a prosecutor to lose a case. They'd have to be mad to think there was any need. They lose themselves. Anyway, I was thinking, yellow all over. Let the light in.'

Ah, my generous girl, he thought, with the dark hair, and the dark flat and a liking for light. Bailey thought of his own current work, more darkness than light, plenty of jokes. A solicitor for the Crown and a senior police officer should never meet like this to discuss the décor of their lives. They had tried to keep their professional roles apart since their personal fortunes were inextricably mixed, half the week at her place, days off in between, half the week at his, in a muddled relationship, full of affection and argument, waiting for a better formula to occur to both of them at the same time. Bailey looked at Helen. If it ain't broke, don't fix.

'Hmm,' he said. 'Yellow's a nice colour. Some yellows, anyway.' The woman he had interviewed this morning had worn a yellow blouse, blood from her broken nose mottling the front. The whole effect had resembled rhubarb and custard. He could not remember the colour of her skirt, only that it was held in her fists as she spoke and her bare arms were patterned with bruises. She loved the man, she said. She did not know why he did this to her. Bailey did not understand why. Even less did he want Helen to understand why.

Bailey loved Helen. Helen loved Bailey. It was as complicated as that. The thought of either of them raising a hand against the other was as alien as the planet Mars. Making a simple suggestion was dangerous enough. The cat, fresh from a roll in damp grass, rubbed against his calves, leaving a green stain which Helen noticed with satisfaction.

'But,' he continued cautiously, 'whether you paint it yellow or not, you'll always have a downstairs flat, therefore dark. Won't you? Why don't you just get in an odd job man and a spring cleaner? Then you'll be able to judge what else you really need.'

She pulled a face and stroked the cat with a bare foot. Bailey had often offered his services as Mr Fixit, carpenter, and, latterly, been rebuffed. He had been hurt by this, sensing in retrospect some tribute to the doctrine of the self-sufficient, liberated woman Helen would never quite be.

'Are you suggesting my home is dirty?'

'No, of course not. Only that you don't have time to clean it. Not clean isn't the same as dirty. The place gets a lick and a promise at least once a month. Why should you clean it anyway? Liberated women get help.'

'From other, unliberated women, you mean?'

'There's nothing wrong with domestic labour. You never mind helping someone else scrub their house, you just don't like doing your own. And if you were otherwise unemployed, you'd be glad of the going rate.'

'A pittance.'

'Regular employment, a mutually beneficial arrangement and clean windows.'

She went inside for more wine and another lager for him. The cat followed, licked up the traces of butter on the kitchen floor with noisy enthusiasm. Bailey's nonchalant figure in the garden was slightly blurred by the dust.

He was not ornamental. He was infuriating but consistent. He was still slightly more defensive than she was. There had never been a courtship, there had just been an event. If it ain't broke, celebrate.

The wine gleamed light golden through a slightly smeared glass; the lager was deep amber. In the evening light after summer rain, the red walls of the living room resembled a fresh bruise. Like the inside of a velvet cave

256

in winter, with the firelight covering all the cracks, it was dull and garish now.

She could make it corn coloured, all over. Get some good old-fashioned, middle-class chintz. Clean up the cat; forget the blind. Start all over again. Make herself and her home both elegant and safe.

Cath's lampshade was yellow. A colour once parchment, a nice shade from a second-hand shop, faded even then, the fringes dark brown. A pig of a light for sewing, but Cath liked it. Not that she could sew here, anyway; she hadn't done such a thing for months. Perhaps it was years. She just sat by the lamp and waited.

The room around her bore traces of effort, now sustained on a less frequent basis. The walls were smudged from frequent cleaning and the patchy renewal of paint. She shuddered to think what was under there. Some of her blood, she supposed, a lot of her sweat and a bucket of tears.

Joe had offered to cook. Ready-made, frozen pancakes with something called chicken 'n' cheese in the middle, about as good for a man as they were for a small woman, accompanied by frozen peas, boiled to death, and the bread and butter which was better than the rest put together, her contribution. She sat listless although aware, ready to spring into an attitude of appreciation, her eyes tracking his progress in the kitchen, stage left, while her head was turned towards the TV screen. When the meal arrived, she knew she was supposed to murmur appreciation, ooh and aagh as if the man was a genius to find a plate; she was already rehearsing the lines, dreading what he might burn, unable to suggest a better method. So far, the mood augured well. Cath did not quite know the meaning of relaxation, but as far as she could, she allowed herself lethargy, listening to his movements and his voice as she slumped, forever guilty in the slumping.

'Anyway, this bloke says to me, Jack, you're a very fine chap. Know an ex-army chappie when I see one. Got discipline, knows how to mix a cocktail even better than I know how to get 'em down, hah bloody hah. That's fine, I said, but the name is Joe, sir, not that it matters, much. And then, Cath, do you know what he did? Right in front of the bar at the Spoon, the bastard downs his drink in one and falls off his chair. Could not rouse the silly old sod. He was a picture, I tell you. Gets this look of surprise on his face, grinning all the time, trying to focus, just before he slides away. Laugh? I could have died.'

She tried to match the pitch of her own laughter to his shrill giggle, managed fairly well, encouraging him to continue. Surely, oh surely, there was a formula for managing her own tongue.

'What did you give him, Joe, to make him fall down like that?' Joe worked in the kind of pub which catered to what he called the gentry. And their ladies, haw, haw, haw. And their bloody sons, baying at one another and sticking crisps in the ear of the next person, all good clean fun with Daddy picking up the bills when they were sick or went outside to kick cars on their well-heeled way to somewhere else. Joe had a love–hate view of the officer class, mostly love, an adulation which also got a thrill from seeing them in the dust.

Cath, tired beyond even her own belief, which marvelled constantly at how exhausted and how hurt a person could be while still remaining conscious, sometimes pretended to share his prejudice. People's problems, she reckoned privately, were all the same, provided you liked them enough to listen.

'I said, what did you give the bloke to make him fall over, Joe?' There was a smell of burning from the kitchenette: the transformation from frozen to carbon, all too easy.

'Vermouth, gin, mostly gin. Oh, a touch of Campari to give it colour; a smidgeon of fruit juice. Mostly gin and French. He downed it in one. For the third time, would you believe?'

The smell of burning increased, a waft of smoke drifted in from the oven, bringing with it an end to relaxation.

'Can I help you, Joe?'

'No.'

Anger stirred. Because he would not let her salvage the food. Because of the vision of some poor, lonely old man, buoyed up to spend his money until he fell off his stool, poisoned by a barman he trusted.

'Joe, you shouldn't have done that . . .'

'Done what?'

He was struggling in the kitchen, couldn't find the thing

258

to strain the peas: it made him mad. Cath could see the end result of all this; she should not carp at his cruel jokes on drunken customers, could not stop, either.

'Done that. What you did. Encouraged that bloke to drink that poison. He relied on you, didn't he? Poor old sod. Poor old Colonel Fogey. Shame.'

There was silence. She turned her head away towards the inanities on the TV screen, wondering too late if there was time to move. Then the food arrived in her lap. Without plate or tray. A heap of hot, burnt pancake and soft peas which burned through the fabric of her skirt into her thighs. She braced herself, with her hair hiding her face while he hit her in the ribs and bosom, finished his flurry with a punch towards the abdomen exposed by the futile defence of her arms across her chest. They were hard blows, repeated for emphasis, making the peas bounce and flutter among the folds of her skirt. The sound from her mouth was simply a grunt as he stopped.

'Pig,' he said, dismissively. 'That's what you are. You even sound like one.'

He retrieved his plate, sat back and ate with his eyes fixed on the screen. For a while she was quite still, then she got up and carried her skirt in front of her, like an apron, her movements silent and unsteady. He did not take his eyes off the television and she did not speak. On her return, five minutes later, she was carrying a plate of bread and butter. Cath ate more bread and butter than anything else.

'What did you do,' he demanded, 'with that food I cooked for you?'

'I ate it, of course. What did you think I would do?' she whispered.

'You might have thrown it away, or something.'

'No, it was lovely. Thanks.' She began to cough, stopped herself because it hurt and would annoy him. Coughing lead to vomiting and that annoyed him more. She had learned to control nausea, to use it as a last resort, since there was an element of fastidiousness about the man. He would not go on hitting while she was being sick, but the downside of that was the knowledge that the presence of regurgitated food always stopped him feeling sorry afterwards.

'They don't feed you,' he grumbled, still not taking his eyes off the screen.

'No they don't, Joe, you're right.'

She nibbled at the bread and margarine spread. Not the stuff of genteel sandwiches, nor the stuff of doorsteps. The sight of it sickened her: pallid dough, golden fat. At work she had another kind of sustenance: bread with nuts, rich brown stuff with real butter layered on with a trowel.

She could have eaten anything out of their fridge if she wanted. She could have told them she was in trouble, but then she was not really in trouble. As long as she was clever and he did not hit too hard or scar her face, and she was able to pretend that the cleaning job was as hateful as the gentry who employed her.

'Joe?' she asked, pleadingly. 'Joe, would you get me a drink? Tea, I mean?'

Joe only drank tea at home. He drank alcohol behind the bar where he worked, noon and evening, not that it showed until he came home, unless anyone could call the odd snarling a symptom. She could imagine what he was like, wondered why they put up with him, hoped that they always would since the thought of Joe without work was tantamount to a nightmare. If he did not work, he would stop her working, but as long as he stayed where he was and she pretended her job never involved any conversation, that was all right. Drinking alcohol at home was not. Together, they preserved the pretence that he never touched a drop; she acted now as if she believed he could not bear the stuff, which, in his way, he could not. His body could not. On a bad day, which meant a day when he had trouble crossing the road, an argument with a customer, or suffered any kind of assault on his pride, the alcohol combined with disillusion to make a poisonous cocktail. It was only the booze which turned him from saint to sinner. He was staring at the screen, his plate empty, his belly unsatisfied.

'Joe? Please? I hurt all over, Joe?'

He wavered, then hooked his right thumb inside his ear and used his whole large hand to cover his face. She watched him, hardening her heart without great success, even while her own fingers moved cautiously across her aching ribs. He always covered his face when he was ashamed.

She went to make tea, bending in the middle to ease the pain, wanting nothing more than her bed. He spoke in a

260

small voice, at odds with his well-muscled frame, in keeping with his height.

'I love you, Cath. I'm sorry.'

She felt his left hand clutch at her skirt as she passed, feigned anger. Inside the kitchen, she tidied with long, slow, regretful movements, coughing, spewing into the sink. Carefully, she chose his favourite mug, put a tea bag inside, poured on the boiling water from the new kettle without a cord. The kitchen gleamed. After a deep breath, which caused as much pain as effort, she took the tea in to him.

He was asleep in the chair, his face wet with tears. She brought the duvet from the bedroom, covered him and left him.

Their own bed was new, with drawers in the base, from which she withdrew a spare duvet, as pristine as the one over his knees. There were other rooms, all of them bursting with goods.

Cath worked hard to achieve this daily promise of oblivion. In the bathroom, postponing the real bath until morning the way they both did unless there was blood, she forced herself to slosh cold water over her warm body and face, recognizing the nature and degree of this kind of pain and doing her best to ignore it. She averted her eyes from the puckered scar on her abdomen, washed carefully and estimated the size of tomorrow's bruises. He never hit her face. Never.

Nothing broken: nothing which quite needed fixing.

'Can anyone remember Cath's phone number? Oh, Christ, where have I put it?'

'Darling, why do you want to know? You don't need to phone her, surely? She'll be here in the morning; besides, she doesn't like being phoned at home, certainly not this late.'

'Late? Time for bed, then,' said Emily Eliot, roguishly, ruffling his hair, winking in the mirror which hung over his desk. He looked up from the papers across the surface in orderly confusion, caught her eye and smiled.

'Not tonight, Josephine. I need another hour on this. What on earth were you doing downstairs? Bit of a row.'

'Oh, sorry, playing Scrabble. Mark was winning, he crows when he's winning, frightful child. Have you really

261

got to work?' By this time, her arms were draped round his neck, smiles meeting in the mirror.

'Yup. You know how it is.'

'Dreadful,' she said mockingly, the kiss placed on his cheek denying even the slightest hint of resentment. 'A wife refused her connubial rights in the interests of paying the mortgage. OK, I know my place, I'll simply warm the bed. Now, where's that number?'

'For the second time of asking, why?'

'Oh, Helen rang. Can you believe, she said she was asking me because we're such an organized household, little she knows.' Emily's laugh was loud, clear and genuine. 'Only she was looking for a cleaning lady. Our Cath was saying she wouldn't mind a bit extra, and knowing Helen, she'll pay the earth, so I wanted Cath's number.'

'At this time of night?'

'Oh, yes, it is, isn't it? Bedtime.'

She stood slightly perplexed, as if she had totally forgotten the urgency. Emily's hectic sense of priorities, her need to fulfill each task as soon as it was suggested, fuelled this house and made it work, with the effect of a huge and elegant boiler. The occasional irritation this caused a hard-working barrister on the up was more than compensated for by the very sight of her and every single one of their children. Emily shared their high energy and that sand-washed look which was pale, interesting, and fiery; a big-boned woman, dressed in an old dressing-gown patterned with dragons cavorting on a purple background. Her hair stood on end: her face was scrubbed and shiny. Alistair pulled her into his lap.

'Give me a hug. You smell gorgeous.'

She plumped herself down while he pretended to groan at the weight and, with her arms round his neck, she squeezed the breath out of him. Then she looked at the papers on the desk. There were bundles of them, loosely undone, with the red tape which had bound them pushed to one side.

'What have you got here, my love? Murder and mayhem?'

'Bit of both. I told you about it.' He did; he told her all about his cases, including the most tedious ones, and, even in the middle of the night, she listened. 'Murder, of course. What else can you call it when you have a fight in a pub,

262

one side loses, goes away, arm themselves and come back? One youth stabbed, but only one man caught. Someone else is getting off scot free.'

'Won't he say who?'

'Nope.'

'Is this one of Helen's briefs?'

'No, Bailey's. These are Helen's.' He waved his hand towards the white-taped bundles. 'Even worse. Domestic violence. Wife-bashers. She seems stuck on wife-bashers at the moment. I wonder if that's connected to wanting a cleaner?'

Emily rose and kissed the top of his head.

'You wouldn't ever bash me, would you? However aggravating I am?' He slapped her large behind gently as she moved away. His hand made a clapping sound against the fabric of the dressing-gown; she felt the caress without irritation. It had the sound of shy applause.

'Bash you? I couldn't, even if you begged. Perhaps, if it was strictly consensual. A long, slow collision. No-one's injured by a meeting of true minds.'

'Certainly they are, if the meeting of minds also involves skulls. And I think,' she added demurely, holding out her calloused hand, 'you could finish that work in the morning.'

They got as far as the door, leaning against each other lightly, the old familiar relief flooding through him. What did men do, if they did not have a partner like this who bullied, cajoled, seduced and led them to bed with the stealth of a courtesan? A chameleon she was, a sometime tigress, tolerant, fierce; she kept them safe.

It was an impractical house, full of nooks, crannies and the assembled possessions of five individuals of varying ages. On the first-floor landing stood Jane, the youngest child, with snot congealed on her nightdress. A plump nine-year-old, moist with sweat and tears, her face framed against her brother's surfboard which rested against the wall, her skin pale and pink in patches. Older brother Mark was dark and handsome at fifteen, her twelve-year-old sister, serenely fair and sophisticated, but Jane's carroty hair grew in twisted, uneven curls about her face, the longest locks sticky with saliva from being sucked into her mouth. Jane was not lovely, although in the eyes of her parents and in the words of their constant praise, she was beauty incarnate.

'It's that thing in my room, again,' she said, trembling. 'That thing, Mummy. He's been there again.'

She flung herself into Emily's arms. Father had his arms round mother's waist; they stretched from there to tickle Jane's damp and curly head.

'Well, what a nerve he's got, coming back after all this while. You'd have though once was enough,' Emily said indignantly. 'Some people have no consideration. Come on, we'd better go and fumigate the beast. You know he loves warm weather. Funny how he never visited when it was really cold.'

Jane snuffled, mollified.

'Cath cleaned my room today. I thought if it was clean, he wouldn't come back.'

'But Cath doesn't know about the perfume, and anyway, he's gone now. We'll just make sure, shall we? And then leave all the lights on, so you know to run upstairs to find Mark or us, OK?'

Emily's voice denied the right to winge. The child nodded, made a sound like a hiccup and then turned away from their tableau of hugging and set off downstairs, confident they would follow. Alistair marvelled, and occasionally worried, how it was that Jane had acquired her mother's authority and graceful, plodding tread. They pounded downstairs with maximum thumping of feet. One of these days they could get the kind of carpet which softened sound: school fees came first. Jane had detoured, with a swiftness which belied her weight, into their own bathroom, where children were forbidden most of the time. She was after her mother's cologne. There was plenty of perfume in this house. Alistair brought it from duty-free shops on those visits abroad which left him sick with longing for home. Then he would buy more whenever he saw it. Nothing extravagant, but always the largest size, a habit of his. The end result was a wife who always smelled sweet, even when knee deep in household dirt, and a daughter with such a passion for *eau-de-parfum* sprays, she used them to control her own childish demons.

The ghost who Jane insisted haunted her room on an intermittent basis—usually as the aftermath of either bad behaviour or greed on her part, her father noted wryly—only did so when the room was a mess. Tidiness and cleanliness deterred him. Perfume killed him off completely. Emily sprayed the room, liberally. It had the same effect as a charmed circle. Alistair laughed and supposed it was cheap at the price.

Helen West fell asleep with the grilles left undrawn across the basement windows, the way she did when Bailey slept alongside her but never dared otherwise, and never told him what he already knew, about her being tough and also constantly scared. The presence of the grilles induced a distinct sense of bitterness and a slighter sense of panic when they were closed. Supposing the threat was fire or flood, something from within rather than without, how would she escape when panic made her fumble? Why was it always assumed that the danger came from outside?

Because that was usually so. Certainly so for her. The memory of that violent intruder, faded by the passage of time, came back not only when she saw someone in a street who resembled him, but also at night, making her sweat. Sometimes she could smell his presence in this room, simply by brushing away her hair, from where it fell over the scar on her forehead.

She could taste the blood in her mouth, squirm at the memory of her own violent reaction and all the helplessness which followed. She turned restlessly, distracting herself with visions of daylight streaming in to a clean and sanitized room, washed bare of all reminders. Yellow. The colour of corn and cowardice; bright enough to exorcize the devil.

Bailey felt for her hand.

'You all right, love?'

'No.'

He drew her close. 'All right. Come in here then. I'll tell you a nice, long story. A good one. Happy endings.'

She wanted to stick her thumb in her mouth, wishing she could give up thinking about present, past or future. You do not need me as I need you, Helen thought, taking the hand gratefully, listening to the voice talking through some silly tale until she would fall asleep.

If it ain't broke, don't fix it.

265

Frances Fyfield
Shadow Play

The odd, vaguely menacing little man called Mr. Logo is a familiar figure in the old court building in London; although he may scare the dark-haired, dark-eyed little girls he follows, nobody can prove that he actually touches them. So he is allowed to return to his everyday life and his blinding obsession with the daughter who ran away from him four years before. Helen West is the Crown Prosecutor who has just failed for the fifth time to make good her prosecution of him. He is off-limits to her now until his next certain appearance in court. Yet, when she strikes up an unlikely friendship with Rose, the compulsively secretive clerk in her office, Helen West unwittingly sets in motion events that will push Mr. Logo's rage and dark passion toward uncontrollable and even lethal extremes....

Available in your local bookstore.